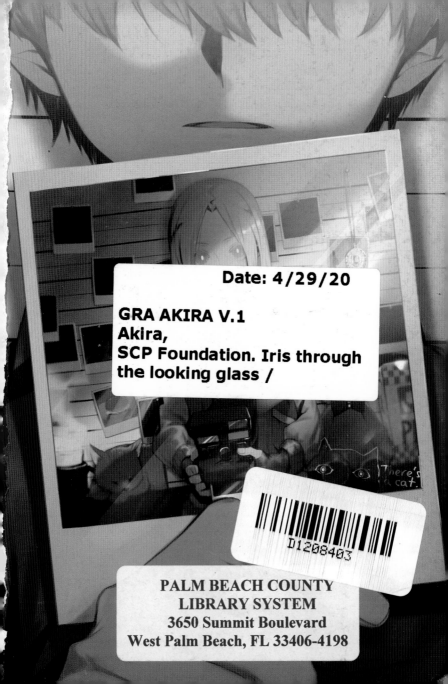

Date: 4/29/20

GRA AKIRA V.1
Akira,
SCP Foundation. Iris through
the looking glass /

D1208403

PALM BEACH COUNTY
LIBRARY SYSTEM
3650 Summit Boulevard
West Palm Beach, FL 33406-4198

THE FOUNDATION DATABASE IS CLASSIFIED
ACCESS BY UNAUTHORIZED PERSONNEL IS STRICTLY PROHIBITED
PERPETRATORS WILL BE TRACKED, LOCATED, AND DETAINED

Confidential

CONTENTS

PROLOGUE [THE GIRL IN THE PHOTOS] —————— P009

SCP-458 [THE NEVER-ENDING PIZZA BOX] ———— P025

SCP-105 ["IRIS"] ————————————— P063

SCP-823 [CARNIVAL OF HORRORS] ————— P113

SCP-294 [THE COFFEE MACHINE] ————— P163

SCP-914 [THE CLOCKWORKS] ————— P185

SCP-131 [THE "EYE PODS"] ————— P247

SCP-529 [JOSIE THE HALF-CAT]———— P275

SCP-348 [A GIFT FROM DAD] ———— P291

MILESTONE [MIRROR WORLD] ———— P309

Content relating to the SCP Foundation, including the SCP Foundation logo, is licensed under Creative Commons Attribution-Sharealike 3.0
and all concepts originate from http://www.scp-wiki.net and its authors. SCP Foundation: Iris Through the Looking Glass, being derived
from this content, is also released under Creative Commons Attribution-Sharealike 3.0. To view a copy of the license, please visit
https://creativecommons.org/licenses/by-sa/3.0/ or contact Creative Commons, PO Box 1866, Mountain View, CA 94042, USA.

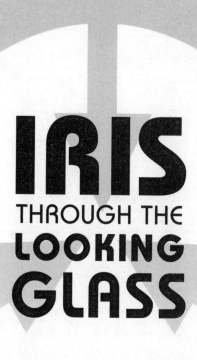

IRIS
THROUGH THE
LOOKING
GLASS

SCP FOUNDATION: IRIS THROUGH THE LOOKING GLASS, VOL. 1
Written by Akira | Illustrated by Sidu
Originally published in Japan by Hifumi Shobo in 2018

"Iris" by DrClef, edited by thedeadlymoose.
Based on "SCP-105 - 'Iris'" and the SCP Foundation
Japanese Branch translations of "SCP-105 - 'Iris.'"
http://www.scp-wiki.net/scp-105
http://ja.scp-wiki.net/scp-105

"The Never-Ending Pizza Box" by Palhinuk.
Based on "SCP-458 - The Never-Ending Pizza Box"
and the SCP Foundation Japanese Branch translations
of "SCP-458 - The Never-Ending Pizza Box."
http://www.scp-wiki.net/scp-458
http://ja.scp-wiki.net/scp-458

"Josie the Half-Cat" Author Unknown.
Based on "SCP-529 - Josie the Half-Cat"
and the SCP Foundation Japanese Branch
translations of "SCP-529 - Josie the Half-Cat."
http://www.scp-wiki.net/scp-529
http://ja.scp-wiki.net/scp-529

"Immortality" by TheDuckman.
Based on "SCP-963 - Immortality"
and the SCP Foundation Japanese Branch
translations of "SCP-963 - Immortality."
http://www.scp-wiki.net/scp-963
http://ja.scp-wiki.net/scp-963

"Builder Bear" by Researcher Dios.
Based on "SCP-1048 - Builder Bear"
and the SCP Foundation Japanese Branch
translations of "SCP-1048 - Builder Bear."
http://www.scp-wiki.net/scp-1048
http://ja.scp-wiki.net/scp-1048

"Neko Desu. Yoroshiku Onegaishimasu"
by lkr_4185.
Based on "SCP-040-JP."
http://ja.scp-wiki.net/scp-040-jp

Content relating to the *SCP Foundation*, including the *SCP Foundation* logo, is licensed under Creative
Commons Attribution-Sharealike 3.0 and all concepts originate from http://www.scp-wiki.net and
its authors. *SCP Foundation: Iris Through the Looking Glass*, being derived from this content, is also
released under Creative Commons Attribution-Sharealike 3.0. To view a copy of the license, please
visit https://creativecommons.org/licenses/by-sa/3.0/ or contact Creative Commons, PO Box 1866,
Mountain View, CA 94042, USA.

This is a work of fiction. Names, characters, places, and incidents are the products of the author's
imagination or are used fictitiously. Any resemblance to actual events, locales, or persons, living
or dead, is entirely coincidental.

Seven Seas press and purchase enquiries can be sent to Marketing Manager Lianne Sentar at
press@gomanga.com. Information requiring the distribution and purchase of digital editions
is available from Digital Manager CK Russell at digital@gomanga.com.

Seven Seas and the Seven Seas logo are trademarks of Seven Seas Entertainment. All rights reserved.
Follow Seven Seas Entertainment online at sevenseasentertainment.com.

TRANSLATION: Jackie McClure
ADAPTATION: J.P. Sullivan
COVER DESIGN: KC Fabellon
INTERIOR LAYOUT & DESIGN: Clay Gardner
PROOFREADER: Stephanie Cohen, Nino Cipri
LIGHT NOVEL EDITOR: Nibedita Sen
MANAGING EDITOR: Julie Davis
EDITOR-IN-CHIEF: Adam Arnold
PUBLISHER: Jason DeAngelis

ISBN: 978-1-64505-177-0
Printed in Canada
First Printing: January 2020
10 9 8 7 6 5 4 3 2 1

SCP FOUNDATION

IRIS
THROUGH THE
LOOKING
GLASS

WRITTEN BY
AKIRA

1

ILLUSTRATED BY
SIDU

Seven Seas
Seven Seas Entertainment

SCP-105

Special Containment Procedures: SCP-105 is implanted with a tracking device and is currently housed at Site-17. SCP-105 is currently allowed Class 3 (restricted) socialization privileges with approved site personnel, granted based on continued good behavior and cooperation with Foundation personnel.... →For details, refer to the section for SCP-105

PROLOGUE
[THE GIRL IN THE PHOTOS]

WHO ARE YOU?

IRIS THROUGH THE LOOKING GLASS

WARNING
:::::::::
THE FOUNDATION DATABASE IS CLASSIFIED.
ACCESS BY UNAUTHORIZED PERSONNEL IS STRICTLY PROHIBITED
PERPETRATORS WILL BE TRACKED, LOCATED, AND DETAINED

Confidential

Content relating to the SCP Foundation, including the SCP Foundation logo, is licensed under Creative Commons Attribution-Sharealike 3.0
and all concepts originate from http://www.scp-wiki.net and its authors. SCP Foundation: Iris Through the Looking Glass, being derived
from this content, is also released under Creative Commons Attribution-Sharealike 3.0. To view a copy of the license, please visit
https://creativecommons.org/licenses/by-sa/3.0/ or contact Creative Commons, PO Box 1866, Mountain View, CA 94042, USA.

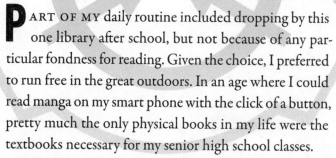

PART OF MY daily routine included dropping by this one library after school, but not because of any particular fondness for reading. Given the choice, I preferred to run free in the great outdoors. In an age where I could read manga on my smart phone with the click of a button, pretty much the only physical books in my life were the textbooks necessary for my senior high school classes.

I never saw much appeal in physical books. My eyes grew tired simply from running across the rows of text. As such, the reason why I frequented this library lay elsewhere.

"Fascinating!" squealed ▉▉▉▉▉▉▉-senpai, standing right in front of a poster with the words "NO TALKING!" written on it in large, bold font. A third-year student (and so a year ahead of me), she was the Vice-President of the Student Council at my high school.

SCP FOUNDATION

Thanks to some ancestors from Canada or the U.S.A., the color of her hair resembled honey in the sunlight. Her eyes were such a vivid ultramarine that it was hard to believe the color was natural. Although her well-defined facial features matched the image of a Western beauty, her wild imagination kept the other students at bay.

"Let's get right down to it, ███-kun," ████████-senpai said, twirling her finger around as she looked down at me excitedly. I was average height for a senior high boy, but she was abnormally tall. To top it off, she made sure to tower over me whenever she spoke, which really laid the pressure on. It was intimidating. I shrank back a bit.

My back rammed against the bookcase fixed to the floor. While I nimbly caught a few books that fell from the shelves, ████████-senpai rattled on. "There are some really strange rumors surrounding this library. People rate it one of the Seven Wonders of the School—and, ah, I'm not sure if you're aware, but apparently this library was originally part of a university that got shut down. It's uncertain whether it was deemed too much of a hassle to demolish after the university was gone or if some kind of intrigue was in play, but it's all that remains standing."

She was a bit hard to follow, that girl. She never really bothered to stop and gather her thoughts; she let her words spill out however they came to mind. But I felt like I needed to at least give the pretense of listening, so I bobbed my head like an idiot.

Indifferent to my lukewarm response, ▓▓▓▓▓▓-senpai continued prattling on, completely unfazed. "That's what makes it one of our school's Seven Wonders. Apparently, the strange rumors surrounding the place date all the way back to when the university was still standing. I'm nuts about paranormal stuff, so I've been looking into it."

Like I didn't know that. That was precisely why I decided to talk to her in the first place: I was currently caught up in some supernatural mumbo-jumbo of my own. I had no idea who else to turn to—certainly not my parents, teachers, or friends—let alone the police. I had no doubt they would just laugh it off, saying something like, "Where did you come up with that crazy idea?"

Grasping at straws, I turned to this upperclassman, a girl who'd been ostracized for never once backing down from her declaration of "I love the supernatural!"

That love was on full display. "This library is incredible! It's a treasure trove of mysteries and creepy rumors! The occult on parade!"

She drew so close that I swore it was bad for my poor adolescent heart—and then she broke into a big grin. Throwing both arms wide open, she looked

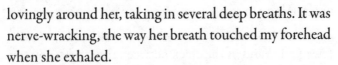

SCP FOUNDATION

lovingly around her, taking in several deep breaths. It was nerve-wracking, the way her breath touched my forehead when she exhaled.

The two of us were surrounded by countless aisles of library stacks. Even though it was an early summer's afternoon, the lighting was dim and gloomy. Blame that on the black curtains lowered over the windows to prevent the books from yellowing. Apparently, the fluorescent lights arrayed along the ceiling were burnt out. They failed to offer any light at all.

Put bluntly, it was one creepy library. Going by the stains and cracks along the walls, it was a rather old building. Mold and cobwebs completely overran places where damp had settled in. The place was practically in ruins. It was hard to believe the building was currently in use.

I guess nobody wanted to set foot in that creepy facility, because I didn't see any librarians, let alone other patrons browsing the aisles. Senpai and I were the only ones there. Her voice carried so well, it actually hurt my ears.

Oblivious to me squinting in pain, she continued her excited rant. "Actually, there are so many weird rumors, I can't even remember them all! For instance, they say there's a demon that will pop out of a book here and grant any one wish in exchange for your soul. And if you crack open this one other unlabeled book, your fate will appear on the blank pages for you to read! If you stick your hand in the crack between the stacks, you can get drawn to another world! There are a whole *bunch* of awesome rumors. Oh, there's even one about a girl ghost who reads all by her lonesome self for all eternity in the girls' restroom—and that room's sealed shut! ...Uh, actually, mind if I go to the little girl's room?" Seeming to think nothing of asking that awkward question, she spun right around.

She was on cloud nine. Seemed pretty safe to assume that her love of ghost stories was the real deal. Personally, I didn't care for that sort of thing. As far as I was concerned, an upperclassman going gaga over scary stories and creepy rumors just looked nuts. I hadn't come here for cheap thrills or ghost stories. Honestly, I was more than ready to leave.

"Now about the strange phenomenon you experienced...the, uh...why don't we dub it 'The Girl in the Photos?' I've never heard of anything like it. You might have something completely new on your hands! Too cool!" she squealed, squirming in delight and pushing her face even closer to mine. I thought I might lose my mind. She was so dang close that her legs and chest brushed up against me.

"Okay," she said. "Okay. I'd like to take a sec to review what you told me, so be sure to correct me if I'm wrong about anything. The other day, you came to this library to do some of your summer homework, correct?" Senpai must have noticed she was getting a little short on personal space, because she slid back a few steps before continuing, "You had to write a personal reflection on a reading assignment, right? What a stupid piece of homework! But since you're a relatively diligent student, you decided to take it seriously and went to the nearest library. That just so happened to be *here,* right? And that's where you encountered the paranormal!"

Senpai picked up one of the books that had fallen earlier and began callously flipping through its pages. "Wasn't there supposed to be a photo stuck inside every single book you picked up in the library?"

That was right. If it was as simple as that, it would be nothing to freak out about. I could dismiss it with the perfectly rational theory that someone who borrowed books from this library used photos instead of bookmarks and forgot to remove them before returning the books. But if that was the extent of the situation, it wouldn't have me so upset. I wouldn't turn to this weirdo for help, either.

"No matter what book you grabbed and flipped open, there was the photo! The result was the same, regardless of which stacks or books you tried! Do you still have one, by any chance?"

No way. They were so creepy, I stuffed them back into the books I found them in. I didn't see any good coming out of holding onto one, and honestly, just making off with them didn't seem right.

"Aw, too bad! If you still had them, I coulda used one to dig up a whole bunch of stuff. Oh, just so you know, it's not like I don't believe you or anything, okay? It's rare to find physical evidence in the world of the occult!" Senpai cackled, before a stern expression suddenly crossed her face. "All of this, well, *could* be explained logically. Someone could have contrived a highly elaborate prank. It just requires stuffing a photo in every book in this library. It's possible for me—or anyone else, for that matter—to pull off with a bit of effort. But that's where things get *really* weird."

Exactly. This was where the story took a turn for the truly paranormal.

"Even after you left...you found a picture of her stuck in *every* book you cracked open. It didn't matter if it was a school textbook, a book for sale at the convenience store, a manga magazine that you borrowed from a friend, or part of the ancient masterpiece collection your parents have on display in the bookcase at home. These photos

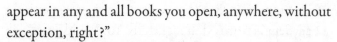

appear in any and all books you open, anywhere, without exception, right?"

Right. There was obviously something weird going on here. No logical explanation could cover this. It was truly a supernatural phenomenon.

Was someone going ahead of me and stuffing photos in every book I might possibly open? I couldn't see what anyone had to gain from that, and it was far too unrealistic for anyone to pull off. I found it hard to imagine there was a person—or organization—that would benefit from me finding pictures stuck inside books.

Whenever I found them, it only served to startle me. It wasn't as if the rate of my pulse and the speed of Earth's rotation were linked, so there wasn't anything to gain from spooking a guy like me.

The possibility that someone hated me to death and was doing this to torment me didn't seem likely, either. The life I led shouldn't incur such spite—I was like any other mundane high school boy out there. Besides, if someone was going to bully me, a better plan would be to stick in something gross, or at least use a more disturbing photo. But each time I found a photo stuck in a book, it was of the same cute girl.

"I assume that girl's an acquaintance of yours...or is she not?" Senpai frowned thoughtfully. You could practically hear the gears turning in her head.

I could give her a clear answer on this one. I was absolutely certain I'd never met the girl before. She was a complete and total stranger. Although I didn't possess a mind so brilliant that I could remember every single person I'd met, nothing had come to me even after pulling my hair out and wracking my brain in an attempt to remember her. I was drawing a blank. I'd definitely never seen her before. I couldn't see how I had anything to do with this unfamiliar girl.

What's more, she was a foreigner, probably a Westerner. Although it was difficult for a Japanese guy like myself to guess the age of a Caucasian, I thought she was probably somewhere around my age, either in her early twenties or late teens. Wearing a kind, warm-hearted expression, her pretty face was reminiscent of a flower in bloom.

Neither her eyes nor her hair were particularly unusual colors, but appeared to be shades rather common for Westerners. That hair extended slightly below the shoulders, generally worn loose rather than kept back, although she would bind it with a cheap-looking hair tie once in a while.

No matter what, there was always an ancient camera in her hands. It gave her a vivacious air, somehow, like a newspaper journalist. Her casual attire showed a disinterest in fashion; many of her outfits were clearly secondhand. She was such a normal, happy-looking girl it seemed weird to call these photos of her "ghost photographs."

Highly intrigued, Senpai crossed her arms and fell into deep thought. Finally, she said, "I wonder who she is. I've never heard of anything like this before... I'm certain she must be related to you somehow. After all, no one else has ever seen the Girl in the Photos. I checked online to see if anyone else shared a similar experience, but no hits came up."

Well, that was less than helpful. I really, truly did not know this girl. Based on their genetic traits, I felt like Senpai was way closer to being "related" to the girl than I was.

After thinking good and hard, Senpai held her head in her hands, its distinct features revealing her own foreign ancestry. She cried out, "Gah, I just don't know! This is too far out there! It would have made things way easier if the Girl in the Photos presented a threat, like putting a deadly curse on you. That'd make this a standard ghost story! But as things stand, I have no idea what this girl is trying to do."

I didn't want to die of some curse! Sure, this was a pretty creepy situation, but it seemed ultimately harmless, so at least I wasn't living in fear. I was simply curious what was up with the pictures...and the girl in them. It was also a bit depressing to think photos like this would appear in any book I cracked open for the rest of my (hopefully long) life. If at all possible, I wanted to do something about this supernatural phenomenon.

"If only you knew who that girl was... Could you try figuring it out? If I know her name and nationality, I might be able to find something online, you know?"

Senpai's question had me at a loss. All of the photographs I'd found thus far shared almost the exact same layout. There were minor deviations between each photo, but the overall image didn't change. There was a girl in the center. The shots were extremely zoomed in; close-ups of her face or the upper portion of her body consumed the majority of the frame.

When a background was visible, it was usually just a boring, gray, concrete wall. A nondescript environment that only vaguely evoked speculation that she could be in a hospital, prison, or research institution.

No one other than the girl ever appeared in the photographs, and she didn't do anything to offer insight regarding her personality. She was either daydreaming, staring at me, or sleeping. They were simple photos akin to the ones used for passports and resumes. Without the sleuthing skills of a great detective, I had no hope of discerning her identity.

"Hmm... Okay, I guess her identity is just one of the things we'll have to start looking into. I'll give you my full support, so don't worry. Let's make the most of your miraculous encounter with the occult in this cut-and-dry modern world we live in! Let's give it our all, partner! Put 'er there!"

Showing absolutely no signs of calming down, Senpai forced me into a handshake and began swinging our arms up and down. Admittedly, it was probably rare to encounter such a bizarre phenomenon in the 21st Century, a time when science flourished. I bet senpai didn't want to let this chance (if you could call it that) slip her by.

Although Senpai was a weirdo who made it no secret she was only doing this to sate her own curiosity, it felt kind of nice getting the whole thing off my chest. Keeping it to myself was starting to wear me down.

"All right! With that settled, let's start our investigation with a few tests." Senpai began carefully checking the book, still in her hands, one page at a time.

"Hmmm... It doesn't look like any pictures are stashed in this one." Senpai took her time, examining it carefully.

"The cover is intentionally designed so that you can't remove it, which makes sense, since it's a library book. I don't see anywhere a photo could be hiding." She proceeded to hand it to me and continued, "So next, I want you to try. Unless you're a top-notch magician, it really will be a supernatural phenomenon if you pull one of those photos out of this book. Oh, I'm so excited!"

I held the book Senpai had just confirmed as photo-free. As she said, it was physically impossible for a photograph to slip from its pages—unless of course, Senpai was feeling mischievous and had decided to play a stupid trick on me by slipping a photo in right before handing it over. I'd never spoken to her before now; I didn't exactly trust her a hundred percent. On the other hand, that meant there was no reason for her to tease or deceive me.

Honestly, I'd never get anywhere if I kept on doubting every little thing.

Feeling a little nervous, I popped open the book and briskly thumbed through the pages.

"Well? Well? Is it there? Where's the photo? Actually, hold up! I wanna document this! I'm gonna record it on my smart phone, so gimme a sec! This is so cool! I hope I get to witness the big moment...!" Senpai was so excited she was practically vibrating—it was downright annoying, but I was too preoccupied with my own issues to pay her any heed.

As I casually flipped through the pages, like I would any other book...I found it.

The photo appeared, tucked into the fold right down the center of the spine.

Cold chills ran down my back.

"Huh? No way! Are you kidding me?"

Senpai got her phone out of her pocket, but filming proved a bigger challenge. The phone slipped right out of her hands. She flailed after it, eyes wide in amazement. I was struck speechless. Just like always, a photo had appeared in the book I was holding. It was flipped backwards, so I instinctively touched the photo to turn it around. The photo was of none other than...

"L-Lemme see! I wanna see! C'mon, ██████!" Senpai cried, her piercing voice growing suddenly distant.

As the sound of her cries faded, a lukewarm sensation slowly engulfed my entire body. It was unlike anything I had ever experienced before, like I was being cupped inside a giant hand.

My gaze fell upon the image imprinted on the small, standard-sized photo.

The mysterious "Girl in the Photos" looked back up at me, wearing a faintly troubled smile.

SCP-105

Special Containment Procedures: SCP-105 is implanted with a tracking device and is currently housed at Site-17. SCP-105 is currently allowed Class 3 (restricted) socialization privileges with approved Foundation personnel. →For details, refer to the section for SCP-105

SCP-458
[THE NEVER-ENDING PIZZA BOX]

WHO ARE YOU?

Confidential

IRIS THROUGH THE LOOKING GLASS

WARNING

THE FOUNDATION DATABASE IS CLASSIFIED
ACCESS BY UNAUTHORIZED PERSONNEL IS STRICTLY PROHIBITED
PERPETRATORS WILL BE TRACKED, LOCATED, AND DETAINED

Content relating to the SCP Foundation, including the SCP Foundation logo, is licensed under Creative Commons Attribution-Sharealike 3.0 and all concepts originate from http://www.scp-wiki.net and its authors. SCP Foundation: Iris Through the Looking Glass, being derived from this content, is also released under Creative Commons Attribution-Sharealike 3.0. To view a copy of the license, please visit https://creativecommons.org/licenses/by-sa/3.0/ or contact Creative Commons, PO Box 1866, Mountain View, CA 94042, USA.

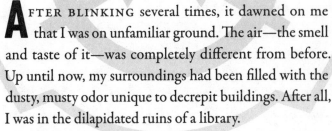

AFTER BLINKING several times, it dawned on me that I was on unfamiliar ground. The air—the smell and taste of it—was completely different from before. Up until now, my surroundings had been filled with the dusty, musty odor unique to decrepit buildings. After all, I was in the dilapidated ruins of a library.

Without any form of air conditioning on hand, simply being inside the humid library in the heat of summer made me work up a sweat. But now I felt strangely cold. To the point I was getting goosebumps, even. The smell drifting in the air reminded me of the poignant stench of medicine in hospitals.

In fact, the room was cramped, like a hospital room. It had gray concrete walls just like the ones I occasionally saw in the background of the photos of that girl.

Although they were clean, the floor, walls, and ceiling were all that same boring gray.

A bare light bulb hung from the ceiling. Next to me was a small stand, like the ones people kept landline phones on. For some odd reason, an antique brooch that looked like it might have archeological value had been thoughtlessly dumped on its surface.

Strangely, I didn't notice any doors or windows. It felt more like I was in a box than a room. Stuck in this cubical room, the wild idea that I'd somehow managed to travel inside the photo hit me.

Vision reeling, I crumbled to the ground. As if on cue, the book with the photo slipped out of my hands and clattered across the floor. I saw now that the title of the worn book was *Through the Looking-Glass, and What Alice Found There*. I'd never read it before, so I wasn't totally sure what it was about.

Stranger still: the photo I was holding along with the book vanished, as if it was nothing more than an illusion, a figment of a dream. In its stead, the girl stood before me.

"███████?" she asked, in something that sounded like English, although I couldn't say for certain.

Dang, it really was the Girl in the Photos... The pictures were always either headshots or three-quarter shots, so this was my first time getting a full view of her.

As suspected, she was a perfectly normal human without so much as an inch of mystique. She was a young foreigner, around the same age as me. Loosely hanging hair spread around and over her shoulders. Her eyes were big and round. She was wearing plain clothes, socks with cute cartoonish bears printed on them, and fluffy slippers. She continued to cradle the clunky camera as if it were a stuffed animal, looking down at me with a troubled expression on her face.

"███████, ████████? ███████████?" It seemed like the girl was asking me something out of concern. But I still couldn't make out what she was saying. I couldn't understand her. Although she was probably speaking in English, the real deal was nothing like what was taught at school. Even if I knew the grammar, I couldn't hold my own in a conversation.

Honestly, it didn't help that my head was a jumbled mess, either. I doubted I could give her a decent answer even if she started talking to me in good ol' Japanese. My mind reeling, I looked like a goldfish, flapping my mouth open and shut. I couldn't make heads or tails of what was going on!

As if prompted by the sight of me in such a sorry state, she kindly offered me her hand. My back had given out on me, after all. Gingerly grabbing her fingertips, I could feel her body heat. I knew exactly how normal people felt, and she felt no different.

"Who are you?" the girl asked in a slow, clear voice, carefully punctuating each word.

Hooray for junior high-level English! Even I could understand that! She was asking who I was. But seriously, that was what I wanted to ask *her*.

In any case, I was somewhat relieved by her rather friendly disposition, so I decided to go ahead and introduce myself. I was planning a pathetic attempt at communicating by mustering all of the English vocabulary I knew, but before I could—

Someone whacked me with all their might on the back of the head. I swiftly fell unconscious.

So, when I regained consciousness, I briefly thought I was still dreaming. But I really was in a place that was completely foreign to me. The grimy ceiling didn't match the one in my bedroom, which I knew like the back of my hand. The place stank of ammonia. I anxiously shot up, trembling.

Where the heck was this? It wasn't the same cramped room I was in right before I got knocked out. The place screamed prison cell, with an area roughly 9'×9'. I was lying in a simple bed bolted to the ground. It was furnished with a scratchy blanket and sheets, along with a hard pillow. Facing the end of my outstretched legs was a narrow entrance fitted with iron bars. The air on the other side was bustling with the presence of people and their voices. The room only had one light bulb, small enough that I could probably wrap one hand around it. If that weren't bad enough, the darn thing kept flickering on and off.

Perhaps the lights were turned off outside the room. It seemed that way, anyhow, because it was so dark that I could hardly make anything out. I strove to comprehend the situation I found myself in, timidly hugging the blanket that had been placed over me. Where was I? What happened? It didn't make any sense!

My mind swirling, I quietly got off the bed to make my way to the barred door. It didn't occur to me until then, but apparently someone had changed my clothes while I was out cold. Prior to now, I'd been wearing my high school uniform, like always. After dutifully attending class, I'd headed straight to the library with that weird girl.

Although I had no recollection of changing, I was currently wearing an unfamiliar khaki outfit that reminded

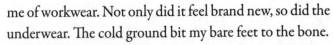

me of workwear. Not only did it feel brand new, so did the underwear. The cold ground bit my bare feet to the bone.

Not only did someone change my clothes while I was unconscious, it felt like my body had been washed squeaky clean as well. All of my skin stung, like I'd been given a body scrub, and I smelled of soap. It beat waking up to find myself sullied, but it still put a bad taste in my mouth.

Upon approaching the door, I wrapped my hands around the iron bars and tried to shake them. They wouldn't so much as budge. Directly across from me was another small cell just like mine, hosting a middle-aged man who was also wearing khaki workwear. He was sitting on his bed with his head resting against the wall, muttering who-knows-what.

Based on the man's red hair and facial features, it was safe to assume he was a foreigner. He was extremely muscular and appeared to have some sort of strange tattoos ringing his neck. It was painfully obvious he wasn't the sort to trifle with, and I sincerely doubted he understood Japanese, anyway. Lacking the courage to call out to him, I simply stood there dumbly.

What was this place? I decided to try unraveling that mystery. Did I get mixed up in some crime? Had I been abducted by some random criminal who was keeping me imprisoned? But to what end? And why me?

It all felt so surreal. I wanted to believe it was all just a dream. But the cold floor, the pervasive *discomfort,* and the throbbing where my head was struck when I got knocked out—all of it was very much real. But if this wasn't a dream, what was it? At my wit's end, my mind shut down; I wanted to break down into tears.

"████ ...?" came a voice from nowhere. Even as I jumped, the sound of footsteps grew closer. I didn't have to wait long before someone suddenly showed their face on the other side of the iron bars.

It was the Girl in the Photos. After all this time, I still didn't know her name. She was still wearing the same outfit I saw her in before I was knocked out, but her camera wasn't with her this time. That struck me as horribly strange—I had this weird mental image that her and the camera came as a package deal.

Although I didn't even know this mysterious girl well enough to call her an acquaintance, I also felt an inexplicable closeness after seeing her countless times in the photos. Perhaps she felt the same, for she began to speak to me rather casually.

"████. ████, ████?" She spoke in what truly did sound like English, but I couldn't understand any of it.

Seeing that I was having trouble, the Girl in the Photos nodded her head several times before walking out of view.

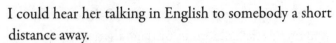

I could hear her talking in English to somebody a short distance away.

A few minutes later, the Girl in the Photos returned in much the same manner as she originally came and offered me a big grin. When she did, the barred door slowly began to open. Evidently an electrically controlled automatic door, it opened on its own. Seeing as I was holding the bars at the time, this made me literally jump back in surprise.

"."

The Girl in the Photos anxiously waited for the door to fully open before looking up at me and waving me over. I was afraid that I might have misinterpreted what she meant, but gingerly stepped out into the corridor anyway.

I looked around me. The darkness impaired my vision, but apparently there was an endless series of small rooms—like the one I was in—akin to solitary confinement cells. There was neither rhyme nor reason to the age or ethnicity of the people sleeping or chatting inside the cells, but they had one thing in common: They all donned the same khaki workwear.

Distracted by that, I fell behind the girl, who was already making her way down the corridor. She only stopped to look over her shoulder once and jerked her chin as if to say, "Aren't you coming?" I silently followed her like a good little puppy.

When they noticed us, the people in the cells began to shout and reach out for us through the gaps in the bars.

"███!" the Girl in the Photos scolded them, looking like a peeved cat. Intent on hurrying me along, she marched up to me and snatched my hand. She practically dragged me away from there!

I still didn't have a good grasp on the situation I was in, but simply holding the Girl in the Photos' hand strangely calmed me. I doubted she meant me any harm. In fact, I could tell she was on my side.

The girl led me around for a few minutes. I wasn't sure if this was a prison, a hospital, or even a research facility, but whatever it was, the building seemed massive. It was impossible to count all of the doors dispersed across the plain, nearly identical corridors. They broke off into a seemingly infinite number of branches. Many of the doors had the letters "SCP" written on them. I had absolutely no idea what that meant.

After walking to the point my feet were starting to grow a bit sore, the Girl in the Photos came to a stop. There was a randomly placed door in the corridor with a device that resembled an interphone built into the wall next to it. Standing on tiptoe, the Girl in the Photos held something like a cardkey up to the device. It must have served as some form of verification, for the door slid open with an electric buzz.

"Come in," she said, again in English simple enough for me to understand. She curled her fingers toward the palm of her extended hand in a beckoning gesture.

With her urging me along, I entered the room a few steps behind her. I could only assume she did something, because the lights popped right on. As a result, I was able to get a full view of the room.

From the looks of it, this was a cafeteria of sorts. The place was saturated with the smell of food. Multiple sets of tables and chairs claimed a space roughly the size of a high school classroom. A wall-mounted exhaust fan spun round and round. Someone apparently forgot to clean up after himself, leaving a plate, fork, and coffee cup abandoned on one of the tables.

Seeing as the room was desolate aside from the two of us, it was safe to assume this wasn't mealtime. The girl trudged over to the nearest chair, pulled it out, and plunked right down. She motioned me over with her eyes, so I took a seat directly across from her.

The girl seemed antsy, swinging her legs back and forth as she studied me. "   ," she said, but I couldn't understand her for the life of me. Man, if I knew this was going to happen, I would have taken my English classes more seriously.

She must have found our inability to communicate just as aggravating, because she scrunched the bridge of her nose in annoyance as she repeated the beckoning motion, flicking her fingers toward herself. I got the feeling she was saying, "Lean toward me," so I did just that.

The way I leaned in could easily be confused with the gesture for requesting a kiss, so I was a bit nervous. But rather than indulge in any amorous pursuits, the girl pulled out a collar of sorts from somewhere and attached it to my neck! Taken by surprise, I was like a deer caught in headlights.

The ring hung loosely around my neck. It seemed like a cheap, rubber collar. I was flabbergasted, unable to discern what would compel her to do such a thing. But I was in for an even greater shock mere moments later.

"Are you able to understand me now? Do you comprehend what I am saying? A response would be most appreciated!" Although somewhat stilted, she was speaking in Japanese. Actually, it sounded like she was still talking in English, which was converted to Japanese for me to understand without any time lag, I think... Bluntly put, it was really weird, and hard to describe. Had putting on this strange collar made me suddenly proficient in English? It was a bizarre—almost magical—experience.

"Huh? Was it no good after all? I didn't want to use The Clockworks if I could avoid it, since the results are so unpredictable, but none of our Japanese-speaking personnel are present and we don't have any translation devices on hand." The Girl in the Photos kept going on about stuff that went over my head.

So I cut in, responding to her in Japanese. Although it came out faltering, I tried to tell her not to worry; that for some odd reason, I could understand the meaning of the words coming from her mouth.

She broke into a broad smile and gave an overexaggerated sigh of relief. "Thank goodness! It would be inconvenient if we couldn't ascertain mutual understanding. It makes anyone—even a humanoid SCP object—substantially easier to deal with if you can hold a conversation," she explained, throwing in a few terms I didn't recognize.

Once finished, the girl pulled out of her chair. She went to the other side of the counter along the wall and began making a ruckus, shuffling things around.

"Do you like coffee? I have to load mine with gobs of sugar and milk. Oh, are you hungry? At the very least, I could warm up a frozen dinner for you," she offered, holding a siphon in one hand.

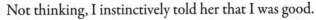

Not thinking, I instinctively told her that I was good.

"It is hard to pick up little nuances with this. There is no need to hold back, inhabitant of Japan," she said. Not exactly what you'd call a perfect translation. She took her time preparing the coffee.

As if an afterthought, a way to kill time, she finally got around to sharing her name. "I guess we should start with introductions. I am Iris Thompson, although I am also called SCP-105. If possible, please just call me Iris."

The Girl in the Photos offered a moment's silence to indicate it was my turn now. I hastily told her who I was.

"███████? You're called ███████, right? In Japan, is that a common name? It sounds so mysterious...! Sorry, but you *are* Japanese, aren't you? It certainly sounds like that's what you're speaking, anyway."

I acknowledged that she was right. And then I proceeded to tell her briefly about myself.

"Uh-huh, I see. So you attend ███████ Senior High School in ███████ Prefecture, Japan. One moment, please. I want to jot this down... Hmmm, due to hearing 'translations' of what you said, I'm not sure I heard the names correctly. If I could locate them, I might be able to discern where you came from."

Apparently, the pot of coffee came out a success, because Iris came back with a cup in each hand. She walked over carefully, trying not spill any. "Here you go." She handed me a cup, holding onto her own as she hunkered back down in her chair.

"By the way, this place is located in ███████, ███████ in the United States of America—not that you'd know where that is. It isn't marked on the map, after all. This is a covert facility working under the *cover story* that it belongs to the government. In fact," Iris said, "This is a stock-standard research facility for the SCP Foundation."

It seemed like she was observing my reactions as she spoke. She probably thought she was stealthily analyzing me, but her inexperience was showing through. It was so obvious what she was doing, it was actually somewhat cute. Our eyes happened to lock, and she quickly turned away.

"Speaking of which," Iris wondered, "Have you ever heard of the SCP Foundation?"

I'd been wondering about that sequence of three alphabet letters ever since I first saw them earlier. They seemed like initials for something, but I was unfortunately ignorant as to what.

"Oh... So you don't know? Really? Well, if push comes to shove," she whispered to herself, "We can always administer amnestics and implant false memories." What a blood-curdling notion. "I suppose there's no harm in going over it."

She shifted to face me head on. "Okay, so to keep this brief, I'll just give you a quick outline...about the SCP Foundation."

"Mr. ███████—uh, may I just call you ████████ instead?" Iris started out with a rather trivial question.

When I nodded my head to indicate that I didn't mind, she broke out into a giant grin.

"I appreciate it. I realize it's coming on a bit strong when we just met, but I hate acting all stiff and formal. Whenever I put my best manners on, I get a cramp in my cheeks from all that fake smiling." As if to prove it, she pulled her cheeks out in imitation of a forced smile.

Each and every one of Iris's expressions were rich with emotion; her movements were large and exaggerated. I guess foreigners were generally a bit over the top compared to Japanese in that regard.

As such irrelevant thoughts were passing through my head, Iris suddenly looked very serious. "At any rate, ██████, tell me. Do you believe in God?"

That rang pretty oddly to my Japanese, atheist ears. Why would she ask such a question...? Was she a church missionary? Thoughts like that ran through my head as I shrunk back a bit.

Seeing my reaction, Iris nodded knowingly and threw out more questions. "Then do you think aliens exist? Do you believe in the existence of monsters, demons, ghosts, fairies, angels? What about other non-human life forms, or superior beings? Have you personally witnessed magic, miracles, psychic powers, or other supernatural phenomena that ignore the laws of the natural world? Or do you believe it's possible for such phenomena to occur?"

Although Iris slung questions at me one after another, I was unable to throw any answers back. In all honesty, I was a little scared. Despite the friendly, down-to-earth impression she gave, Iris was starting to spout out incomprehensible nonsense along the same lines as that occult-fanatic upperclassman. And she just kept going on and on! It had me pretty freaked out.

Aliens? Psychic powers? What the heck is this chick going on about? That crap only existed in movies and comics. Here in the real world, all of that was impossible. Back when I was little, there was a time I believed there might be something out there beyond the scope of rational thought. I even believed in Santa.

But as I underwent my compulsory education, I obtained a certain degree of knowledge and experience. With that, I came to learn the "supernatural" was all just fabrications concocted in someone's head, or a bunch of baloney.

I was a modern-day high school boy with a good head on his shoulders. I wasn't about to fall for any of this nonsense. Neither gods nor demons dwelt in our world, and a person couldn't move a pebble with his mind. Scientists already finished explaining all of the things once revered as divine ages ago, leaving the world bereft of any mystery or mystique.

...But not so fast. I *was* experiencing something strange that neither logic nor science could explain. I was right in the midst of a surreal situation, like something out of a fairy tale.

No matter what book I picked up, there was always a photo tucked inside. And now I was holding a conversation face-to-face with the mysterious girl—Iris Thompson—who always appeared in those photos. If I took her words as truth, I was in a research facility clear on the other side of the world, off somewhere in America. This whole situation was so surreal, it felt like a dream. Was it possible for something so mysterious to happen in this world of ours?

"Please remain calm and hear me out," Iris said. She waited for the cascade of thoughts to finish racing through my mind before continuing.

"I've noticed you are an extremely normal, sensible person, based on your reactions. I believe I had a similar reaction when I was first told about the SCP Foundation, myself. I laughed it off as stupid, only to turn around and think of my brush with the strange. I was dumbstruck when I realized what they meant," she explained earnestly, twirling her finger the whole time like a conductor's baton, finger moving with the ease of habit.

"Skipping straight to the point, monsters and all of that paranormal stuff that surpass all rational thought really do exist. Just counting the ones I know, there are one, two, three... Honestly, I know too many to count on two hands," she said. She opened both hands and ticked something off on her fingers before giving up and turning to look me square in the eye. "That goes to show just how many of these things are out there."

These things? As in aliens, ghosts, and people with psychic powers? They really existed?

"Yes. For example, The Old Man is capable of causing any solid matter to corrode at a touch. It's particularly fond of killing people with its corrosive power... There are superior beings akin to the gods or demons portrayed in mythology that surpass mankind in any number of ways... And a researcher who could make countless duplicates of his mind. He travels the world by possessing various people and things..." Iris listed these spine-chilling examples in her adorable voice.

It was too much to swallow. An onslaught of unnerving stories all at once. If not for my personal experience with the strange and inexplicable, I would have thought she was spinning wild tales and laughed it off. But I was far from laughing, now. I gulped in fear.

Betraying not a single sign she'd been joking, Iris continued, deathly serious. "All manner of mysterious beings and things are referred to as 'SCP objects.'"

SCP. There was that strange acronym that I'd observed multiple times throughout the site. Although I figured they stood for something, they rang new and unfamiliar to my ears. I was still struggling to grasp the gist of them.

Seeing me struggle, Iris offered a simple explanation. "Basically, the 'S' in 'SCP' stands for 'Secure,' the 'C' stands for 'Contain,' and the 'P' is for 'Protect.'"

Thanks to the translation collar (was that what it was?), I heard the words in English but understood them in Japanese, making her explanation extremely easy to follow. "Right. The goal of the organization is to swiftly and safely secure SCP objects—anomalous occurrences and objects extending beyond human comprehension—to isolate them from the general public and contain them, then properly observe them, and protect them."

Uh-huh. So, it was like a crossover between a spy organization for the supernatural and guards for a vault. Hm, that might not actually be a good analogy... I couldn't think of a similar organization on the spot with my limited knowledge.

Whatever! Precisely *because* the SCP Foundation was isolating the eerie from conventional society, normal folk like us didn't even realize they existed. Yes, anomalies existed in the world. But the SCP Foundation was hiding them from the masses as they thoroughly secured, contained, and protected them.

"We—it feels weird for me to say, 'we,' but anyway— we are a secret organization carrying out the mission to secure, contain, and protect anomalies, or SCP objects. Hence, in accordance, we are generally referred to as the SCP Foundation," she said. The strand of difficult words made it hard for me to follow.

"The SCP Foundation, as implied by the name 'Foundation,' is built upon a foundation of massive financial resources, which serve as the substrate for its international operations. There are research sites like this one scattered across the globe, each heavily staffed with researchers and other personnel."

While I strived to digest that information, Iris plowed right on. "There are countless agents who travel the world and blend into society to conduct investigations rather than remaining permanently stationed at any one site. I'm certain the Foundation has extended its reach to Japan and spread its roots there as well."

It had? But seeing as it was a secret organization, there was naturally no way a normal high school boy such as myself would know. This was the sort of far-fetched conspiracy story that would make my occult-crazed upper-classman flip out. It was hard to believe...and yet, here I was, in one of the research facilities run by that strange organization operating behind the scenes in the world of the supernatural. It made me feel awkwardly out of place, like I'd stumbled into a movie.

Simply hearing about all of it filled me with such fear that I began to tremble. I wasn't sure what she mistook the trembling for, but Iris poured more coffee into my cup.

"Really," she said in a cute little voice, "You shouldn't have too much caffeine, or you might have trouble sleeping tonight." She stuck her tongue out. I found the sight comforting and relaxed a bit. I heaved a long, heavy sigh of relief.

It didn't seem like she had anything to gain by deceiving me with absurd stories, so at least for the time being, I was going to take her words at face value. Besides, we wouldn't get anywhere if I questioned every little thing.

The main thing I didn't understand was how I wound up inside the research facility for such a creepy organization. Did I teleport here from the library? Everything pertaining to my arrival, from the how to the why, was unknown to me, filling me with unease.

Evidently not a fan of bitter coffee, I observed Iris drop several sugar cubes in her drink right before my eyes. She proceeded to stir it. As the Girl in the Photos, I sincerely doubted she was unrelated to the strange things occurring to me. I decided to be open about my concerns.

"We don't have the answers to any of that ourselves," Iris replied, her brows pinched in consternation. "In fact, my goal is to discover who you are, as well as how and why you appeared in our research facility. But you aren't sure yourself, are you?"

No, I was totally clueless.

"I see. This could prove problematic... I subjectively— not objectively—perceive you aren't a bad person. That is my biased, personal opinion. There is no saying how the other personnel will appraise you." Iris folded her arms and grumbled to herself as she wracked her brain.

"Humans fear the unknown. Seeing as your identity is unknown, excruciatingly thorough and elaborate safety procedures will be enacted unless you are impartially deemed Safe," she said.

Hmm... I bet this was an issue with the translation collar, which was probably altering her words to convey minor nuances in her speech. Whatever the case, the slew of difficult words made it challenging for me to wrap my mind around what Iris was saying. Honestly, it made the way she talked sound unnatural. I had no doubt she was talking perfectly normally in English, but that didn't help me much...

"I suspect the standard SCP containment procedures will be put in place. Bluntly put, you will be locked in a completely enclosed room. If you try to leave, explosives will detonate, and chemicals will dissolve and sterilize everything in the room, or something along those lines." Iris mumbled the details of the horrifying processes before closing her eyes and contemplating in silence for a moment.

"I'd hate for that to happen to you," she said as she opened her eyes, offering an awkward smile. "As such, you're staying in my room as of today."

From my perspective, she'd just randomly blurted out the most insane idea.

A cute girl just told me to stay with her. Normally I would be overjoyed, expecting fun times ahead, but not under these circumstances. I wasn't exactly a hormone-crazed beast. Thrown off-kilter, I wasn't sure how to respond.

"Yep, I've decided that will be for the best. I'm going to go let the Doc know, okay?"

Apparently, Iris's earlier statement wasn't a question like "Would you like to stay with me?" but the order "You're going to stay with me!" Without so much as waiting for my response, she darted off to the back of the room.

I bet this cafeteria-like room probably had something like a kitchen or staff office in the back. From the sound of it, an intercom was installed in there. I could hear Iris's cheerful voice carry on for a time after she dialed the "Doc" up. Due to the distance, I could only catch snippets of what was said.

With nothing better to do, I sipped at my coffee. The awkward downtime allowed my mind to suddenly resume rational thought. Fear and unease came crashing down upon me. What time was it now? Without any clocks or windows in the cafeteria, I couldn't tell. My internal clock said the sun had already set and it was well into the night...

I wondered if my family was worried about me. I bet they thought I went missing. That senpai I was with probably let them know what happened, and then they

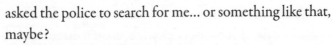

asked the police to search for me... or something like that, maybe?

If I truly was in the United States, it was a first-world country, so there should be plenty of telephones. Maybe I could make an international call to my home and let my family know I was all right. I was of a mind to ask Iris when she returned.

But if everything Iris just told me was true, this was a research facility run by the secret organization, SCP Foundation. It was a covert facility hidden from the eyes of the public. Seeing as the Foundation viewed me as a suspicious man of unknown origin, it seemed unlikely they would allow me to simply call home.

I wondered what was going to happen to me going forward. Was the Foundation going to do terrible, painful things to me? Although it had nearly slipped my mind, someone had already whacked me on the back of the head and locked me in a room akin to a prison cell. I probably shouldn't get my hopes up for a warm welcome as an honored guest.

My fears were growing worse by the second. Iris's presence and the way she treated me with her own brand of warm, quirky kindness were my only saving grace.

"Sorry to keep you waiting," Iris apologized, casually waltzing back after a fairly lengthy call. "I received permission, so you can stay with me starting today. I put in a request for a change of clothing and other basic necessities. I'll show you to my room in a bit, okay? But first!" She revealed her pearly whites in a happy grin for some odd reason. "Aren't you hungry? It's awfully late, but if you don't mind, why don't we grab a bite to eat? I've had an unusually hectic day, so I could use the calorie intake."

Iris's sentences came out sounding as weird as ever, but I understood the gist of what she was saying. And come to think of it, I actually was hungry. I went to the library with that upperclassman after school, which would put it around 5:00 P.M. Although I didn't know the exact time now, if it was around midnight...that meant roughly seven hours had passed. That was plenty of time for a young, healthy high school boy such as myself to completely digest the contents of his stomach.

"Great! It makes for an odd sight when one person isn't eating and the other is stuffing her face," Iris said, grinning happily. She brought something over to our table. "Are you okay with pizza? I feel like I'll get fat eating it at this hour, but it seems good enough, since it's quick and free!" As she said that, sure enough, she placed a pizza box down on the table in front of me.

It was a perfectly normal, thin, square box that appeared to be made of cardboard. The logo to a pizza chain

SCP FOUNDATION

I recognized yet couldn't place was printed on the box, along with the word "PIZZA" in large font. After such a bold declaration, I'd actually be surprised if there *wasn't* pizza in that box.

"I'm going first," Iris declared. She must have been famished—she licked her lips hungrily before popping the box open. A normal, steaming-hot pizza was inside. It looked awfully good. The pit of my stomach began to growl.

"Man, I figured this is what I'd get." Iris made that strange remark as she brought out the large plastic plates tucked under her arms. She placed one in front of each of us.

Effortlessly picking the pizza up with both hands, she plopped it on the plate in front of her. The whole darn thing! I was hoping she'd share with me, but apparently, she intended to devour the entire pizza on her own, and took a massive bite out of it. The melting cheese stretched, and stretched...

"This is the best!" Iris cried blissfully, chomping her food before gulping it down. "I always get a small with thin, wheat crust. Olives are a must! The rest varies on the day, but it's always a healthy pizza that isn't too heavy or spicy," she explained, before giving me a puzzled look.

I wasn't sure what she wanted from me. Seeing me grow flustered, she burst out with an "Ah!" of realization.

She put down the partially eaten pizza and wiped her mouth with a paper napkin that was already at the table when we first arrived.

"Feel free to help yourself," Iris offered. She closed the lid of the empty pizza box and pushed it up to me. Jeez, like offering an empty pizza box would do me any good. I was hungry! I needed more than a gesture.

"Oh, right. You don't know about this, do you? Okay, fair enough. That little detail totally slipped my mind." Iris batted her eyes exaggeratedly. "Although you probably can't tell at a glance, this is also an SCP object. Yep, this here pizza box. We always keep it here in the canteen, so I grabbed it," she said, indicating the box with her hands, but I was still a bit confused.

That was an SCP object? A mysterious object that defied human logic?

"Doesn't look like it, does it? I know how you feel, but the thing is, it really is one." Iris continued on eloquently, her meal forgotten. "This box is SCP-458. In other words, it is the 458th SCP object identified by the Foundation. It is known as 'The Never-Ending Pizza Box.'"

It had a rather fun name. And here I'd thought that all these so-called SCP objects were terrifying, after Iris's earlier explanation. Infinite pizza! My tension oddly melted at hearing the idea. I burst out laughing!

"What's so funny? This is a very impressive, mysterious SCP object in its own right! It's extremely convenient. Not just me, but all of the on-site personnel love it!" For whatever reason, Iris seemed pretty keen to defend the virtues of the box. She jutted out her lips in a pout.

"Well, I guess it isn't surprising, after all of the intimidating things I said. There are also harmless or amusing SCP objects that are more like parlor tricks than anything dangerous. But just because the Foundation deems them harmless doesn't mean they aren't incomprehensible anomalies, so never take them lightly."

As if an afterthought, she began rattling off another slew of technical terms. "For the record, SCP objects are divided into the three classes. 'Safe,' 'Euclid,' and 'Keter,' based on how difficult they are to contain. In many cases, the containment difficulty is directly proportional to the SCP object's level of danger."

Iris swung her finger around as she offered a detailed explanation. Almost too detailed, really. "Let's say we were going to contain an SCP object in a box. If we could put it in the box and everything was okay, it's Safe. If we could put it in the box, but who knows what would happen if we did, it's Euclid. If it wouldn't go, we couldn't get it in, or it popped out after we put in the box, it's Keter. I believe that sums it up."

I wasn't quite sure whether or not I understood the analogy.

"The Never-Ending Pizza Box is Object Class: Safe. It is considered particularly harmless. On top of that, it is terribly handy to have around," Iris said. Smiling like a mischievous child, she pointed at the perfectly ordinary-looking pizza box and urged, "Go ahead and open it. I'm sure you'll be in for a surprise."

Although a bit flabbergasted, I did as I was told. I opened The Never-Ending Pizza Box. True to her prediction, my eyes nearly popped out of my head. Nestled in the box was what appeared to be a hot pizza, fresh out of the oven.

But that was impossible! Iris had just grabbed one herself! But then she closed the lid, only for me to open it and find another pizza in the box, a box that should by all rights have been empty. To top it off, this was even a different type of pizza from the one she got. Bigger than hers, thick crusted, it was heavily loaded with seafood and broccoli.

What the heck? This didn't make any sense!

"Didn't I tell you? It defies all logic; hence, it's an SCP object." Iris tilted her head back. It felt like she was gloating, for some reason.

She cheerfully pulled a folded sheet of paper out of her pocket. Unfolding it, she looked down, and hummed contemplatively as she read over the note. Curious what it said, I tried to sneak a peek only for Iris to snap, "No!" in a surprisingly stern voice.

"You aren't allowed to look. In a sense, I am allowed some personnel privileges, so I've got authorization. This is a report documenting details pertaining to this SCP object. Or to be more precise, a copy of the report. Technically, it's explicitly prohibited to make copies, but I had to cheat a bit since I can't remember every little detail." Iris left me mystified, once again setting her eyes on the piece of paper, or report, I guess.

She began to read aloud. "SCP-458 is a large-sized pizza box from the pizza chain ████████, of their ████████████ variety. It is made of simple cardboard, measuring 25.4cm by 25.4cm by 2.54cm."

Although the string of numbers meant nothing to me, I figured this meant it was a normal pizza box.

"What makes SCP-458 an oddity is that, while appearing to be an ordinary pizza box, when it comes into contact with human hands, it instantaneously replicates the holder's subconsciously preferred choice of pizza, down to the favorite sauce, cheese, crust, and topping."

If that was true, this really was a bizarre phenomenon.

Or rather, it was like something out of a fairy tale. It seemed like tales of boxes or bags that produced an infinite supply of stuff appeared frequently around the world. I could swear I'd heard stories like that somewhere before. But the pizza aspect had a strangely modern edge that detracted from the fairy tale vibe.

"Although merely conjecture, it is believed The Never-Ending Pizza Box could create a near infinite supply of pizza. It is a miraculous item that could save countries suffering from food shortages. But even though test results deemed it Safe, its classification as an SCP object prevents us from being able to take it to the outside world," Iris said with a dry smile, her eyes looking off into the distance.

"After all, the Foundation's goal is strictly to Secure, Contain, and Protect. They don't care if it's something wondrous that could help better mankind. As a rule of thumb, it will stay locked up forever under their close observation, never getting to see the light of day. The Foundation owns you until the day you—" she suddenly cut herself off and blatantly changed the topic. "So that's the type of pizza it makes for you, huh? I can see you're a seafood lover! May I have a bite?"

Having already gobbled up her own pizza, Iris was going after mine. Jeez, she didn't need to steal my food.

Wasn't this thing supposed to spit out an infinite quantity of pizza? Why not just pop the lid again?

"Hee hee! Well, actually, it seems this thing isn't horribly flexible. When it does its thing, it always makes a whole new pizza! I don't have enough room to eat that much," she said sadly.

Feeling a bit bad for her, I gave her just one slice of my pizza. Beaming with happiness, she gobbled it down.

"Huh, so this is your favorite type of pizza... One of the interesting features about this box is that it appears to possess a form of telepathy. It uses that ability to ensure it creates the perfect pizza for its holder." Iris spoke cheerfully, but then her face suddenly twisted into a frown. "That darn Dr. Bright—uh, there's a person by that name, someone you might even call a mad scientist—he experimented on SCP-458 by having a bunch of people and sentient SCP objects pop it open just for the fun of it. Supposedly, he was curious to see what he could learn from tracking what kinds of pizza would appear."

Dr. Bright... When she mentioned his name, her expression changed entirely. It was a meaningful scowl, seething with hatred—but at the same time, etched with understated terror.

"As a result of those tests, we've found that the box

cannot produce toppings indigestible to humans. So these are, overall, perfect pizzas—safe to eat, delicious, and healthy! But since pizza is high in calories, be careful not to pig out on them."

Apparently, she was inclined to bring things to an end, now that we were done eating. Iris stood up. She wiped her mouth with the paper napkin and shot me a smile.

"At any rate, the world is full of strange things—SCP objects—like this. We have quite a few here in this facility," she said.

I got the feeling that the pizza box was no accident. Iris had brought me in contact with an SCP object that would serve as a concrete example to support her explanation of the basics. Ever since we first met, she'd been nothing but nice to me. It was surprising, honestly, for her to be so nice. We weren't family or anything. I was a complete stranger. Someone she'd just met.

...Why was she going out of her way for me?

I received my answer sooner than I expected.

"By the way, I mentioned that I am referred to as SCP-105 earlier, didn't I? I am also contained in this facility as an SCP object, since I have a somewhat special ability." So said that perfectly ordinary-looking foreign girl, self-deprecatingly, standing there with her hands on her chest.

Then she pointed at me. "The Foundation has decided to call you SCP-105-C. As you can probably tell from the name, they believe you are either an accessory or somehow related to me as SCP-105," the Girl in the Photos said cryptically. "We aren't just strangers."

SCP-105

Special Containment Procedures: SCP-105 is implanted with a tracking device and is currently housed at Site-17. SCP-105 is currently allowed Class 3 (restricted) socialization privileges with approved site personnel, granted based on continued good behavior and cooperation with Foundation personnel…→For details, refer to the section for SCP-105

SCP-105
["IRIS"]

WHO ARE YOU?

Confidential

WARNING

THE FOUNDATION DATABASE IS CLASSIFIED
ACCESS BY UNAUTHORIZED PERSONNEL IS STRICTLY PROHIBITED
PERPETRATORS WILL BE TRACKED, LOCATED, AND DETAINED

Content relating to the SCP Foundation, including the SCP Foundation logo, is licensed under Creative Commons Attribution-Sharealike 3.0
and all concepts originate from http://www.scp-wiki.net and its authors. SCP Foundation: Iris Through the Looking Glass, being derived
from this content, is also released under Creative Commons Attribution-Sharealike 3.0. To view a copy of the license, please visit
https://creativecommons.org/licenses/by-sa/3.0/ or contact Creative Commons, PO Box 1866, Mountain View, CA 94042, USA.

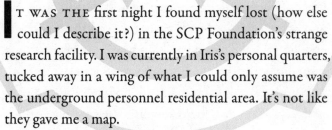

IT WAS THE first night I found myself lost (how else could I describe it?) in the SCP Foundation's strange research facility. I was currently in Iris's personal quarters, tucked away in a wing of what I could only assume was the underground personnel residential area. It's not like they gave me a map.

Either Iris didn't believe in collecting much stuff, or there were restrictions on how much she could own as an SCP object. Whatever the case, her room was extremely barren. It wasn't what I imagined when I pictured a normal girl's room. It lacked any kind of cute, feminine touch.

It was a pretty nice-sized room, just a bit smaller than the classrooms at my high school. Simple wallpaper was plastered on the walls and unappealing carpeting was laid out across the floor. A metal office desk, a locker, and a bed with a pipe frame like something taken from a hospital were placed throughout the room in an arrangement that pleased the eye.

The room was clean, but overall there were so few things that it didn't exactly need tidying to begin with. I thought the place could use some stuffed animals or knick-knacks.

I could tell Iris worked to make the freakishly uninviting room acceptable for a young woman to live in. The books with marked pages, clothes strewn along the walls, wads of paper, juice boxes with the straws sticking out, and other odds-and-ends gave it a lived-in vibe. It was enough to make me aware that I was in a girl's bedroom. Even under the circumstances, I was a bit nervous.

Figuring she didn't want me snooping around, I did my best to keep my eyes focused on Iris. Despite all the times I saw her in the photos, most of them were taken head-on, so it was somewhat refreshing to her other angles.

"███████, how do you customarily decide something in Japan?" Iris asked as she turned to face me after furiously throwing something that she didn't want me to see (maybe panties or her diary...) into the locker. Not really catching her drift, I was at a loss as to how I should answer.

Iris shrugged and patted the bed twice with the palm of her hand. "Bluntly put, there is only one bed in this room. It is, after all, my private room. And sleeping together would not, logically speaking, be very desirable for either of us, would it? Therefore, it is imperative we determine who will obtain the right to sleep upon the bed! Do you understand?" she said, coming across polite and logical, but also rather hard to understand. It was true there was only one bed...and sleeping together would be *bad*.

We weren't in that sort of relationship. But if you asked me to describe the nature of our relationship, I'd struggle to find any answer at all.

At any rate, this was Iris's room, so she should get to sleep on the bed. I was like a freeloader, bumming in on her. Besides, it didn't seem right to enjoy a good night's rest while making a girl sleep on the floor.

There was a good chance I was originally supposed to sleep in that musky cell...and Iris was inviting me into her room out of the kindness of her heart. Getting to stay here was more than enough. I noticed there was a sofa, so I could borrow a blanket and sleep there. I wouldn't be able to sleep fully stretched out on one that small, but it beat rolling around on the floor.

Personally, I was more concerned about sleeping in the same room as a girl, which felt foreign to me. Could I actually fall asleep while hearing the sound of her breathing? I wasn't too sure I could. Simply the thought of it made my pulse race. As a normal, hormonal high schooler who didn't have much luck with girls, this situation was bad for my heart.

"I see, but you really don't need to hold back on my account, 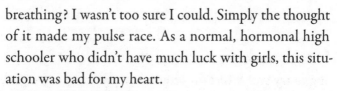," Iris said, her brow knit in concern after hearing out my jumbled opinion. "You're a bit reserved... You don't give your own unvarnished opinion very much, do you? Be more assertive! Do all Japanese come across this way?"

Although she didn't seem happy with the situation, Iris pulled the blanket from her bed. Moving as nimbly as a little animal, she carried it over to me and plopped the blanket in my arms.

"It's too late to argue over the finer details of life. I'm exhausted, so I'm going to bed. Sorry, but please sleep with the blanket on the sofa for today." Pulling open the locker she probably used as a wardrobe, Iris said, "First thing tomorrow, I'll request they either deliver an extra bed or set up a room for you... I'd like to change into my pajamas, so could you turn around?"

As soon as I heard that, I quickly averted my eyes. A moment later, I could hear the sound of cloth rustling. I guess she was changing... Oh, jeez! How did I end up in this situation?

If Iris was going to change right there, then I was going to try and divert my attention as far away as I could. I studied the things in the room in the order they entered my line of sight. The date displayed on the digital clock atop the office desk matched the day I went to the library. I'd randomly teleported (had I?) to a research facility supposedly located in the U.S.A., but that didn't mean I'd traveled to the past or future, too. Well, I guess that was good news.

I realized a bunch of strange things were probably contained within the confines of this research facility. Nevertheless, my normal, lower-middle class mind couldn't handle crazy mumbo-jumbo out of a sci-fi flick happening left and right.

...*What was this?* As my eyes drifted around the part of the office desk that held the digital clock, something caught my attention. True to my stereotypical image of a foreign girl, there was a large corkboard hanging on the wall next to the desk with several photos pinned to it. A bunch of framed photos were also placed across the desk nearby.

Come to think of it, Iris was the Girl in the Photos. She was almost always holding a camera in the photos.

It was such a magnificent, high-end looking Polaroid camera that I was under the vague impression she was either a professional photographer or a hardcore hobbyist.

All of the photos were taken from unique angles, but there were only a handful to be seen. I guess she wasn't snapping away all day, even if she was a shutterbug. With nothing better to do, such relatively trivial thoughts ran through my head.

As far as I could see, there was nothing but landscape photography. That came across to me as the mark of a true hobbyist. Most people liked to take pictures of other people, or themselves, be it in commemorative photos or selfies... Or was all of that unique to Japanese culture?

At any rate, each of the pictures were beautiful. All of them depicted places I had never been. I didn't recognize most of the locations, but I did particularly notice one. It was probably the Grand Canyon. It was one of the greatest, most wondrous vistas around, a place that America took great pride in. As I recalled, that majestic canyon was among the biggest in the world. I'd seen what it looked like on TV. I guess Iris actually went there in person and hit the shutter. As someone whose life was just home and school, I was a bit jealous of her.

...*Huh?* Something didn't feel quite right. I made my way to the corkboard. At first, I thought it was due to the lighting, but one of the photos shone white, preventing me from seeing what it was. It wasn't as if there was a dire need to learn the contents of the photo, but I had nothing better to do while waiting for Iris to finish changing and was somewhat curious.

As I drew near, the answer became clear. No wonder I couldn't tell what it was a picture of. For some reason, it was the only photo pinned backwards.

Either Iris didn't want to look at it and intentionally pinned it up backwards, or she pinned it that way by mistake... If the former, it wouldn't feel right to look without permission, but ultimately my curiosity got the better of me. I reached out for the photo, flipped it over, and took a peek.

It was an impulsive act driven by sheer curiosity. For a long time to come, I would regret ever touching the photo at that moment.

The picture was *crimson red*.

For a split second, I thought it was covered in red paint or something. Or if not, that maybe Iris made a mistake during the shoot that caused the photo to come out red... But neither of these were the case. This shade of red was...blood. It was the color of human blood.

Apparently, this was a murder scene. The grotesque photo showed blood splattered all across the room. Parts were blacked out, as if blood had splattered the camera lens. Thanks to that, I couldn't clearly discern the contents of the picture.

At the very least, it seemed like it was a photo of some kind of room. A common Western-style living room. A pair of human legs looked as if they were growing out of the corner of the photo. Covered in bloody gashes and twisted at unnatural angles, they probably belonged to a corpse.

What the hell? What was this creepy, disgusting photo doing in here...?

"...Is something the matter?" Iris asked. She must have sensed something was amiss, for she turned to face me... or so I thought. I didn't get the chance to find out.

As if the spray of blood in the photo came pouring out, my vision was drowned in the color red. I stumbled, staggered—like a man gone drunk—before falling unconscious.

The air tasted different. My surroundings were filled with a nauseating stench, denser than anything I had ever breathed before. Fighting the urge not to barf, I had to cover my mouth with my hands.

My eyes batted rapidly—I was utterly dumbstruck. This was a completely different location. I was just in

Iris's fairly comfortable, albeit stark, bedroom. Now I was standing somewhere else altogether, like I'd randomly teleported there.

I was struck with a strange sense of déjà vu, despite the fact I had never seen this place before. Oh, duh! I'd just caught a glimpse of this room in that picture... It was the same Western-style living room. Compared to Japanese living rooms, it was pretty spacious, but things were strewn about like a hurricane had blown through.

Popcorn was scattered everywhere. The curtains were tattered and torn. Gouges raced along the walls, floor, and ceiling. The light had fallen from the ceiling and shattered. The club chair was overturned. The piano legs were broken. Dirt was spilling from the overturned houseplant's pot. Cracks ran through the big-screen TV. And then there was all that blood.

Everything was dyed crimson with blood. This was probably the source of the awful stench wafting in the air. It was abnormal, a miserable odor that I would probably never smell if I stayed in peaceful Japan.

Ignorant of the situation and what had transpired, I simply stood there stupefied, unable to so much as force out a scream... And then I heard groaning. Filled with hesitant trepidation, I turned toward the sound of the voice.

In the corner of the room, a man drenched in blood leaned against the wall, his legs sprawled out before him. In the corner of this vandalized room, he was knocking on Death's door.

There was no way he would survive. I didn't know what happened, but I could see his legs and hands were twisted in unnatural angles, and he was bleeding profusely from multiple lacerations across his body. The wounds were made by some kind of sharp blade. Cracks in the wall behind him spread like a spider web, his head substantially caving in on itself.

It looked like a giant monster with jagged claws had crushed this guy before bashing him into the wall... I was no doctor, so I couldn't say anything for certain, but it looked pretty obvious these injuries were fatal. But this man, whom I still didn't know by name at the time, was very much alive.

"*Nnngh*," he muttered incomprehensibly, under his breath.

After a moment's hesitation, curiosity got the better of me. I began to walk toward the man's side. There wasn't much distance between us, but my feet felt heavier with every step. My legs were unsteady, making the path to him long and drawn. I felt dizzy.

Overwhelmed by the strangeness of it all, it took all

I had just to keep from toppling over to one side or the other. Even the slightest jolt would be enough to completely knock me out.

He eyed me through the strands of bloody bangs plastered to his face. "...Run."

Now that I looked more closely, I saw that the blood-drenched victim was actually a young man around the same age as me. I wasn't good at guessing the age of Caucasians, but he might even be younger than me. With his head dropped against his chin and his face covered in blood, it was hard to discern any distinguishing facial features. To top it all off, the room was fairly dark. Apparently, the only light bulb in the room was shattered across the floor, and it was evening outside. Thanks to that, I couldn't see very well.

The same should have been true of the other boy. With all of the blood he'd lost from those severe injuries, he was probably barely hanging on to consciousness. I wouldn't be surprised if he only vaguely sensed someone was standing in front of him.

For some reason, he desperately repeated that one word. "Run. Run. Run."

Thanks to the translation collar around my neck, I was barely able to understand him as he said, "Run. Iris, he's here to kill us."

What could he mean by that...? But I was in no position to debate about the meaning of his words. The next moment, it felt as though something large wrapped itself around my body. And then it pulled me with great force. As it did, I briefly blacked out.

"█████, ████ ! Are you okay? Please say something!"

Once again, my environment changed in the blink of an eye. I'd returned to Iris's room without even knowing it. The stench of blood dissipated as I was embraced by a gentle, bittersweet fragrance.

"What happened? Can you explain in detail? First, let's take some deep breaths!"

The sound of Iris's voice calling out to me sounded awfully close. And little surprise there! Apparently, Iris was holding me tight against her chest. In an unfortunate turn of events, I was laying on top of her! My nose was buried in the cleavage of deceptively ample breasts left exposed by her pajamas.

This was bad! Sensing greater danger than when I was in the room drenched in blood, I slapped my hands on the floor and hastily put some distance between us. I slid on my butt all the way to the wall.

"...Are you okay?" Iris asked, an expression of genuine bewilderment on her face as she looked at me. She nonchalantly straightened her pajamas after noticing they were slightly disarrayed from our encounter and titled her head quizzically.

"The facts I observed are as follows: You just vanished from this room for the duration of a dozen to several dozen seconds. The photograph appeared to absorb you right before my eyes," Iris explained, squatting down—who knows why—while twirling her finger in the air.

"I was so surprised, I walked over to identify the photograph that absorbed you. Whereupon I saw you moving around inside the photo," Iris continued. Somewhat awkwardly, she said, "This is the one." Pinched between her fingertips, she waved the abnormal photo of the blood-drenched room.

"Shocked, I tried touching the animated image of you in the photo. Although it appeared you were moving, there was a possibility my eyes were playing tricks on me. I wanted to verify things for certain. And despite me making it all sound intelligently planned, this was all done purely on impulse, not out of conscious thought."

As if seeing something mystifying, she studied me intently and went on. "When I touched your image, you popped back out. Due to the difference in our physiques,

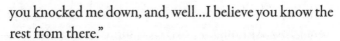

you knocked me down, and, well…I believe you know the rest from there."

The scene in the photo she indicated was identical to the blood-covered room I was in only moments ago. Did I truly go *inside* the photograph…? Was that even possible?

"I speculate that is what transpired, but I don't understand the mechanics behind how. While this photograph is of great enough value and danger that it would prove problematic if discovered in my possession, it has never exhibited the ability to draw people inside," she said.

Apparently, Iris didn't care to touch the photograph a great deal. Deftly rising, she quickly flipped it upside down and left it on the desk for the time being.

"In which case, it would suggest that instead of the *photograph* being special, it is *you* who possesses the ability to travel between the photo-world and reality. When you were placed under initial observation, a similar phenomenon was noted."

When I was placed under initial observation? I wonder if she meant when I first teleported to this research facility. Come to think of it, I felt a similar sense of something warm wrapping around my entire body or coiling around me back then, too.

"Hmmm, I'm afraid conjecture is all we have at this point in time," Iris said. Folding her arms, she groaned, scowling. "Let's ask a trustworthy researcher about this tomorrow. Although I possess personnel clearance, I am not much different from a regular civilian. You should seek assistance from a researcher well-versed in a relevant area of expertise. But it's late now, so I'd like to go to sleep for tonight," Iris finished with a dry smile.

The very next moment, a surprisingly loud round of applause pealed through the air like a firecracker.

"Wonderful!" a resounding young man's voice boomed.

Iris and I practically jumped out of our skins as we turned to face the man. It was like he'd teleported in! He was a physically fit black man somewhere in his thirties. For some reason, he was wearing an outlandishly bright red polo shirt and black pants that glistened with sparkles. I probably shouldn't let it bother me, since this *was* another country, but he was wearing leather shoes, right there in the bedroom! As if that wasn't enough, his head was crowned with a top hat. In contrast to his otherwise gaudy fashion sense, he wore a crisp, white lab coat.

Who was this...? Although my head was reeling, Iris took one look at the man and spat out a rude "Geh!" Distaste for the man was written all over her face.

Seeing her reaction, he shut one eye, as if to say he would turn a blind eye to her. The man continued his applause until he was satisfied. Then he bowed elegantly with hat in hand.

"Sorry to intrude at this late hour! But rest assured, you need not stand on guard, for I am not an assassin! Nor am I an angel or demon! Let alone a magical girl or ninja!" Something must have struck his funny bone, for he burst into a fit of laughter.

"If any of those are more to your taste, I'll change after I redo my big entry. So? How would you like me to look?" There must have been another glitch in the translation collar, because it emitted a strange noise when he said, "change." Whatever he said probably meant something along those lines, but it was unable to translate it perfectly...I guess. Not that I was an expert on the device or anything.

"Dr. Bright," Iris groaned in an exhausted voice, her thumb pressed against her forehead. "I thought you weren't allowed to visit adolescent humans at night in their private rooms. In fact, weren't you prohibited from interacting with adolescent humans at all, due to the bad influence you have on them?"

The term "adolescent humans" seemed like an awfully strange, roundabout way of putting it, but the English word I heard simultaneously issued from Iris was actually "teenagers." It wasn't a word generally used in Japanese to describe that age group.

At any rate, the strange researcher she referred to as Dr. Bright broke out into a broad smile, for some reason. "Oh, Iris! You're as adorable as ever! Don't tell me you not only believe 'The Things Dr. Bright is Not Allowed to do at the Foundation' is an official document recognized by the SCP Foundation, but also expect me to obediently adhere to the rules in that amusing joke of a list! You're so cute!"

"At any rate, isn't it unreasonable to barge into the private space of someone of the opposite gender without setting prior arrangements and receiving permission to enter first?"

"Aha ha ha! You could hold an exhibition displaying all of the unreasonable things collected here, so I'm quite intrigued by what precisely you deem 'unreasonable!' Do please explain it to me logically, so I can ignore it with the elegance of a true gentleman! I will boldly let it go in one ear and out the other...with style."

"You ███████!" Iris shouted ear-bleeding profanity at Dr. Bright, but it must have exceeded the capacity of the translation collar, for it didn't convert the word into something I could understand.

After laughing for a while, Dr. Bright turned his attention to me. I was partially zoned out, pointedly steering clear of their conversation. But when his eyes fell upon me, I was struck by an indescribable cold chill. It was like a finger ran down my spine.

"...Look, I don't know what brought you here, but I bet it's nothing good. Could we resume this at another date?" Iris said, slipping protectively between me and Dr. Bright. "I am honestly extremely tired."

"As you wish! Come, fly into my arms! I'll cradle you to sleep, widdle Iris! My adorable Iris! Daddy will sing you a sweet lullaby!"

"You are not my father. Why, that was genuinely offensive. The next time you make any suggestions that we are related, I will use whatever physical or legal means necessary to completely obliterate your very existence," Iris vehemently spat at Dr. Bright, while he held his arms wide open as if urging her to dive into his chest. Honestly, I was somewhat taken aback by her attitude.

Iris treated me well. She was an overall good person who came across as kind and straightforward. But she treated Dr. Bright on par with a pest caught in the house: with undiluted disgust.

"Okay, it looks like I went a bit too far. You're so uptight, Iris!" Dr. Bright shrugged casually. "Which makes it all the more surprising you've dragged a boy you hardly know into your bedchambers! Do you merely come *across* as uptight, when you're actually secretly one of those creatures so deliciously convenient to us men, commonly referred to as ███████ ?!"

"Ah, if only I was permitted to use a gun."

The two went on bantering back and forth. There was a lot of vocabulary that seemingly couldn't be translated. Scenes like this frequently appeared in foreign comedies, but it was surprising to see people actually talk that way in real life. While it was hardly appropriate given the situation, I couldn't help but feel astonished.

"Heh heh. I can't have you shooting and killing me. It's such a headache, how people seem to think they can kill me at the drop of a hat just because I'm essentially immortal. Where have my rights gone?" Dr. Bright jeered, "Will I find them if I go to the Lost Child Center?"

Never at a loss for words, Dr. Bright continued right on, throwing in some words I didn't understand as he went. "Anyway, in order to sate my academic curiosity—what I'm saying is, it was necessary to my work as a researcher—I planted bugs throughout your room, Iris. Or should I call you SCP-105?"

Hearing this, Iris screamed in such a loud voice I

thought she was trying to break the walls down. "Remove them right now! Right this instant!"

"...But all joking aside, it's only natural for the Foundation—for this facility—to keep mystery boy SCP-105-C—tentative as that moniker may be—under observation. His background is currently unknown." There was that weird title for me again. I definitely wasn't used to it yet.

"I peeked in on you to get a grasp on the situation in here. Comprende? The other personnel are so obsessed with keeping things squeaky-clean, they blocked out their beloved Iris during the changing scene! So have no fear on that account. They really did, honest to God!" Dr. Bright wasn't exactly doing much to inspire confidence.

His mouth kept right on flapping. "Anyway, I've formed a hypothesis regarding his existence. In order to prove it, I would like to conduct a variety of experiments—or to put it more softly, tests. As such, I want you to bring him to my lab first thing tomorrow morning! That was all I came here to say!" He turned before we had a chance to argue, making his lab coat flare (unnecessarily) out behind him.

"Of course, you're free to reject my request, but I'd advise against it, myself. No matter how much you dislike me personally, there is no changing the fact that I am the

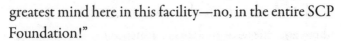

greatest mind here in this facility—no, in the entire SCP Foundation!"

He spoke with an odd confidence, his grin so wide it seemed contrived.

"If you want to know the truth, feel free to ask me! I'll thoroughly explain anything and everything, from 'one plus one' all the way to the simple question 'Did the chicken come before the egg?' From philosophical questions such as 'Why are humans born?' to the ins and outs of where babies come from! None other than *moi*, Dr. Bright, will shed light on all your questions!" He burst into a loud cackle as he opened the door, like any other human being, and walked right out. It felt as if a storm had just blown through.

After Dr. Bright left, Iris and I went straight to bed. Night broke, ushering us into the next morning. This didn't turn into one of those scenarios where I wake up in the morning to sigh in relief at the discovery it was all just a dream. Instead, my eyes snapped open like usual and I had breakfast with Iris.

We ate in the canteen she took me to yesterday. It was fairly crowded with personnel coming in to eat breakfast, or on their way out, having just finished. If their curious stares and the way they were whispering about me behind my back were any indication, everyone here already knew about me. It was a bit unnerving.

This secret research facility supposedly located in the U.S.A. might as well have been another world, as far as I was concerned. The snippets of conversations I overheard went over my head more often than not. Their vocabulary was filled with technical terminology. So when one of the personnel-looking people in the canteen looked at me and said, "What's a Class D doing in here?" I had no idea what to make of it.

After breakfast, Iris addressed that question while we were walking down corridors that seemed to extend forever. She said, "Detailed classifications are assigned to SCP Foundation personnel based on occupational duties. Three major titles you should know include field agent, researcher, and Class D personnel. There are also heavily armed soldiers, but we don't interact much with them in our daily lives. We also have on-site security officers stationed here at all times."

Although Iris seemed rather listless when she first awoke, eating breakfast must have gotten her blood sugar back up. The pep was back in her voice.

"As you can surmise from their name, field agents

live undercover as normal people while they investigate anomalies related to SCP objects and report their findings to the Foundation. Researchers hole up in facilities such as this one and study the objects field agents find."

Iris pulled up the ID card hanging from a lanyard around her neck to show me as she said, "I'm also technically classified as a researcher."

Sure enough, "Iris Thompson/Researcher/Class 3B" was printed on the ID card. Printed in font even larger than her name, the characters "SCP-105" stood out far more than "Iris Thompson."

"Class D personnel are, uh, gosh, they're hard to explain. Honestly, their peculiar existence would generally be considered intolerable by most moral standards." Iris awkwardly skirted around the explanation, so I still wasn't exactly sure what they were.

Apparently having no intention of elaborating further, she hurried on, "You were knocked out immediately after you were found here yesterday and stripped of all your clothing. I suspect a researcher is inspecting them as we speak."

Come to think of it, I'd been struck on the back of my head and knocked unconscious after I first teleported (?) to the research facility yesterday. Now that the pain was gone, I'd nearly forgotten all about that.

"We couldn't leave you naked, so we changed you into a spare Class D uniform we had on hand. That's why the low-clearance-level personnel not informed about you back at the canteen mistook you for Class D personnel."

Pointing to my clothes, Iris said, "That is the Class D uniform right there."

She was referring to the khaki workwear someone changed me into at some point yesterday. I could have sworn that back when I was at that prison-like place, the inmate-looking people I caught glimpses of were also wearing this... Apparently it was the standard uniform for these Class D folk.

Hardy and flexible, it was actually fairly comfortable. But not all that great for sleeping in. I'd taken off the workwear and slept in my underwear with the blanket over me last night.

"I put in a request, so I believe normal clothes should be delivered to my room shortly. You can change later! It isn't wise to wear a Class D uniform more than necessary," Iris said, enigmatically.

I wasn't particularly picky about my clothing, so I was fine with staying in this.

"Moving right along! I wish with all my heart we could avoid turning to him, but you can't make an omelet without breaking eggs. Do you have that idiom in Japan? I'm afraid we have no choice but to take Dr. Bright up on last night's offer and go see him. We have to thoroughly investigate who and what you are."

Iris led me through the facility's nigh identical corridors, occasionally making a turn here or there without ever getting lost. I had no reason to argue and didn't care to leave her side after she'd treated me so well, so I obediently tagged along. Iris's presence served as a shining beacon of comfort in this confusing situation.

"Although Dr. Bright is an unpleasant individual who takes delight in pranks, he is overall brilliant and highly knowledgeable about SCP objects," Iris explained, her voice dripping with distaste as she said his name.

"In general, researchers display great passion and interest in their field of study, and Dr. Bright is...no exception. Fortunately, you probably fall outside of his specialties, so you should be okay."

I wondered what Dr. Bright's specialties were. Our brief conversation last night wasn't enough to offer insight on his true disposition, so it was hard to guess. Going by my superficial first impression, I didn't even think he looked like a researcher. The sole aspect that hinted at his classification was the random lab coat, but even then, he came across more as a comedian than a researcher.

"He's another difficult case to explain... Due to his strong connection with the SCP object known as 'Immortality,' Dr. Bright exists as something no longer quite human. Actually, he's bound to tell you all about himself whether you—what's this?" Iris cut her explanation short, her eyes growing big and round.

She suddenly stopped dead in her tracks, making me nearly crash into her. When I asked what was wrong, Iris unexpectedly dropped to her haunches.

"Wow! Lookie over there, ███. This is our lucky day. There is Bill," she said.

Bill? Who was that? With questions like that running through my mind, I followed her line of sight. And boy, was I in for a surprise. A teddy bear was lying in the middle of the otherwise stoic corridor. It was an adorable stuffed bear. The fluffy fur looked so realistic, I thought it was an actual animal for a split second. But then when I looked closer, I saw it was just a teddy bear. What was a teddy bear doing out here? Did someone lose it?

"No, this is an SCP object. As I recall, it's SCP-1048, Builder Bear. I like to call it 'Bill' for short," Iris said, happily holding her hand out to the teddy bear apparently named Builder Bear.

As if by magic, that perfectly normal-looking stuffed animal, Builder Bear, suddenly moved. It deftly rose onto its round little legs and walked to Iris to snuggle up against her.

Did that stuffed animal just move?!

"Yes, as you can see, Builder Bear is a stuffed bear mysteriously able to move on its own. Manufactured from the same materials as a normal teddy bear, there are no mechanical parts inside. Yet for reasons unknown, it is able to move around as if it were alive," Iris explained. She looked overjoyed as she rubbed her cheek against the stuffed animal.

"Since that is the extent of its anomalous existence, it is perfectly harmless. Deemed Object Class: Safe, it's allowed to freely roam the facility. It's studied as an SCP object since we don't know why it moves, but we generally think of it as the SCP Foundation's cute mascot."

They even had a *mascot*? Well, I guess the SCP Foundation's motto only specified that they "Secure, Contain, and Protect" anomalous entities that surpassed human comprehension. Not all of them would necessarily be dangerous monsters or harbingers of calamity. The mere sight of a girl happily hugging a stuffed animal melted my heart. It was a pleasant, peaceful interlude in the day.

"Oops, this is no time to get distracted. Let's head on over to Dr. Bright's lab... Bye-bye, Bill," Iris said reluctantly as she gently placed Builder Bear on the ground.

Once its feet were firmly planted on the ground, Builder Bear slightly bent at the waist in a bow before waddling down the corridor. Was it really moving on its own, not via remote control? I could barely believe my own eyes. But if I stayed in this research facility, I bet this was just one of many similar encounters waiting for me. It made me realize anew that I was in a mind-boggling world above—or perhaps beyond—all comprehension.

"It's so cute!" Iris squealed.

Iris watched Builder Bear hobble down the corridor until it disappeared around a corner. Bursting with energy from all the cuteness, she roughly began yanking my hand.

"Let's hurry. We're most of the way to Dr. Bright's lab," she urged.

I nodded and was about get moving, my hand still caught in hers...but a cold chill running down my spine made me spin around. That was when I noticed it. Although we thought it was long gone, Builder Bear was peeking its head around the corner. With those lifeless, black eyes, it was staring intently at us...like a carnivore hunting for prey.

"...Is something wrong?" Iris asked. She seemed confused as she followed my line of sight, but Builder Bear quickly ducked back around the corner before she did. Its head didn't pop back out again.

When I fell silent, trying to find the right words to describe the intensely creepy sensation I'd just felt, Iris gave my hand a hearty tug.

"You should brace yourself. Dr. Bright is a bonafide prankster who takes delight in surprising people. I wouldn't put it past him to have a bucket of ketchup ready to fall on us the moment we open the door," Iris warned with a straight face.

Well, I guess we were currently occupied with Dr. Bright. I didn't need to concern myself with Builder Bear. Having come to that conclusion, I quickly forgot all about the strange vibe I had felt.

Dr. Bright's lab was a complete mess. It probably had either the same floor space as Iris's room, or maybe even a little less, a row of computers claiming one of the walls. There was a workbench placed across from the computers with keyboards, test tubes, a brightly colored American comic, a confusing jumble of electronics, and a massive model collection in disarray.

The floor was also in horrible shape. There were countless stacks of magazines, and the trash can was overflowing with hamburger wrappers and crumbled documents. A familiar Japanese handheld game console and one of those toys that you spin around with your finger were carelessly strewn across the floor. Folded clothes were left out in piles.

I thought the sight seemed familiar, but then I realized it reminded me of the room of one my senior high buddies back in Japan who was an otaku. It didn't resemble a lab by a long shot.

The room was designed so Dr. Bright didn't have to leave when he needed his shuteye. Next to the entrance, there was a small door, which seemed to lead to a full bathroom. If the sound of the running water was any indication, Dr. Bright was in the middle of taking a shower. In fact, hazy steam was even spilling out of the room.

"How could he take a leisurely shower after making us come all the way over here?" Iris grumbled in annoyance, glancing at the narrow bed claiming a section of the room. There was an array of comics and junk there too, but she bound them in the comforter and shoved the whole lot off to the corner to clear space to sit down.

SCP FOUNDATION

"It's too much effort to come back later, so let's wait here for him," Iris said, slapping the spot next to her twice.

Catching her drift, I went to sit next to her. We were so close, our shoulders rubbed. It made me a bit nervous, but it couldn't be helped. This was a cramped room! Not only was there nowhere else to sit, there was hardly any room to *walk*.

Hardly talking, we were stuck twiddling our thumbs. After a while, the shower shut off. I couldn't help but hear the rustling of someone drying off with a towel. And then the bathroom door burst open.

"Sorry for the wait! I thought I heard something, but did you honestly come first thing in the morning, Iris?" The voice struck me as odd. It was a woman's voice, but the manner of speech sounded just like Dr. Bright.

My head snapped toward the bathroom in surprise, just as the owner of the voice jumped out the door. It was a woman, not Dr. Bright, randomly talking in a high-pitched voice. A beautiful woman in her prime. Sensuality wafted from her shapely body. I had no idea what country she was from, but her black hair was long and lustrous while her eyes were as crimson as if she sucked blood.

To top it all off, she was practically naked, wearing nothing but the towel wrapped around her. Probably due to just hopping out of the shower, her slightly flushed limbs were still damp—I froze like a deer in the headlights. Noticing my reaction, the mysterious beauty enjoyed screaming, as if on cue, "Eek! You're such a pervert, big bro!"

...Say what? While I was left too stunned to react, the mysterious beauty blinked in confusion several times.

"Huh? What's this? I didn't get much of a rise out of you! I guess the expressions in anime and manga are exaggerated, after all. Well, it *is* biologically programmed in humans to freeze upon suddenly encountering the unexpected! It's not all that often that 'truth is stranger than fiction!'"

"...Dr. Bright," Iris snapped, sounding completely exasperated. "What purpose does this serve?"

"A philosophical question! I can't answer that, since I am a *scientific* researcher, not a philosopher. But if I were to answer nonetheless, well, it's my usual fun and games."

The mysterious beauty laughed heartily, flapping her hands in the air before returning to the bathroom. Back up! Didn't Iris just call her Dr. Bright? I could have sworn Dr. Bright looked like a completely different person when I met *him* last night. Their gender and race were totally different. What was going on here...?

A bit later, the mysterious beauty referred to as Dr. Bright reappeared after taking her(?) time getting dressed. They shared the same fashion sense as the black Dr. Bright I met last night. For some odd reason, they were garbed in an ostentatious bright red dress, as if about to depart for a ball. The bra strap intentionally slipped over the tip of one shoulder was a rich black. This strange beauty clad in the black and red color scheme grabbed a folding chair that was set off to the side, unfolded it, and sat crassly with their legs spread wide open. Then they smiled elegantly at Iris and me as we sat huddled cozily together on the bed.

"I didn't give you a proper introduction yesterday, so I might as well start over with my name," the mysterious beauty began—soon proving that the only feminine thing about them was their appearance. "The SCP Foundation has the immense honor of employing me, Dr. Jack Bright, the greatest mind in all the world! Feel free to simply call me Jack, uh... ███████, was it?"

Even though I didn't recall sharing my name, they somehow knew what it was. It went to show that the Foundation was taking measures to keep an "unidentified" person such as myself under observation without my noticing. In which case, this mysterious beauty who called herself—himself(?)—Dr. Jack Bright was cleared to view the data collected on me through such means.

"Hmmm. I expected Iris to go over this beforehand, but my existence is somewhat unique. I can copy my personality onto other people. But that doesn't really paint much of a picture for you, does it?"

Dr. Bright (or so I'd decided to call him...her?) picked up a handheld game console on the floor and popped out the cartridge with the ease of familiarity.

"Let's say this cartridge is the personality belonging to me, Dr. Bright. Couldn't you insert the cartridge in any of these handheld game consoles scattered across the world and play the same game? It's the same concept," Dr. Bright explained.

I wondered what exactly that meant. But at least I got the general gist of what Dr. Bright was saying.

"That is what has happened to me, due to the unique characteristics of SCP-963, Immortality. If you get that general concept, you're good," Dr. Bright said, before leaning forward to emphasize all that cleavage.

"I thought you would appreciate feasting your eyes on this beauty rather than that Class D brute while we talked. I did this with you in mind, so you're welcome to show some appreciation! I mean, aren't you Japanese into this sort of thing? What do you call it again, *moe*? Anyway, that! Aha ha ha!" The longer Dr. Bright prattled on about irrelevant garbage, the more they got under my skin.

"I actually would have preferred a cuter little girl, but I have the damndest time getting permission to possess young children! If only I'd had the chance to possess a wider variety of ethnicities, ages, and nationalities before the Foundation came to fully understand my unique characteristics!"

"...Dr. Bright, I'm sick of listening to your drivel. Can you move on to the main agenda?" Iris sounded more than a little annoyed as she put an end to Dr. Bright's tirade, one that would undoubtedly have continued on forever if left alone. "We didn't come all the way here to have a fun chat. If you expect people to call you 'Doctor,' please live up to the title."

"Of course, I am well aware of what the job entails. I'm sure you still have plenty of questions, but I'll have to tell you more about myself in detail at another date and time...under the covers! Aha ha ha ha!"

In retribution for all of Dr. Bright's inappropriate comments, Iris grabbed a slipper off the ground and chucked it at the beauty. Upon elegantly dodging the slipper, Dr. Bright made a show of sensually crossing their legs.

"Anyway, no one at the Foundation foresaw the existence of SCP-105-C—that's you, ▇▇▇▇▇—and hence, our research has only just begun. I don't possess all of the answers myself, so I would like to conduct each test with the utmost caution and care as we uncover your true nature," Dr. Bright declared.

"That is actually something I would appreciate," Iris reluctantly agreed, nodding. "So long as you promise not to dissect him or subject him to dangerous experiments, I would be willing to offer my cooperation. I'm afraid the two of us don't have what it takes to find the answers on our own."

I was of a similar mind. I was completely ignorant as to how or why I wound up in this American research site. Although I was worried about leaving my fate in the hands of this mad scientist, if Dr. Bright could give me the answers to my questions, I had no qualms about helping.

"Uh-huh. If possible, personally, I'd love to conduct amusing tests until I've gotten them all out of my system, but each and every SCP object is invaluable—truly one of a kind! I have absolutely no intention of ruining one in violent experimentation," Dr. Bright proclaimed.

A rather serious expression washed over Dr. Bright's face as they looked at me with an intellectual gleam in their eyes. They continued, "If you two are willing to offer your assistance, I'll make headway by leaps and bounds. Now that I've established communication with my test subjects, I can proceed with this case with greater peace of mind than the majority of SCP objects, seeing as I won't have to constantly fear for my life."

The strange researcher licked their lips before saying passionately, "So where should we begin?"

After that, Iris and I gave a detailed report of all of our experiences leading up to that moment. Dr. Bright occasionally interjected with a question, but methodically typed away at the PC without interrupting us for the most part. I guess they were compiling an interview log or writing a report. It was far more tedious and lackluster than I'd imagined... I'd been bracing myself for some sort of extreme test.

"Fascinating!" Dr. Bright declared once we finished giving our reports, eyes shining like a child. "Heh heh! We've gleaned essentially all there is to know regarding SCP-105, Iris, so the Foundation deemed it unlikely we would discover new elements regarding her. I'm thrilled to see you've given us yet another new mystery!"

"That wasn't my intent," Iris groaned, sounding genuinely annoyed. "And why are we being treated as a set?

What is the relationship between ▮▮▮▮ and me? Even if it's just a hypothesis, could you tell me why?"

"Sure. He—▮▮▮▮—is considered a new anomaly generated by the SCP object known as SCP-105, 'Iris.' At least, that's what the higher-ups have decided for the time being. That's why he is tentatively named SCP-105-C," Dr. Bright explained, before taking a short pause and turning to Iris. "How much have you told him about your own unique trait?"

"Hardly anything... There wasn't any time yesterday. And today we woke up, got dressed, ate breakfast, and came straight here. I never had the chance to tell him," Iris explained apologetically.

In all honesty, I currently saw Iris as just a straight-forward girl who treated me warmly. As of yet, nothing about her came across as an anomalous SCP object.

"I see. But if we're going to collaborate on this investigation and research henceforth, we should make learning that a prerequisite instead of leaving him in the dark. As I said before, the two of you are contextually viewed as the same anomalous phenomena... Would you like me to provide a brief explanation?"

Dr. Bright motioned to Iris with the palm of their hand as they said, "She—Iris Thompson—is an ESPer, in a sense. Science cannot begin to explain her paranormal abilities."

Really? When I shot Iris a sidelong glance, she nodded her head.

"It would be much quicker if I could actually show you... But I'm not supposed to use my powers very much. So I don't have SCP-105-B, which is necessary to activate my powers, or any of the photos taken with it on hand," Iris said.

"Couldn't you activate your powers to a certain extent with a normal photo?" Dr. Bright asked.

"It's not impossible, but it doesn't always work. It really needs to be my camera and a photo taken with it."

Their exchange went right over my head, but Dr. Bright nodded. "I thought that might be the case, so I took the liberty of removing SCP-105-B from its safety deposit box beforehand."

With the childish grin of someone who'd just pulled off a little prank, Dr. Bright slipped their hand under the bed and pulled out an attaché case. It popped open with surprising ease. Nestled inside was none other than the ancient camera Iris was always holding when I saw her as the Girl in the Photos.

"Ah, my camera!" Iris exclaimed, eyes bulging. She effortlessly pulled the camera out of the case and cradled it. Apparently that camera meant a great deal to her. She touched it with loving care.

"Heh heh! I explained that it was necessary for testing and filled out the paperwork to formally retrieve it. I received permission without a hitch. To be fair, you never stir up any trouble and this camera isn't particularly dangerous. The fact that I was the one retrieving it was actually considered more of a cause for concern," Dr. Bright explained, looking touched as they watched Iris.

"As you can see, SCP-105-B is a perfectly normal camera. It's a Polaroid OneStep 600 camera that was manufactured in 1982, although I doubt that means anything to you. It does not appear to have any out-of-the ordinary physical characteristics and appears to be, for all intents and purposes, a normal Polaroid camera, operating normally for all persons aside from Iris."

Sure enough, nothing about that camera stood out as abnormal. As a modern-day man accustomed to taking pictures with my smart phone, it was full of rustic charm, but I probably would have felt that way about any antique.

"Iris, why don't you try your powers on something?"

"Oh, okay... I'll just take a quick snapshot."

At Dr. Bright's suggestion, Iris rose and moved about the room, eyeing it like a highly experienced cameraman,

before taking a quick picture. The flash went off, its blinding light making me close my eyes for a second. Since it was a Polaroid camera, it popped out a picture that quickly developed.

Apparently, Iris took a picture of a model on Dr. Bright's workbench. It was a masterfully sculpted monster. Not just me, but anyone from Japan would be able to recognize the character of this model: Godzilla. For just a quick snapshot, the tremendous impact of the photo suggested that Iris's camera work was phenomenal. Nevertheless, it was just a photo. There was nothing peculiar about it.

"Please watch this photo carefully," Iris said, showing the picture to me as she returned to her spot on the bed.

"Allow me to lend a hand," Dr. Bright offered, stood up, and walked over to the real Godzilla model. Then they waved their hand in the air. "Can you see me?"

I was blown away! In the photo, Dr. Bright's hand was traveling by the image of Godzilla. They started horsing around, jumping across the photo and making goofy faces.

"Now do you see? In Iris's hands, the photograph changes from a still image to real-time video," Dr. Bright explained.

I had to admit, the photo in Iris's hands looked less like a photograph and more like a small screen displaying a video. The images in the photo were actually moving! That was all there was to it, but that alone was mysterious enough.

"I can also reach through the photograph and manipulate objects within reach of the original point at which the photograph was taken...like this," Iris said.

When she pressed her hand against the surface of the photo, something peculiar happened. A black hole—or something that looked like one—opened up next to the Godzilla model she photographed. From the black hole, out came what appeared to be Iris's hand. With the tip of one finger, she flicked the model over.

"Ah, how could you?! That's the extremely rare *Godzilla vs. Biollante* edition!" Dr. Bright cried hysterically, but Iris ignored the researcher and smiled at me.

"It might be a bit confusing, but these are my powers. They come in pretty handy. Distance has no influence on them, so even after we leave this room...even if we went to the other side of the planet, I could still manipulate the contents of this room through the photo," Iris explained.

She turned to shoot Dr. Bright a triumphant grin, threatening, "I can move everything within reach of the original location of the photo. If you do anything unsavory or try tricking us into any weird tests, I will crush your beloved models one at a time, Dr. Bright."

"You wouldn't! You're a monster! A child conceived by a ▓▓▓▓ murderer who ▓▓▓▓ a swine!" Dr. Bright roared. Either the translation collar was having trouble with the crass vocabulary or it couldn't understand what the words meant, but I could tell they were dissing Iris.

"Ugh! I need to move anything that would prove problematic if broken outside of Iris's range—out of her reach," Dr. Bright exclaimed with teary eyes, running every which way, a bundle of models lovingly cradled in their arms.

As Iris happily watched that go down (I was a little freaked out from catching a glimpse of her scary side...), she returned to the topic at hand. "▓▓▓▓, you were appearing in all of the photographs I took of late with SCP-105-B—this camera—for experimental purposes."

With the topic turned to me, I straightened my back and gave her my full attention.

"I swear, I do not remember seeing you when I took the pictures. Nevertheless, you always appeared in them without fail... In order to pursue the truth behind the mystery of that strange phenomenon, I followed the instructions of the researcher with me and touched you."

Iris pushed on, informing me that all happened yesterday.

"When I did, I somehow *pulled* you out of the photo...

Although I can manipulate things I touch in the pictures, I have never been able to pull something out. Ever. It's unprecedented...and we don't know what to make of it."

"Our current objective is to investigate the mechanism behind how this works," Dr. Bright chimed, joining the conversation now that they were done moving all of the models to a corner of the room.

"You only appeared in photos taken by Iris. Furthermore, she was able to pull you out of the photograph when utilizing her ability to manipulate the photo-world. Taking these facts into consideration, you were tentatively named SCP-105-C as an anomaly related to SCP-105."

Upon returning to the folding chair, Dr. Bright studied me, a passionate gleam in their eyes as they continued, "I wonder what you are...? For the record, after you were knocked out, we checked your clothes, personal possessions, and every inch of your body. We even took blood and DNA samples for testing, but all of the results so far claim that you are a normal human."

Yeah, no surprise there. The thought that they took my blood for analysis while I was out cold was terrifying, but I was a perfectly normal human. Nothing strange had

SCP FOUNDATION

ever come up in any of the school physicals. I was just like any other normal high school boy out there.

"And as a fascinating case in point...didn't you enter a photo last night?"

We told Dr. Bright about that incident when giving our detailed reports earlier. Last night, the moment I casually touched a photo that was turned over, I got zapped to that blood-drenched room. Then a man covered in blood, breathing his last breaths, talked to me. Ingrained deep in my brain, I could still hear his voice: "Run. Run. Run. Iris, he's here to kill us."

Who was that man? How did he know Iris's name...? Why was he so grievously injured?

"Just to make sure, was this the man covered in blood?" Dr. Bright placed a laptop on their lap and fiddled with it for a moment before turning the screen to face me. It displayed a large portrait of some man's face.

I wasn't sure why, but Iris's face crumbled in sadness at the sight of it. Although I was curious, I turned back to the screen and nodded. I didn't get a clear look at the man's face since his head was lowered and his visage was covered in blood, but it was probably the same person. The eyes, nose, and mouth were all the same. I wasn't very good at telling foreigners apart, but no matter how much I wanted to, I would never be able to forget what I saw in that bloody room... I could say with fairly strong confidence it was the same person.

"I thought so," Dr. Bright said, twisting their lips as they nodded knowingly. "Information regarding him is classified, so I can't divulge his name, but he was someone Iris knew. Several years ago, a terrifying SCP object murdered him."

I see... So he passed away. I wasn't surprised. It was obvious just by looking at the man that his injuries were fatal. But hold up; he was killed several *years* ago? Didn't he just talk to me last night...?

"That was a photo of the crime scene. Or to be more precise, the camera was at the scene of the murder and happened to catch the final moments when it was knocked or dropped to the ground. In other words, there was a chance he was still alive when the picture was taken," Dr. Bright said excitedly, teeth showing in a too-wide grin.

"This could be the last picture taken of him still alive. After intense pleading and dogged negotiations, Iris made several concessions in exchange for keeping it on display in her room."

"......"

Iris was struck speechless. It felt as if she were on the verge of tears—my heart went out to her. Honestly, I thought that photo was too grotesque to keep on display in her room. And in fact, she constantly kept it flipped over, as if she herself didn't want to see it... If she went to such lengths to obtain a photo she didn't even want to look at, it was safe to assume that guy meant a great deal to Iris.

"Yes, yes...! I think I'm beginning to understand. The synapses in my gray matter are on fire again today," Dr. Bright declared with a satisfied nod, before pulling a photo from the pocket of their lab coat. "I should know for sure if we conduct a little experiment. That having been said, ▮▮▮▮, would you be so kind as to touch this photo for a second?"

Iris seemed a bit rattled at the moment and I was busy worrying about her. Distracted, I did as asked without thinking. Dr. Bright probably had this whole conversation scripted out beforehand, probing us along with this goal in mind. I fell right into that mad scientist's hands—and touched the photo.

Iris noticed before I did it. She cried out: "Don't!"

She tried to warn me, but it was too late.

I briefly blacked out, and my surroundings changed.

SCP-823
[CARNIVAL OF HORRORS]

SCP-105

Special Containment Procedures: SCP-105 is implanted with a tracking device and is currently housed at Site-17. SCP-105 is currently allowed Class 3 restricted socialization privileges with approved Site personnel, granted based on continued good behavior and cooperation with Foundation personnel. →For details, refer to the section for SCP-105

IRIS THROUGH THE LOOKING GLASS

WARNING ....

THE FOUNDATION DATABASE IS CLASSIFIED
ACCESS BY UNAUTHORIZED PERSONNEL IS STRICTLY PROHIBITED
PERPETRATORS WILL BE TRACKED, LOCATED, AND DETAINED

Confidential

Content relating to the SCP Foundation, including the SCP Foundation logo, is licensed under Creative Commons Attribution-Sharealike 3.0 and all concepts originate from http://www.scp-wiki.net and its authors. SCP Foundation: Iris Through the Looking Glass, being derived from this content, is also released under Creative Commons Attribution-Sharealike 3.0. To view a copy of the license, please visit https://creativecommons.org/licenses/by-sa/3.0/ or contact Creative Commons, PO Box 1866, Mountain View, CA 94042, USA.

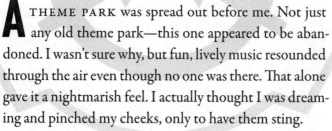

A THEME PARK was spread out before me. Not just any old theme park—this one appeared to be abandoned. I wasn't sure why, but fun, lively music resounded through the air even though no one was there. That alone gave it a nightmarish feel. I actually thought I was dreaming and pinched my cheeks, only to have them sting.

I looked around me. Theme parks weren't exactly places I went to a great deal. I could only vaguely remember when my parents took me as a child to a certain famous theme park that built a branch in Japan. Nevertheless, I saw them enough on TV to tell that this was one.

As a large-scale theme park, it appeared to have all of the usual attractions (was that the right word?) I might expect to find. There was a rollercoaster in the center

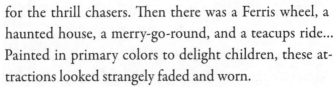
for the thrill chasers. Then there was a Ferris wheel, a haunted house, a merry-go-round, and a teacups ride... Painted in primary colors to delight children, these attractions looked strangely faded and worn.

All of the attractions and stalls that entered my sight were rotting away, rust corroding the metal parts. The handful of benches I noticed were filled with holes or broken down the middle. Fruit flies buzzed around the fountain, which was filled with either lichen or sludge.

Overall, the place was in ruins. And as I first suspected, not a soul was to be found. Not even Iris or that yappy Dr. Bright were with me anymore. Taking that into consideration, I began to form an inkling of what happened.

I'd gone inside another pictured, hadn't I? Right before my vision switched to this scenery, I'd touched that photograph Dr. Bright held out to me. What if that served as the trigger, making me go into the picture just as I had the previous night with the room covered in blood? The idea that I could enter photos was nothing more than a theory proposed by Dr. Bright, and I still didn't get how that worked... But assuming that was what happened helped ease my nerves some. Scientific formulas and mathematical equations might not be able to prove this anomalous occurrence, but this wasn't my first time experiencing it. I knew how to get back this time, too.

When Iris touched the image of me in the picture last night, I returned to her room—I was drawn back to her. I had no choice but to believe she would pull me back the same way again. Looking up at the sky, I tried shouting her name countless times.

But she didn't help.

She didn't even call back.

I started to get nervous. I swung my head wildly like a lost child, calling out for her as if I were searching for my mom. But no matter how long I waited, there was no sign of me returning to that lab.

What should I do? I was suddenly in a bind. I felt like the world before me was going black.

It didn't seem like I was in any imminent danger, but I couldn't simply stand there forever. In the worst-case scenario, it wouldn't be too long before I started to starve.

Although the mysterious theme park looked like desolate ruins, it was nonetheless a creation of the modern, civilized world. It wasn't as if I was dumped in a jungle or desert. For the time being, I needed to get out, find someone, borrow their phone, and call for help. If this was a developed country, the police or whatever form of law enforcement they had ought to be able to help me out. Fortunately, the translation collar was still fixed about my neck, so communication shouldn't be a problem. I wasn't sure if the device would work if this wasn't an English-speaking country, but lucky for me, English was said to be the international language...

Anyway, I was going to find someone and borrow their phone. Then I was going to call someone dependable. Having decided on my course of action, one that admittedly relied far too heavily on the benevolence of others, I found the confidence I needed to take my first step.

"Freeze!" yelled a deep voice, as something hard pushed up against my back.

"Slowly raise your hands," the terrifying voice ordered from behind me. Unfamiliar with such situations, I foolishly tried to turn around out of habit.

Raised in the gun-free society of Japan, it wasn't drilled into me to immediately do as told when someone said, "Raise your hands." Alas, my actions proved all too rash.

Sounding like a beast, the person behind me roared something incomprehensible to the translation collar. He flung me to the ground and was straddling me a second later. He pulled my arms behind me and tied them behind my back. A moment later, my entire body was struck with unbelievably sharp pangs of pain. I cried out in agony.

"Shut your trap!" he snapped sternly. Scared, I fell silent.

Someone was sitting astride my back, putting all his weight on me. If that weren't bad enough, he was applying pressure with something lumpy, maybe his knees. Damn, that really hurt…! The places I scraped on my cheeks and lips when I was knocked over stung, making it hard to form any coherent sentences.

What was going on? What was this? I was so confused!

"Huh? Isn't he Class D?" came the surprised voice of a flippant-sounding young man. Something hard (was it the muzzle of a gun?) was pushed firmly against my head, preventing me from looking up to see what the owner of the voice looked like.

"You're right, that is their uniform. Huh?" the person on my back (a middle-aged man, seemingly) responded. From the sound of it, several people had surrounded me during the course of all this. Their voices flew back and forth over my head for a while. "That's strange. I didn't think any Class Ds were sent on this mission."

"But that's our uniform. Look, you can see the Foundation logo," the flippant-sounding man said as he flipped up the collar of my khaki workwear. Apparently, the Foundation's logo was printed on it somewhere around there.

Seeing that, the man plunked on my back exclaimed in surprise, "Well I'll be... Wait, I'll contact the Foundation. It's possible this Class D is a survivor from another team we weren't advised about. Likely we aren't the first to investigate the Carnival of Horrors."

The Carnival of Horrors...? Yeah, that didn't inspire confidence.

"Damn! I can't establish a connection. What the hell is going on? Can either of you get through on your radios?"

"No good here, Sir. Honestly, I don't see why we don't just ask him. Push comes to shove, we can shoot the Class D twerp if he does anything suspicious."

"He might be Class D, but a human life is still a human life. I don't think we should treat him like a consumable resource. For the record, I can't get through either, Commander."

That last voice belonged to a young woman. All of them seemed to be speaking in English, but thanks to my translation collar, I was able to make out what they were saying.

"All right... C'mon, on your feet."

The weight of the person sitting astride my back let up. I guess the "Commander" climbed off of me. After having him weighing down on my lungs, I couldn't help but cough as I slowly stood up. Although it was a bit late now, I held my hands up as I rose.

"Huh? Isn't he just a kid...?" the owner of the flippant voice said, suspiciously furrowing his brow. Apparently, he had been standing right in front of me the whole time. His fuzzy hair was the color of carrots, and freckles speckled his baby-faced features. A Caucasian man, probably in his late twenties. His clothing was something a soldier might wear—he was clearly in the armed forces.

The man was wearing a camouflage jacket and matching pants. His helmet was in a similar print. There was a pouch and handgun strapped to his waist. Some model of machine gun was slung over his shoulder. I wasn't sure why, but he had leather straps wrapped over his body fitted with countless shells of ammo.

"A lot of Asians look younger than they are," came the crisp woman's voice. When I turned to face her, I saw she was a woman in her early twenties wearing essentially the same attire as the man with the flippant voice. She had dark brown skin and dark eyes with a bluish tinge. Her black hair was tightly tied back. I have no idea what they represented, but I noticed heart tattoos on both of her hands peeking out of her jacket. She was keeping a lookout, hiding in the shadows of one of the flower gardens. Though there wasn't a flower to be seen, there. The mounds of reddish-brown dirt indicated the flowers either withered away or were never planted to

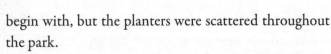

begin with, but the planters were scattered throughout the park.

"Nah, he really is just a boy. I can tell by the way he's acting. I'd say he's about the same age as my kid back home," the person referred to as "Commander" said with a groan.

The commander was a brawny giant of a man who came across as overall harsh. His hair and eyes were the color of the desert. A deep crease ran across his brow along with a scar. Clad in military fatigues, with a helmet identical to the other two, he was outfitted pretty similarly at a glance. Yet all of his guns were broken in—they showed the nicks and wear of use. It gave the impression he was no stranger to the battlefield.

These three were the only ones near me, but all of them were overpowering in a way I had never experienced in my peaceful high school life. They gave off dangerous vibes. The air felt heavy.

"Who are you? Are you with the SCP Foundation?" the commander asked on behalf of the unit in a tone that broached no nonsense.

Pathetic as it was, I started trembling as I answered incoherently. I think I stuttered something as shaky as a child first learning to speak. I only managed something along the lines of stringing out my name, Iris's name, and Dr. Bright's name... But it had a dramatic effect.

The commander groaned with disgust. "Dr. Bright?"

As if those were the magic words, the tension in the air suddenly dissipated, replaced with apathy. It was as if they thought remaining wary of me was a stupid waste of energy.

"That man's shenanigans can be a pain in the ass. I bet he deployed a Class D outfitted with observation equipment since he couldn't participate in the survey. Unauthorized, I'll wager," the commander groaned.

"Now that you mention it, I got the feeling he was chomping at the bit to come," mentioned the flippant man.

"A troublesome ally can be far worse than any foe," the woman said.

All three spat their baleful comments before turning to me with sympathy in their eyes. And then they said things along the lines of, "You've had it rough, haven't you?"

Huh? What was this all about...? What was so horrible about Dr. Bright? I didn't know what was going on, but it filled me with foreboding. I got the feeling I should be a little more careful about dealing with that mad scientist, going forward...

A bit later...

As things worked out, it was ultimately decided that I would move out with these three. They claimed they were soldiers in service of the Foundation Task Force Rho-71, AKA, the "Origami Toads."

The SCP Foundation employed countless such task forces (just like in the military), which were dispatched to deal with emergencies. It commanded vast military forces equipped with cutting-edge weaponry, enough that it could easily neutralize an entire area the size of a small town.

Come to think of it, wasn't the SCP Foundation a massive secret organization that covered the entire world...? It sounded so absurd—like something out of a manga—that it made me want to laugh, but the three before me were obviously trained soldiers. The guns they were equipped with were probably the real deal.

Nonetheless, the commander claimed sardonically that their guns wouldn't do them a bit of good against a truly dangerous SCP object. Even so, any of them could probably break my neck in a matter of seconds, so I had no choice but to quietly do as they said.

They seemed to think I was a Class D dispatched on a whim by Dr. Bright. They let me off pretty much un-scathed since we were on the same side, and allowed me to accompany them. Their attitude toward me softened and they actually treated me fairly well. They were surprisingly nice people.

Still, I couldn't help but wonder what the deal was with Class D personnel... Iris never did give me a proper explanation, so I didn't know what their classification entailed. Although I was curious, this didn't seem like the right time to ask. The three soldiers were quietly making their way through the theme park as they whispered or made various signals.

They let me move with them, but they had no intention of protecting me. Their brisk pace seemed to say, "We'll leave you behind in a heartbeat if you can't keep up." I was a normal high schooler; naturally, I never went through boot camp. Just struggling to keep from getting left behind had me winded.

"...Commander, why don't we take a quick breather?" The woman soldier saluted before offering that proposal, out of concern for me.

"I personally think we should pull out. This place gives me the heebie-jeebies. For an amusement park, it isn't very amusing. The whole place is like one big haunted house." Rather than the commander, it was the young soldier who responded, taking the lead with a harsh grimace on his face. They never told me their names, so their roles were the only way I could distinguish them.

"Hmmm."

The commander came to a halt and called into his walkie-talkie several times.

"I still can't get through. If at all possible, I would like to rendezvous with the rest of the unit. If we don't find anyone after sweeping the area, I'll consider pulling out," the commander said.

From the sound of it, other members of their squad were sent here as well. I could only assume as much from the snippets of their conversation I happened to overhear. But for some reason or other, they got split up and were currently in the middle of wandering this abandoned theme park, trying to regroup. But why? Why were fully outfitted soldiers sent to such a forlorn, decrepit theme park?

"I take it you weren't told anything," the female soldier kindly indicated, assuming as much from my perplexed expression. She sounded polite, treated me with consideration, and was a woman besides. The combination somehow reminded me of Iris.

I wondered what Iris was doing at the moment. Why was she leaving me in the photo (I thought) instead of pulling me back out? Was there also trouble on the other side—the world outside of the photo?

I was merely growing apprehensive and a little lonely, but the woman soldier mistook the look on my face for fear. In an attempt to bolster my courage, she offered me a heartening smile. "It'll be okay. We're professionals, trained to handle any situation. I'm sure you'll make it back safe and sound."

"Even if he does, the only thing waiting for him back there is his own execution. The kid's Class D," the young soldier said ominously, laughing as if it were the funniest thing in the world.

Execution? What was he talking about…?

"Hey, cut the chitchat," the commander snapped at the two like a schoolteacher. A moment later, he sighed. "Don't forget we're in the middle of a mission. But I have to admit, we won't get anywhere walking around aimlessly. That open café will serve as base while we take a quick break," he said, jutting his chin toward a place that certainly resembled one. Out of business for ages, the creepy store was reduced to a jumble of tables and chairs, the tattered and torn tablecloths fluttering like the hands of the deceased.

"I wouldn't get my hopes up for a good cup of coffee… but at least we can use it as shelter while we try to get our radios up again. If at all possible, I want to make contact with the others. If it doesn't seem feasible, we'll resort to more primitive methods, like burning some of this crap to send smoke signals."

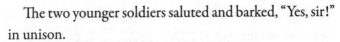

The two younger soldiers saluted and barked, "Yes, sir!" in unison.

What a relief! I was glad to hear we were going to take a break. Utterly exhausted simply from following them, it was music to my ears. The soles of my feet started aching quite a while ago.

"You don't seem to know anything, so I'm going to quickly fill you in." The woman soldier slowed to match my pace. Her eyes were fixed on the other two, who rushed ahead to the open café. They began rummaging through the chairs—probably to find ones with the structural integrity to support a person's weight, so they could sit and rest.

"This theme park is SCP-823, also known as the Carnival of Horrors. The entire park is a dangerous SCP object with the Object Class: Euclid."

The entire park was an SCP object, an anomalous place that surpassed all logic...? It didn't seem like one so far. It was creepy, but only because it was in ruins.

"That's right. At a glance, it looks no different from an abandoned theme park you could find anywhere," she agreed.

I didn't think you could find something like this just *anywhere,* but I didn't disagree out loud. She was only explaining out of the kindness of her heart, and I wanted to learn as much as I could. If I remained ignorant, my fear and anxiety would only increase.

The woman soldier spoke in an emotionless voice that reminded me of a TV announcer. "It was shut down and abandoned after several violent events resulting in the deaths of park attendees. To be precise, 231 attendees were killed, and another seven injured or maimed."

I could barely believe my ears. That was a huge disaster... The number of lives lost here was in the triple digits. Why? How in the world did that happen?

"Every one of the deaths was bizarre. For instance, the unicorn on the merry-go-round broke from its support beam and plunged toward an attendee standing in front of it. The attendee died, impaled by the unicorn's horn."

It was hard to believe she seriously meant someone actually died in such an implausible way. What would get put down on the death certificate? "Died instantly due to impalement by unicorn?" What would he tell everyone when he got to the other side? But seriously, this was no joking matter.

"For reasons unknown, an attendee on the freefall ride 'Scream Machine' removed his safety harness and jumped

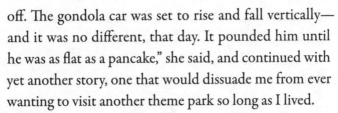

off. The gondola car was set to rise and fall vertically—and it was no different, that day. It pounded him until he was as flat as a pancake," she said, and continued with yet another story, one that would dissuade me from ever wanting to visit another theme park so long as I lived.

"If the nature of the accidents was limited to those examples, they could be attributed to design flaws in the attractions... However, there were other incidents. Stranger ones."

Talking must have joggled her memory, for she quickly moved from one incident to the next. "For example, a couple on the teacups ride inexplicably *melted* while it was spinning at high speeds... When the ride came to a stop, the cup was full of their boiling blood."

That was definitely crazy. There was no rational explanation for that.

I was starting to understand why the park had earned its Euclid classification.

"There was also an instance where a ride operator saw all of the passengers on the Ferris wheel turn into infants when it suddenly spun backwards one rotation. It proceeded to resume turning in the correct direction, but at an accelerated speed. This time, all of the passengers disembarked as seniors," she said, adding that several of them consequentially passed away due to old age.

There was no hope of rationalizing something like that. I was smack in the middle of a theme park where such strange things happened one after the next. Overcome with horror, I began to tremble.

Afraid she went too far when she saw me shaking in my boots, the woman soldier covered her mouth with both hands and fell silent. She flashed me a quick look with her eyes that seemed to say, "I'm sorry."

"These aren't the most pleasant stories to hear, are they…? Anyway, the theme park shut down after there was a slew of such incidents. Since its closure, pretty much all of the tourists and urban explorers who occasionally wander in here have fallen prey to it and died. Not even the Foundation knows exactly how many victims it has claimed."

Why would anyone wander into such an obviously dangerous theme park? I'd be way too scared to go anywhere near it.

"Well, some foolish kids like it for the thrill, since it's a famous horror spot. It's also located by a rather densely populated town. Some people try to slip through as a shortcut."

The commander grunted. "That's precisely why the SCP Foundation can't wipe it off the face of the Earth with an air strike, even though it's an obviously dangerous

SCP object. It'd take a toll on the civilian population and surrounding town." He was happy to join in the conversation now that he'd found some decent chairs. He offered one to the lady soldier and even one to me before he plunked down.

"The Foundation's immediate containment protocol to keep people away is to purchase all of the land and buildings surrounding the Carnival of Horrors—this theme park—to physically seal it off from the outside world. That, and establish a media blackout. But I think that's not near enough, personally," he said.

"The Foundation's motto is to Secure, Contain, and Protect," said the woman. "Just because it's dangerous doesn't mean we can destroy any SCP object at the drop of a hat... But I feel like I'm preaching to the choir."

Oh, wow! There was an idiom I recognized! I bet the translation collar converted the English idiom to a Japanese equivalent. Horribly off-topic to think about it at that moment, though.

The commander didn't seem to mind that I wasn't paying attention. He continued the serious conversation with the woman soldier. "I realize we can't just eradicate the thing, but we're still striving to analyze the anomalous events that occur within the Carnival of Horrors and devise countermeasures to neutralize them.

That's why we were dispatched. We're to assess the situation and learn as much as possible about the Carnival of Horrors."

Although the woman soldier agreed with him, she weakly shook her head. "But so far, it feels like we've been grasping at straws... To top it off, we were somehow separated from the rest of the unit. We're cut off from the outside, too, since none of our radios work. It's like we're stranded in this theme park. What is the plan from here, Commander?"

"I'm still working on it. As I've said, it's been my priority to regroup, but this is starting to smell fishy... It might be wise to pull out while we still can," the commander admitted, slightly contorting his dependable, rock-hard face with regret. He let out a heavy sigh.

The next moment, the sound of screams and gunfire filled the air.

The soldiers reacted with lightning speed. Startled by the roaring bangs, I blanked out like an idiot.

The woman soldier grabbed my head. "Duck," she screamed—and flung me to the floor.

Meanwhile, the commander readied the machine gun formerly slung over his shoulder. He crouched low to take cover behind the barricade (When did they build that thing?) made of a pile of tables and chairs.

"Let's hear a sitrep!" the commander ordered.

I have no idea how he got there so quickly, but the flippant soldier was a good distance away from us, scanning the area. As the commander issued his order, he gave the thumbs up as if to say, "Okay!" He pulled a pair of binoculars from the pocket where he stored them in his fatigues and homed in on the direction of the sound.

"This is bad, sir!" The blood drained from his face. He crouched in the shadows of the flower garden—one of many in the park—that was right by the open café. "Several missing team members spotted! Located at 10 o'clock by the...what do you call those? House of Mirrors? Anyway, they appear to be engaged with something by that building!"

"Can you get a visual on what they're fighting?" the commander asked harshly, but the flippant soldier only briefly replied, "Negative!"

Throughout all of this, the woman soldier held my head pressed against the ground. My eyes were swirling in confusion. Although I'm sure she meant to protect me from the danger of a stray bullet, it felt like my skull was going to crack after getting smashed to the ground so many times in one day.

"Wh-what should we do?" the woman soldier asked the commander. She whispered, "Stay down," before creeping over towards her superior.

The commander contemplated the situation, a deep crease running down his brow for a moment or two before he reached his decision. He ordered, "We can't abandon our allies. Men, battle positions. We're going to rescue them. Advance toward the House of Mirrors using the gardens and buildings for cover."

The younger two replied, "Yes, sir!" with looks of determination on their faces. They were real soldiers. On the other hand, I couldn't even pick myself up off the floor. Terror held me down, a physical weight. I felt humiliated—I was even trembling. I completely lost myself to the pressure of a true battlefield, a place unlike anything in video games and manga.

"......" The woman's mouth trembled partially open as if she wanted to say something, but she didn't have the time to coddle me. Their operation was quickly underway.

With unbelievable speed, the three set out. Within a few blinks of the eye, they were disappearing into the distance. I guess they went to the House of Mirrors, off to fight an unknown *something*.

Wh-what should I do...? They really did leave me behind like it was nothing. None of them ever told me to "Come," and I would probably just get in their way if I tagged along... Would it be best to stick with them after all?

The idea of getting abandoned in a place like this was disheartening. But still, the screams and gunshots we just heard resounded across my mind, drowning me in a sense of unfamiliar terror. If I went with them, I could face even greater horrors. After all, this entire place was an SCP object, an anomalous land from Hell.

Honestly, I wanted to wait it out with my head buried in my knees, but I doubted that would actually solve anything. For a while, all I could do was let my jumbled mess of incoherent thoughts and emotions fly every which way...as I wondered why I had to go through this living hell, and what I should do next.

Out of the blue, a sound came from nearby. I near jumped out of my skin. It sounded like something sharp was scraping against metal. I hesitantly turned to see what it was and nearly dropped my jaw.

The shape of an arrow was etched onto the floor of the open café. My memory wasn't the most reliable at the moment, but I was pretty sure that wasn't there a minute ago. Graffiti had been scribbled with unnatural suddenness across the floor. Finding it strange, I crawled over—ever so cautiously—to examine the arrow.

I was dumbstruck! Not only was there an arrow, but also a single word...seemingly carved into the ground with a screw. The word...?

"GO!"

Was it telling me to proceed in the direction of the arrow? To top it off, it was signed "Iris Thompson."

"Iris Thompson" was written in English, so I wasn't entirely sure if I was reading it right. But I think it spelled Iris's full name...maybe?

Iris, the mysterious Girl in the Photos... A girl deemed an SCP object, doomed to an unfortunate fate. Did she manage to manipulate the photo-world (I assumed the inside of this theme park was in a photo) to leave me that message?

As I fell into silent contemplation for a spell, I waited to see if she would carve another message (or at least I assumed the first one was from her). None were forthcoming. On the other hand, the area suddenly became extremely noisy. The various rides throughout the park randomly turned on. The rollercoaster's empty cars roared as they raced along the track; the teacups spun wildly. The speakers set all over the park blasted jaunty music that conveyed no sense of joy—only horror.

Bereft of workers or attendees as far as I could see, it was as if the theme park itself had awakened from slumber. Everything turned on at once. The majority of the attractions were worn from age and use; they cracked with each movement, making horrible grinding sounds that assaulted my ears. The sound of screams and gunfire grew louder, mixing with the music and creaking rides.

I thought I heard familiar voices among the screams. Filled with uneasiness, I slowly rose. My entire body hurt, but not enough to keep from moving.

I could have sworn those last screams belonged to the three soldiers from earlier... Rather than kill me on the spot as a stranger who screamed "suspicious," they were kind enough to let me stick with them and bring me up to speed. Were those good-natured people facing a hopeless struggle?

That didn't sit well with me. I had no idea what I could do to help, but I wanted to repay them at least a little for the kindness they showed me. And seeing as the arrow also happened to point in the direction of their screams, I had all the reasons I needed to head over there.

I wasn't entirely sure what I could do, but at least I knew this was what I *wanted* to do. If that arrow was a message from Iris, I could expect to find some glimmer of hope by doing what it said. After all, Iris was my ally. I only just recently met her, so I knew it wasn't terribly rational, but I knew it in my gut.

As the cacophony spread around me, I gingerly tiptoed in the direction indicated by the arrow. Compared to the soldiers, the way I moved was outright pathetic.

The sound of the screams came from across a large building (obviously a souvenir shop gone under) not far from the open café. Upon reaching the store, I decided to hide behind the building and assess the situation.

What was going on? Were those soldiers all right? I hoped to find the answers to all the questions racing through my head.

The sight I beheld only served to throw me into greater confusion.

"Aaagh! Eeeyaaaaa! Eeeeyaaaaargh...!" one of the three soldiers—the flippant one—screamed so hard that his voice cracked, spraying machine gun fire wildly. His entire body shuddered from the recoil. The bullets roared so loudly that I thought my eardrums were going to burst.

Along with the peal of the machine gun's rapid fire, the sound of something shattering echoed throughout the air. There was a fair bit of distance between us, so I didn't have a good view. But from what I could see of the backside of the flippant soldier, he was firing at the House of Mirrors directly in front of him.

Each burst of shells gouged out chunks of the House of Mirrors' walls, which collapsed to the ground. The bullets marred and shattered countless mirrors on the other side. Glistening, the shards of glass shined as they danced through the air.

Apparently, the machine gun packed quite a punch. Just one of those things was enough to make the building look like flimsy Swiss cheese ready to topple. With a loud bang, the bright-colored sign proclaiming "House of Mirrors" fell to the ground.

Arriving to the scene a bit late, the other two—the commander and the woman soldier—looked like they were trying to talk to him, despite cringing over his abnormal behavior. It was impossible to make out what they were saying clear over by the souvenir shop. Of a mind to draw closer, I was about to take my first step, when...

"What the hell?! What the hell was that?!" The sound of the flippant soldier's shouting made my pulse race. He must have been shouting at the top of his lungs for me to hear him with such clarity.

"He was devoured, *inside* the freaking mirror! By some

goddamned monster! Dammit! Dammit! Dammit! ▇▇▇▇ had a wife and son! This is bullshit!" the flippant soldier screamed, mentioning a squad member by name as he continued to fire wildly.

Completely unhinged, he barely acknowledged the other two calling out to him. A trained soldier in his own right, he'd come across as calm and collected in this eerie theme park...until now. So what in the world had he seen? What had he witnessed that was capable of rattling, warping, and ultimately unhinging his mind?

He continued firing his machine gun until he completely unloaded the clip. Even then, he continued to scream and cry, oblivious that he was out of ammo, long since burning through it all. It was a bit quieter without the rapid-fire bangs of his machine gun, allowing me to barely catch what the other two were saying.

"Hey, what happened? Calm down and tell me. What did you see?" the commander asked in a calm yet slightly strained voice.

Snapping back to his senses, the flippant soldier was about to respond to the commander. But before he could, something wrapped around his neck. I have no idea what the heck it was. I could only describe it as some sort of murky liquid from out of this world. It wrapped around the flippant soldier like a frog's tongue, binding him.

"......?!"

By the time the soldiers responded, it was too late. The next moment, the flippant soldier was being dragged into the House of Mirrors at lightning speed.

"Eeeyaaagh...!" His scream hung in the air, slowly fading away.

I was able to see what became of him. It looked like the flippant soldier was *absorbed* into one of the mirrors inside the House of Mirrors...and vanished.

Was that really what I'd just seen? It didn't make any sense.

However, the next anomaly was already waiting for us, leaving me no time to puzzle over the last. Not all that far off, it was visible from my perspective. The creature was approaching the commander and woman soldier, who were left standing before the House of Mirrors. With their eyes stuck on where they last beheld their team member, they were in too great a state of mental disarray to notice it.

The thing walking toward the two soldiers appeared to be someone in a mascot suit. It went to show all theme parks and amusement parks had their own mascots... It had a creepy design that resembled a caricature of a gaudy pink hippo, its mask distorted, as if warped under extreme heat. It was sluggishly hobbling over to the soldiers.

The thing might have been able to pass off as cute once, but something about it didn't feel right. At the top of my lungs, I warned the two soldiers to look out to their right. They glanced at me in surprise for a split second before turning toward the mascot with their guns in position. However, they didn't immediately open fire.

This was the park mascot. There was a possibility someone was inside that suit. And no matter how suspicious a person might seem, it wasn't in their nature to shoot on sight as long as that possibility remained.

The commander demanded in a harsh voice, "Who are you?! Don't come any closer! If you're human, answer me! If you don't do as I say, we will not hesitate to shoot!"

Unfortunately, that was a painfully careless response. Inside the uncharted territory of the SCP object "Carnival of Horrors," we were essentially in the belly of an unfathomable monster... There was no telling what dangers awaited those who didn't act quickly. It wasn't as though they were unaware of that fact, but their common sense—their human nature—made them hesitant to pull the trigger the moment their eyes fell on the mascot. And that wasn't good.

As if in response to the commander's questions, the hippo mascot howled in an eerie voice. In contrast to its hippo-like appearance, it had the piercing screech of a demonic bird.

"KREEEEE!"

As it screeched, it began to charge with the speed of a great beast. It was hard to believe the hippo mascot had moved so lethargically until that moment. Barely able to follow it with my eyes, it moved with the speed of a professional baseball player's pitch.

But with a gasp, the commander barely managed to react in time, quickly firing his machine gun at the creature. A moment later, the woman soldier shot a flurry of bullets from her own machine gun, which she held pressed against her hip. Not a shot missed. The mascot was showered in a spray of direct hits. But it didn't stop. Hardly even flinching, it kept charging forward. There wasn't so much as a single hole marring the surface of the suit.

The machine guns each of these soldiers carried were powerful enough to tear apart the House of Mirrors, yet the hippo mascot never wavered or dropped speed as it closed in on the commander.

"Wha—?!" the seasoned soldier cried, eyes bulging in surprise for a split second.

The next moment, the mascot thrust out its hand (front leg?) and snapped his neck.

It was over in seconds.

In the blink of an eye, the middle-aged man—the commander—lost his life. We'd been conversing only minutes ago. I saw him go down with my own two eyes, but it was over so fast, I was struggling to process what happened. He was dead? Killed? By a hippo mascot...?

"Aah! Waaaah!" the woman soldier screamed in terror, hitting the mascot with point-blank rapid fire. Even then, it didn't seem to have an effect... It was like she was shooting at a hallucination.

"Stop—run!" The commander mustered the last of his strength, defying death despite his broken neck, to force out those two words. With tears welling in her eyes, the woman soldier gave an anguished nod. Following the commander's final order, she took off running.

It was probably sheer coincidence, but she was racing toward me. Completely unmanned, her eyes were imbued with fear... Behind her, the hippo mascot plucked off the commander's head as if it were picking grass. In a fountain of blood, his decapitated body swayed as it fell back to the ground.

That was about when the woman soldier reached me, her eyes growing round as she finally noticed me.

Without so much as a moment's hesitation, she firmly grabbed hold of my hand.

"Come with me! It's too dangerous here! We need to run for it!" she practically screamed hysterically as she dragged me with her. I had no choice but to go along, desperately struggling not to trip or stumble.

The woman soldier held my wrist so tightly it felt like my hand was going to fall off. If I could feel pain, it meant this wasn't a dream. But the situation felt more like a nightmare than anything...

There was a strange sound that piqued my curiosity, so I chanced a quick look over my shoulder. What I beheld was so trippy, I wanted to burst out into hysterical laughter. The hippo mascot drew the commander's decapitated head toward its mouth as if to give a kiss. Then it appeared to be blowing air into the head.

As it did, I could barely believe my eyes as the commander's head began to blow up like a balloon. His rough, gnarled, yet handsome face inflated dramatically. His eyes popped out of their sockets and dangled. The hippo mascot tied off its masterpiece—a grotesque, human balloon—with string. Having completed its task, it wandered off somewhere, the balloon bobbing airily on the string.

Save for the flesh and gore, it could have been any theme park mascot anywhere.

It was insane...all of it. In that theme park, none of the natural laws applied.

The horrors only continued from there. The theme park—the Carnival of Horrors—had slaughtered over 200 people, and now it revealed its true nature. It showed us one terrifying attraction after the next. Each one was a nightmare that claimed lives in horrible tragedies. They were so atrocious and cruel, it made me nauseous... I never wanted to set foot in another theme park so long as I lived.

There were several decapitated corpses riding the rollercoaster with the sign "Thriller Chiller." Some must have died a long time ago; their bodies were rotten and festering. But then others were still fresh... Outfitted in the same fatigues as the soldiers, I could only assume they were the missing team members.

At the exit of another ride with the sign reading "Tunnel of Love," piles of bodies were merged at multiple points as if fused together. There was also the merry-go-round, rotating endlessly with bodies skewered on the support beams. Chunks of flesh that looked like human innards were frying on grills at food stalls. Tormented expressions haunted the faces of the men and women trapped under the oddly red-tinged ice of the skating rink... And those were only a few of the things we saw.

It felt like a sick joke as the numerous attractions appeared before us no matter where we walked, filling us with a wealth of dark emotions each time. After seeing more horrors than I could take, my mind started to grow numb.

Faring no better than I, the woman soldier probably didn't even realize she was still holding my hand anymore. She quietly muttered to herself, "This is Hell. This is Hell on Earth... I want to go home. I want to go home. I want home!"

Eventually, she swayed and collapsed to the ground, her knees crumbling under her, more from mental fatigue than physical. With her hand still wrapped around my wrist, I fell to my knees with her. That seemed to remind her of my presence, for the woman looked at me in mild surprise.

"█████..." the woman said, calling someone's name before tears began streaming down her cheeks. She sat and cried, sniffling like that for a while.

Unable to call her name, unsure of how to comfort her, and lacking the strength or energy to do anything, I simply sat there in a daze. I couldn't even cry. It all felt so horribly surreal.

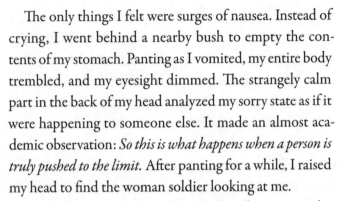

The only things I felt were surges of nausea. Instead of crying, I went behind a nearby bush to empty the contents of my stomach. Panting as I vomited, my entire body trembled, and my eyesight dimmed. The strangely calm part in the back of my head analyzed my sorry state as if it were happening to someone else. It made an almost academic observation: *So this is what happens when a person is truly pushed to the limit.* After panting for a while, I raised my head to find the woman soldier looking at me.

"...Here," she said, sounding dead and empty as she removed a bottle from her secured waist pack to offer it to me. It was mineral water. I guess she wanted me to rinse out my mouth.

I gratefully filled my mouth with the water, gargled, and spat it back out. I didn't even have the strength to swallow it down. I was so sick of it all.

"I wonder if we're the only survivors," the woman soldier (come to think of it, I still didn't know her name) whispered half-heartedly as she gently patted my back.

"I don't want to end my life here, not in this stupid theme park... Mom, Dad, ███████, I want to see you... I can't take it! I can't! I can't," she cried, in an increasingly incoherent train of thought. After hanging her head between her shoulders for a minute, she popped back up with a look of determination.

She faced me head on and leaned forward to grab my hand tightly again. "Let's get out of here. Since the commander is dead, that would make me the highest-ranking officer among those who infiltrated the Carnival of Horrors. I am the commanding officer here now. So follow my orders." Her voice cracked but was clear with determination.

"We are going to head toward the main entrance, the one we used when first infiltrating the theme park. I don't know if we can make it out...but all we can do is run in the hope that we can," she said, and then added as an afterthought that fighting wasn't exactly an option.

"What in the world are SCP objects, anyway...? Why do monstrosities like these exist? What the heck are they? What was God thinking when he made them? Ha ha! There is a theory that even God is an SCP object," the woman said, laughing as if it were a hilarious joke, but she might simply have been on the verge of cracking completely.

"Hey, kid... If I die on the way, and you still manage to get out of here alive, I'd like you to tell Mom, Dad, and ███████ back home about what happened to me."

███████? I repeated the word that sounded like a name, bringing a faint smile to her lips.

"My younger brother. Even though you're different ages and races, you remind me of him. It's probably

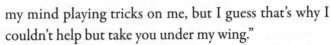

my mind playing tricks on me, but I guess that's why I couldn't help but take you under my wing."

The two of us rose, hand-in-hand.

"My family and I were refugees. We were chased from our first home, so we've had to rely on each other to get by. But my parents sustained injuries in the war that have left them bedridden, and my brother is still too young to work long hours. I'm the one and only lifeline for my entire family... That's why I don't want to die," she whispered, her eyes looking out into the distance.

"My life insurance will go to them if I die, but I'm not sure it will be enough to support a family of three forever... That's what has me so worried and scared. Kid, I don't even know your name, but please check on my family as much as you can in my stead," she asked, her head lowered solemnly as we slowly trudged on.

"And if there are any problems, please help them... I know this might be challenging for you as a Class D, since you never know if you'll live to see tomorrow, but you're my only hope and prayer."

She brought the heart tattoo on the hand not holding mine—her right—to just above her heart... As if offering a prayer, she said, "God, please don't let this cruel world bring further harm upon my loved ones."

Those were the last words I ever heard the anonymous woman say.

Before I knew it, my surroundings shifted. Something warm embraced my body, and a second later, I was somewhere else entirely. I'd grown familiar with that sensation. I knew what had happened. Iris pulled me out of the photo.

After blinking several times, I looked around me. I was back in Dr. Bright's messy lab. It was exactly the same as before I strayed (seems like a decent word to describe it) into that eerie theme park, the Carnival of Horrors.

I made it back! As that fact sank in, my knees gave out from under me. I was so relieved that I sunk down helplessly to the ground and nearly burst into tears. The realization I might not have made it back was overwhelming.

Strictly speaking, Dr. Bright's lab—a laboratory run by the SCP Foundation—was still like another world to me, so it wasn't like I'd truly made it back to my normal life. But I'd just been in a terrifying, nightmarish place. A place where I could lose my life at any second. Compared to that, an otaku's room filled with comics and video games was like Heaven on Earth.

"██████? Are you okay? I'm so sorry!" Iris exclaimed, staring into my eyes worriedly.

Struck with such fondness—even love—at the sight of her, I nearly gave her a hug. But still suffering the aftereffects of my terror, I wasn't able to lift a finger. Trembling, I took several deep breaths in an attempt to calm myself. The nightmare was over. It was supposed to be over. I could relax now.

"Well done! My, you were great out there! I would have joined you if I could. Alas, I had to give up when it became evident I couldn't—not that it kept me from trying! Ah, but after so many failures, I had to face facts. Too bad, so sad!" Dr. Bright spoke with unsettling enthusiasm as they swiveled in their chair before the workbench of junk to face me. That painfully bright red dress flared out as they turned.

"The experiments are far from over, but it would appear my hypothesis that only you can enter the photos was correct! I would love to experience the sensation myself, so I'm going to present Immortality to you as a reward for doing such a fabulous job! Congratulazioni!"

Even though I'm pretty sure they said "congratulations," either Dr. Bright's pronunciation was funky, or the word was translated to sound weird. Acting goofy as ever, the mad scientist gave a big grin as they removed the necklace resting on their bosom in the blink of an eye and approached me.

I could swear I saw that necklace somewhere before... Oh yeah, it was the antique brooch near me when I very first appeared in this bizarre research site. It appeared to be a rather expensive piece. A bunch of diamonds surrounded an oval, crimson gem—perhaps a ruby. The chain and brooch itself were either white gold or platinum.

Seeing this, Iris made a face of disgust. "Doc, you're joking, aren't you? I won't let you get away with that!" she snapped and moved in front of me with arms spread out as if to protect me.

Dr. Bright cursed, "Damn!" although they didn't sound terribly disappointed, and elegantly crossed their legs. "Yes, I was kidding, just kidding! It was a gag to lighten the mood! Do you know the best way to handle situations like this? I believe it's best to laugh! Aha ha ha ha...☆"

I had no idea what was so funny, but after laughing for a while (much later, I was informed they were paraphrasing a famous mecha anime, but I really couldn't care less), Dr. Bright's expression turned blank as rapidly as if they were a robot shutting down.

They placed the strange necklace back around their neck and stared at me intently. Those were the eyes of a researcher. That cold, unfeeling gaze made me remember that as weird as they were, they were nonetheless a scientific scholar worthy of the title "researcher."

"Thank you. I was able to conduct a most fascinating test, 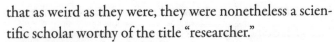," Dr. Bright said, quickly flashing a smile and bowing elegantly from their seat.

"I'd like to compile my report, so I'd appreciate it if you could tell me what you experienced in the photo. You're such a mystery! I've yet to discern how your powers work. But that's what makes this so much fun!"

In the photo... So, I really was inside the photo. Nevertheless, everything I experienced in the Carnival of Horrors was extremely vivid and real. The pain of hitting my face on the ground. The stench of blood. The warmth of the woman soldier's hand...

When she ran across my thoughts, I grew concerned for the woman soldier. What became of her? Even though she nearly lost her mind to fear, that brave woman nonetheless led me by the hand as we tried to escape from that theme park. Did I make it out, leaving her behind? That seemed extremely callous somehow.

"Naturally, she is dead," Dr. Bright informed me indifferently in a surprisingly businesslike voice. "The cause of her death is shrouded in mystery. She was discovered with a broken jaw and her rib cage was cracked open. Teeth and pieces of her heart were retrieved from her trachea.

It is currently unknown whether she died of suffocation, or shock due to blood loss from the open chest wounds. It is also theorized she committed suicide."

......

I didn't know what to say. I mean, I had feared this might happen. So she didn't make it. She didn't get to return to her family after all.

Feeling disconsolate and miserable, I lowered my head. Tears filled my eyes. Before the might of such an outrageous anomaly as the Carnival, my existence felt horribly small and insignificant.

This was no time to wallow in my sorrows. I needed to fulfill the request she asked of me. She wanted me to look after her family and help them if I could...

"That would prove difficult. In fact, it would be outright impossible to accurately carry out her request," Dr. Bright said with a wry smile. "The photo you entered was actually taken decades ago. Her parents already died of old age, but her younger brother is still alive and well."

Decades ago? Not only did I enter the photograph, I traveled back in time...? This was getting weirder and weirder.

"That is what makes you an SCP object," Dr. Bright pointed out, seductively brushing back their glossy hair. "The exact nature and capabilities of your powers are still unknown, but I would like to explore them. I'd appreciate your continued cooperation on these tests."

"I'm against it," Iris weakly contended, but Dr. Bright wasn't the least bit shaken.

"Of course, you have no right to refuse. Your cooperative behavior with the SCP Foundation has earned you a certain degree of freedom, but you are fundamentally test subjects. You cannot defy us if we wish to use you in an experiment. You're free to turn me away if you truly don't want to work with me, but we would probably implement changes in your containment procedure," they threatened, before plowing right on.

"On the other hand, I will guarantee your safety as long as you are cooperative with my tests. You'll be under the great Dr. Bright's wing! I don't think it's a waste of time for me or either of you to learn about your powers and their unique characteristics." As Dr. Bright said this, they checked their watch (the type with cartoon characters little girls in Japan flip out over) and sighed in satisfaction.

"At any rate, it's gotten quite late... You may call it a day. We can discuss this in detail at a later date. ███████ appears absolutely exhausted. Try not to push yourself too hard," they said considerately, but their eyes were shining with intellectual curiosity. I was struck with a sick, sinking fear they were going to grab me and gobble me up.

"Come to my lab again tomorrow. We can hold off on the nitty-gritty stuff until then... Good night, you two! ♪" Dr. Bright span back around in the chair. They began typing something furiously into the PC, so I hastily threw my question at them.

Not so fast! There was one thing I wanted to know. It was about that woman soldier's brother who was still alive. Where was he now and what was he doing? At the very least, I wanted to pass on her final words. I wanted him to know how desperately she tried to make it out of that hellish theme park to return to her family... If I could tell someone in her family at least a little about the bravery and kindness she demonstrated, I felt it would give meaning to the time I spent wandering through that theme park in lost confusion.

"I see. It's just as I predicted. You entered a mysterious photograph found at the site of a massacre where there were no survivors and caught a glimpse of what happened during the incident... I had high hopes you would be able to unravel some of the secrets surrounding SCP objects that no amount of legwork could hope to uncover."

Dr. Bright spoke seriously before popping out with the most outlandish comment.

"And for the record, you don't need to ask about her brother. You've already met him! When you very first met me, Dr. Bright, *I* was a black man—her brother! Having lost most of his original personality, he's practically a completely different person now. I don't see much point in going to tell him what happened."

What were they talking about...? Come to think of it, Dr. Bright was a completely different race and gender from when we first met. I still couldn't wrap my head around the mystery shrouding this person.

"I'm sure he'd be grateful. The death of his sister always weighed heavily on him. The entire reason why he decided to become a researcher here was to uncover the truth of how she died. I'm sure you've made him happy just by uncovering what his sister did and said before she passed," Dr. Bright said, a shadow of grief crossing their face. They sighed.

"With your help, we could draw just a little closer to unlocking the secrets behind SCP objects shrouded in mystery, just like with the Carnival of Horrors. It would reduce the number of lives lost or destroyed from encounters with the unknown, if only a little. Would you help me to that end?"

Once again switching to a terrifyingly serious expression, the strange researcher said, "███████, all of the SCP Foundation's researchers are welcoming you with open arms."

In all honesty, I wanted to go home right that instant.

SCP FOUNDATION
IRIS THROUGH THE LOOKING GLASS

SCP-294
[THE COFFEE MACHINE]

SCP-105

Special Containment Procedures: SCP-105 is implanted with a tracking device and is currently housed at Site-17. SCP-105 is currently allowed Class 3 (restricted) socialization privileges with approved site personnel, granted based on continued good behavior and cooperation with Foundation personnel... →For details, refer to the section for SCP-105

WHO ARE YOU?

Confidential

THE FOUNDATION DATABASE IS CLASSIFIED
ACCESS BY UNAUTHORIZED PERSONNEL IS STRICTLY PROHIBITED
PERPETRATORS WILL BE TRACKED, LOCATED, AND DETAINED

Content relating to the SCP Foundation, including the SCP Foundation logo, is licensed under Creative Commons Attribution-Sharealike 3.0 and all concepts originate from http://www.scp-wiki.net and its authors. SCP Foundation: Iris Through the Looking Glass, being derived from this content, is also released under Creative Commons Attribution-Sharealike 3.0. To view a copy of the license, please visit https://creativecommons.org/licenses/by-sa/3.0/ or contact Creative Commons, PO Box 1866, Mountain View, CA 94042, USA.

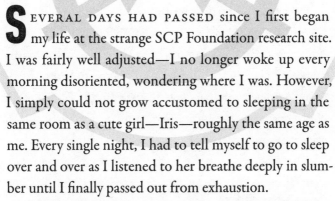

SEVERAL DAYS HAD PASSED since I first began my life at the strange SCP Foundation research site. I was fairly well adjusted—I no longer woke up every morning disoriented, wondering where I was. However, I simply could not grow accustomed to sleeping in the same room as a cute girl—Iris—roughly the same age as me. Every single night, I had to tell myself to go to sleep over and over as I listened to her breathe deeply in slumber until I finally passed out from exhaustion.

If that weren't bad enough, I was stuck sleeping on the sofa. It wasn't exactly the best place for getting a good night's rest. All of that combined with the drastic change in environment made me horribly sleep-deprived, and my head felt heavy.

One look at me that morning, and Iris proposed, "Let's go get some coffee to wake up."

I rubbed my bleary eyes as she practically dragged me behind her. When we reached our destination at the end of some corridor in the facility, I beheld *it* for the first time.

"This is The Coffee Machine," Iris explained in a crisp voice like a tour guide, still wearing her pajamas.

It was early morning in the research facility. Perhaps the on-site personnel still weren't up yet, for there was a quietness hanging in the air. The zone where we primarily worked was mostly underground, so the sound of birds chirping never made its way to us from the outside. We could hear only the faint, deep, hollow rumble of the air conditioning system.

Uh...? The gears in my head were struggling to turn so soon after waking. A bit delayed, it clicked that Iris had invited me to coffee and brought me here. We were going to buy coffee from this vending machine.

"You don't have to buy it. Personnel can use the machine for free," Iris chirped.

Guess it wasn't much of a *vending* machine anymore. Although the smart-aleck remark popped in my head,

I didn't have the energy to actually say it. At the moment, I was dead on my feet.

"Hee hee! I hope they deliver your bed soon," Iris said with a giggle, patting my head comfortingly.

I couldn't have said it better. After appearing in this research facility—practically summoned to another world—things happened to shake out with me staying in Iris's room, but I still didn't have all my basic necessities. It took forever to receive new clothes (I awoke one morning to find a box stuffed with clothes my size sitting outside our door), so I could finally kiss that khaki workwear goodbye. But I was still missing most of the furniture that I needed.

"The security level here makes prisons look relaxed. You have to go through endless red tape to bring something in from the outside world," Iris said with a shrug.

"Everyone pulled together and donated things like clothes for you, but I'm afraid no one happens to have much in the way of spare furniture like beds. We had to send away for one," she explained, and added with a smile, "It should arrive in a few days, so hang in there."

Personally, I felt that once my furniture was fully set up in her room, it meant I was stuck sharing a room with Iris for good. If possible, I would have preferred the Foundation give me a room of my own. It wasn't

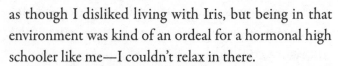

as though I disliked living with Iris, but being in that environment was kind of an ordeal for a hormonal high schooler like me—I couldn't relax in there.

"Hmmm, I don't see that happening. It's not like we have any spare rooms. For the record, my room is a containment cell specifically made for SCP objects. There isn't exactly a surplus of similar ones."

I didn't know that. Even though she looked like a normal girl, Iris was an incomprehensible SCP object in her own right. She had the ability to manipulate objects inside the pictures she took... Though aside from that, she was a perfectly normal, harmless, kinder-than-average girl.

"Furthermore, I'm under the impression the Foundation wants to keep us contained together since it believes you and I are connected. It would simplify neutralizing us if the necessity arose."

Now there was a terrifying notion. Iris nonchalantly moved on to the next topic.

"Anyway, I would like to propose we take turns using my bed until yours arrives. You don't appear to be sleeping well on the sofa," she said, looking up at me in concern.

That wasn't it! The reason I wasn't sleeping well was mostly her fault, not the sofa's.

Besides, it was Iris's room, and I was essentially free-loading off her. I truly believed with all my heart she had the right to the bed.

When I explained this to her, Iris folded her arms and grumbled in dissatisfaction. "Okay, I understand your stance. So how about this? We'll hold a simple duel in which the right to sleep on the bed goes to the winner! Seize the right to a good night's sleep!"

I felt like she was taking this down a weird path...

"If I lose, I will have no qualms with sleeping on the sofa. How does that sound? This is the most I'm willing to compromise!"

Well, I guess I was game if it would make Iris feel better. I imagine she felt awkward and guilty over constantly sleeping like a baby on the bed. With that in mind, I decided to accept her challenge.

Honestly, I was starting to miss the luxury of a bed... If mine was supposed to arrive in a few days, I would only wind up stealing her soft bed for a couple of nights in the event I won each round. Plus, it was said people showed their true colors in games and contests. I thought competing in this silly little game would be a good way to learn more about this girl I still knew nothing about.

"The nature of the duel is simple. We do combat using The Coffee Machine," Iris said, jutting her chin toward the towering vending machine. She had an air of satisfaction, as if this had been the reason she'd brought me here all along.

It wasn't until now that I truly looked at the vending machine in question. It seemed like a normal vending machine that could be found anywhere, although it was a bit different from the ones I was accustomed to in Japan. If I had to describe it, I'd say it reminded me of the freestyle beverage dispensers at restaurants. Instead of bottles or cans like most vending machines, it dispensed cups that it filled with your drink of choice.

Vertically elongated, the entire machine was just... grody, giving off an impression of old age and decay. For being so old, it had a strangely cutting-edge touchpad built into the center of the machine that constantly emitted a pale light.

There was no panel indicating what drinks were available for purchase. Next to the touchpad, there was a simple coin slot. Located by the coin slot was printed "50¢." I wasn't familiar with that symbol. Did it mean "cents"? How much was fifty cents in Japanese yen? Roughly fifty yen?

"Like I said, you don't need to cough up any money.

See the coins stuffed in there? Anyone who wants a drink can use those coins," she said.

Now that she pointed it out, I saw there was a semi-transparent plastic container next to The Coffee Machine filled with fifty-cent coins (or so I thought).

Seeing as the coins were still good money, I was afraid someone might swipe them... Were the people here indifferent to that sort of thing?

"Even if someone stole all of the coins in the basket, it wouldn't amount to much. Considering the risk of getting called out for thievery, no one is going to try to fatten their wallet... And if a member of the staff commits a crime, they could always get dismissed in disgrace. Anyway, I think you get the idea." Iris yet again presented terrifying notions and grabbed two of the (apparently not fifty-cent) coins from the container.

"Now then, we're going to use The Coffee Machine in our battle for the bed. Are you ready? There is no going back." She tried to sound intimidating, but I could tell she meant it as a joke. Apparently, Iris could be quite the tease.

Still, what sort of "duel" was fought with a vending machine? Seeing as we had money to burn, and the stakes were pretty low, I didn't see what was wrong with deciding on a coin toss.

"No!" Iris put her foot down; I guess she really wanted to go through with her plan.

"We're currently able to communicate due to the translation collar...but that was created with an SCP object called 'The Clockworks.' There is no guarantee it can produce another. You should prepare yourself in advance for the inopportune possibility it breaks," she said.

I wasn't sure how to react. It felt like the conversation had suddenly shifted. When I cocked my head in confusion, Iris further elaborated, "As such, ███████, you should work on learning English. At the very least, it would be in your best interest if you could speak conversational English without the assistance of your translation collar."

She made a solid argument. The translation collar around my neck was so convenient, I didn't feel much urgency, but I was in an unfamiliar foreign land. It was essential to study the local language. Seeing as English was the international language, obtaining a degree of proficiency certainly wouldn't hurt. And in truth, I had no idea what the principle was behind how this translation collar worked. There was no telling when it might lose effectiveness or stop working properly.

Still, her train of thought was disconnected. I couldn't see what linked the battle for the bed, studying English, and The Coffee Machine. If I was going to study English, I would be pouring laboriously over a textbook and dictionary... Or did she want me to learn by practicing my conversational skills with the native English speakers?

"You should start by building your vocabulary."

With an impish grin, Iris waved her hand toward the vending machine as she said, "As you can see, The Coffee Machine has a touchpad. If you use it to input the English term, it will dispense any number of drinks."

Wow, I had no idea vending machines could do that nowadays... Not one to buy drinks from vending machines all that often, I didn't think the interfaces had gotten so fancy.

"No, this isn't normal. The Coffee Machine is able to dispense essentially any and every drink input in English."

Any and every...? Did she mean that literally?

"I mean that literally. It can dispense any liquid. It can give you a cup of plain old coffee, or anything else from that matter, from human blood to molten gold."

That...wasn't normal. It was impossible! And then the thought hit me like a train. Was this perfectly ordinary-looking vending machine another SCP object?

"Yes, this is SCP-294, also known as The Coffee Machine," Iris affirmed in satisfaction, like a teacher standing before her prized student.

"This vending machine can produce any liquid imaginable... So each of us gets one turn inputting the name of a drink in English," she explained excitedly, clearly enjoying herself. "And then we offer the drinks we ordered to each other. The winner is determined by who finishes their cup. Whoever fails to drink it all loses. If neither of us finishes our cups, whoever has the most left over loses. Those are the rules. Understand?"

In other words, whoever drank the most of whatever was offered to them won. Wait! In that case, what would happen if we both emptied our cups? A draw?

"In the event of a draw, we'll hold extra sudden death matches until it's settled. We'll simply have to continue presenting more drinks until the winner becomes clear."

Iris spun her finder around as she added, "For the record, The Coffee Machine always fills twelve-ounce cups. Seeing as there is a limit to how much the human stomach can hold, we will definitely have a verdict within a few rounds."

If it came to that, I would have the advantage, thanks to the difference in our builds. But even so, I'd have a hard time downing two full cups. If I really pushed myself, I

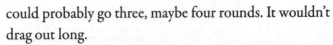

could probably go three, maybe four rounds. It wouldn't drag out long.

"Please try to avoid drinking to your full capacity. Too much liquid intake is bad for your body. Even consuming too much water can prove lethal. This rule is only in place to avoid draws. We could allow draws, but I'm afraid that in the event of a draw...the two of us would have to share the bed."

Oh, that would make it even harder to get a good night's sleep than if I lost. Honestly, I wasn't expecting this to be the sort of fun game you'd play at a drinking party... I was simply relieved it wasn't something crazy like a battle to the death. In fact, this actually sounded fun.

"Okay, so you can only punch words in English into the machine. As you come up with the drinks you want to order, you can learn English! But my native mastery of the language gives me an unfair advantage, so let me know if there are any words you would like to use. I'll show you how to spell them."

Ah-ha! So that was where studying English came in. Everything was coming together now. This was like an educational game for little kids. Admittedly, I'd balk if she ordered me to sit down and study English in earnest, but it seemed like I could enjoy learning it casually this way.

"Well, it's not like there is any rush. Take your time picking things up. Not just English, but also information about the objects secured here in the facility."

I nodded in agreement with Iris and we began the relatively trivial battle for the bed.

"I will relinquish the first-move advantage," she offered. I didn't think there was much of a first-move advantage in this game (after all, it was just a matter of drinking whatever was handed to us), but Iris made it sound like she was some great champion.

"I know a surefire way to win these duels...but this is our first round, and all. It wouldn't be fun if we already knew how it was going to end, so I will refrain from using it this time."

She was really annoying me! If I was doing this, I wouldn't hold back any punches. Otherwise it'd take away the fun of the game.

As various ideas raced through my brain, I double-checked with Iris that The Coffee Machine could produce any kind of drink imaginable.

"That's right. Oh, but let's make alcoholic beverages against the rules. I don't think it would be appropriate

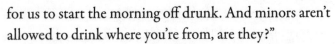

for us to start the morning off drunk. And minors aren't allowed to drink where you're from, are they?"

Come to think of it, I wasn't entirely sure how old Iris was.

"I am seventeen years old. I should actually still be attending high school."

Ah, that was only a year older than me. That was a bit surprising.

"What do you meaning by 'surprising?' That I come across as mature, so you thought I was older? Or that I seem childish, so you thought I was younger?" There was a bite in her teasing voice as she rubbed her elbows. "Anyway, let's finish quickly and hurry back to our room. The air must be set low; it is freezing in these flimsy pajamas. I do not care to catch a cold."

Yeah, both of us were still in our pajamas... I felt that if she knew this was going to take so long, we should have changed before heading over. But there was no point bringing that up now, so I focused on the duel instead.

Upon deciding what drink I wanted, I stood before The Coffee Machine. Iris said I could ask her what the word was in English, but I wanted to try doing it on my own this first round. I consulted the Japanese-English dictionary stored in my mind, flipped through it for a minute, and inserted two quarters into the coin slot. Then I typed "umeboshi juice" in the touchpad.

Yeah, I was pretty sure that was the correct spelling for "juice..." I remembered learning it in English class. Would it understand what I meant by "umeboshi?" Concerned, I asked Iris what she thought. The translation collar must have properly translated what I was trying to convey (Apparently it translated what I said into words the listener could comprehend, as could be inferred from the fact that we were able to hold conversations), for her eyes grew wide.

"Uh... Um, I could be wrong, but aren't those 'pickled plums?' As I recall, aren't they a type of Japanese plum fermented to make pickles?"

I didn't really think of them as *pickles*... But I guess technically they were. Wait, they were fermented to make pickles? Wow, I just picked up some random trivia.

"I've heard The Coffee Machine will infer the meaning of rather abstract words punched in. Still, I'm impressed you came up with something as bizarre as pickle juice on the spot. I see you're taking this seriously yourself."

Well, I could have gone with something like Japanese plum wine, too. It wasn't like she couldn't handle drinking the stuff...most likely. I was merely going with the idea that she might struggle with something unfamiliar to her American taste buds. In that vein, I figured I stood a good chance at winning if I offered her *natto* gunk, but I didn't want to watch her down that. I just knew it would be nasty to watch, although it would probably be good for her health.

"Oh, here it comes," Iris pointed out.

After waiting only a few seconds, the sound of liquid being dispensed from behind the retractable compartment below The Coffee Machine's touchpad came to a stop. With no chime to alert us that it was done, Iris stuck her hand in when she felt it was ready and pulled out the (supposed) pickled plum juice.

A fairly large paper cup was filled to the brim. The vivid, vermillion liquid looked like a rather tasty drink.

"This smells great...! Heh heh! I think you're going to wind up teaching me a few things about Japanese culture," Iris exclaimed happily, standing before the touchpad with the drink in one hand.

"Now it's my turn."

After a moment to think, Iris began to type with the ease of long familiarity.

The screen said, in English, "sea water."

Huh? If she meant "sea," as in the body of water, and "water" as in the mother of all life, wasn't that *seawater...?* Was this girl telling me to drink a twelve-ounce cup of ocean water...? Was she trying to kill me...? Crap! She was seriously out to win. My carelessness would have led to a bittersweet defeat, or maybe I ought to say salty defeat, if I drank that stuff.

"I could have asked for oil, molten iron, or liquid nitrogen, but decided to go with something that barely seemed feasible," Iris claimed meanly with a straight face. "As your competitor, it's more amusing to watch you struggle drinking the stuff...than it is seeing you instantly tell it's impossible," she said, devilishly. Ah, now I knew how Dr. Bright felt when she knocked over his Godzilla model in the lab.

She could be quite a malicious tease... Iris was generally nice and kind, so I never noticed until now. I thought she seemed more "real" after revealing the less likeable parts of her personality than those people out there who act like robots, only showing their good side. It actually made me think more fondly of her. But that didn't mean I could drink seawater! No way. I gave up.

"In that case, I win this round," Iris said with a smile after she seemingly enjoyed downing the entire cup of pickled plum juice.

"I'd like to add a new rule... Any words used in a prior round cannot be reused. Good luck coming up with liquids that humans cannot drink."

Man, she really did intend to continue holding these battles over who could use the bed going forward. I hoped my bed arrived soon. I needed it A.S.A.P.

"Let's say that if we both order something unpotable, that round won't count. We'll have to input something new and try again. Tee-hee! This is starting to feel like a real game," Iris said, looking like she was having a blast. Seeing her dazzling smile, winning honestly became a matter of secondary—or tertiary—importance.

This is just an aside, but in the end, it took longer than expected for my bed to arrive. Thirteen days passed before it was finally delivered. Iris and I continued our duels every morning until then, but I lost every single one. It got to the point that I ultimately gave up on winning and began inputting the name of drinks I thought Iris would enjoy.

Iris must have realized what I was doing, because she frequently talked about what sort of flavors she liked. Instead of artificial sweeteners, she preferred the sweet flavor of fresh fruits. Having diverged from the duel, it felt like she was requesting drinks from a bartender. The drink that she liked the most was a mixed fruit juice that her mom "occasionally made on a whim." I couldn't stand that stinky stuff, but Iris was happy to drink it.

"It makes me feel like I've learned a little more about you, and that makes me happy," she explained.

As an aside to the aside, which might be a bit redundant, our duel with The Coffee Machine became a strangely massive hit in the facility. There was always a long line in front of The Coffee Machine of personnel enjoying this stupid game, during the course of which, they invented a multitude of interesting drinks. It would take forever to list them all, so I'll just leave that out, if you don't mind.

For the record, the machine was apparently able to dispense drinks even if rather abstract ideas were input. Some examples included "my life story," "a cup of pertinent medical knowledge," and "the perfect drink," and more... A bemused researcher compiled a list for fun, so anyone interested should go check it out.

By the way, I was a bit curious about the surefire way to win Iris mentioned back during our first duel, so I asked her about it. I was just making small talk as I rolled around on my bed, which had finally arrived.

"Seeing as I added the rule that it doesn't count if we both order something undrinkable, I wouldn't call it surefire anything," Iris said as a preamble. But with a brilliant smile, she continued, "It was 'something no one can possibly drink.'"

Wait, that wouldn't even count as a drink anymore!

SCP FOUNDATION
IRIS THROUGH THE LOOKING GLASS

SCP-914
[THE CLOCKWORKS]

SCP-105

Special Containment Procedures: SCP-105 is implanted with a tracking device and is currently housed at Site-17. SCP-105 is currently allowed Class 3 (restricted) socialization privileges, with approved site personnel, granted based on continued good behavior and cooperation with Foundation personnel...→For details, refer to the section for SCP-105

WHO ARE YOU?

Confidential

WARNING ········

THE FOUNDATION DATABASE IS CLASSIFIED
ACCESS BY UNAUTHORIZED PERSONNEL IS STRICTLY PROHIBITED
PERPETRATORS WILL BE TRACKED, LOCATED, AND DETAINED

Content relating to the SCP Foundation, including the SCP Foundation logo, is licensed under Creative Commons Attribution-Sharealike 3.0 and all concepts originate from http://www.scp-wiki.net and its authors. SCP Foundation: Iris Through the Looking Glass, being derived from this content, is also released under Creative Commons Attribution-Sharealike 3.0. To view a copy of the license, please visit https://creativecommons.org/licenses/by-sa/3.0/ or contact Creative Commons, PO Box 1866, Mountain View, CA 94042, USA.

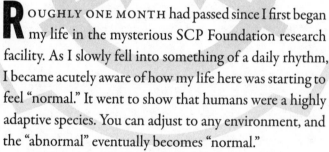

ROUGHLY ONE MONTH had passed since I first began my life in the mysterious SCP Foundation research facility. As I slowly fell into something of a daily rhythm, I became acutely aware of how my life here was starting to feel "normal." It went to show that humans were a highly adaptive species. You can adjust to any environment, and the "abnormal" eventually becomes "normal."

My daily routine included waking up in the morning and eating breakfast with Iris. On the days Dr. Bright led experiments, we devoted ourselves to their testing. But if there wasn't anything scheduled for the day, I wandered around the facility aimlessly. Once evening rolled around, I ate dinner with Iris. Then we'd return to her room and chat or play board games (the only way to kill time in her room) until it was time to take our showers and call it a night.

Days like that cycled endlessly, one after the next. Of course, there were minor variances in the events that popped up on different days, but they were as insignificant as the items lined up on the facility's canteen menu. Nothing drastic worth mentioning ever happened, as the days mostly marched steadily along without any ups or downs.

Coming to expect this as the norm, I fully settled in, letting my guard down and relaxing. I felt completely at home, passing through the days without the least bit of fear or uncertainty. It was just another one of those "typical" days when I met those quirky researchers.

One early morning, Iris and I were walking along the corridors in the research facility after eating breakfast. A researcher in her own right, Iris generally headed out for her own workspace. Supposedly it was a lab somewhere on the site, but I didn't know exactly where since she never took me. On those days she wasn't scheduled to participate in experiments with me, but she was staying with me today.

Therefore, going from past experience, this was going to be a day of testing with Dr. Bright. Since the research site viewed me as Iris's accessory, SCP-105-C, her presence was mandated for any and all experiments using me. The frequency of the tests was irregular, varying anywhere from multiple in a single day to none for several days in a row, making it impossible to know what to expect. Supposedly Dr. Bright decided whether to conduct tests based on their mood that day or whether they were hit by a stroke of genius.

In the event Dr. Bright needed us for testing purposes, Iris would receive notification to that effect early in the morning. It always left her extremely restless and agitated, so I could tell what was happening without needing her to spell it out for me.

After cohabiting (was there a better word for it?) for roughly a month, I could pick up on little signs like that. Iris seemed accustomed to leading me through the corridors now, no longer providing the meticulous explanations she did when we first met.

"Hmmm. Through the course of repeated testing, we've started to form a general understanding of your abilities, ███," Iris said, tilting her head to look up at me. She seemed a bit sluggish in the mornings.

"We've learned that your powers allow you to travel back and forth between this reality and the one inside the pictures," she said. Always one for exaggerated gestures and movement, she swished her hands back and forth, as if she were swimming. "Actually, scratch that. You can enter the photos, but you can't leave them of your own accord... In the event you wish to leave the photo, I must lend a helping hand. Literally," she said, as she opened and closed her hand several times.

"We still don't understand how I am able to do that. Perhaps it is due to my ability to manipulate the contents of the pictures I take... I am able to touch you and anything around you displayed in the picture."

We verified as much through the course of a multitude of tests. While I was in a photo, it looked like it was playing a real-time video to Iris (Since the picture looked like a normal, still image to Dr. Bright and everyone else, it was just as she said, and viewed as an extension of her powers.). And when she touched the photo, she could manipulate the contents displayed in the video/photo. That's how her name was suddenly engraved next to me in the creepy theme park, the Carnival of Horrors. At the time, Iris used the tip of one fingernail to scrawl her name into the ground (or more precisely, she scratched the photo where it showed the ground).

Furthermore, Iris was capable of grabbing the photo-image of me and plucking me out of the picture. So far, we had yet to find alternative methods of expelling me from the photos. I hated to think of it, but if Iris were to die while I was in the photo-world, it was highly likely that I would be trapped in there forever. As a result, she was always present for the tests. She was my one and only lifeline.

"The fascinating—no, beneficial—aspect of this phenomenon…is that your ability to enter photos allows you to observe the events captured in the pictures as they happened," she observed.

Exactly. By entering the photos, I could observe a score of things experienced with my five senses; seeing with my own eyes, hearing with my own ears, and smelling with my own nose. So long as there was a picture, I could conduct a wide array of investigations such as speaking with someone currently dead who was either in or near where the photo was taken.

This ability was highly valued here at the research facility dedicated to the analysis of SCP objects. If there was an SCP object where nearly all of the data was either redacted or practically non-existent to begin with, it only took one photo for me to be able to slip into the photo-world and investigate what happened.

I entered photos regarding various SCP objects each time we conducted tests, and the wealth of information I brought back always verified or overthrew numerous theories. And in doing so, the research concerning those SCP objects steadily progressed.

A picture truly was worth a thousand words. Rather than pull their hair out debating over a hundred possibilities based on insufficient data, it was generally easier to have me go into the photo and see what happened. I wasn't entirely sure what the information I brought back was used for. Seeing as a great deal of it was technical stuff, I probably wouldn't understand even if someone explained it to me, but apparently the SCP Foundation held my ability in extremely high regard.

There was currently no end to the influx of requests from researchers near and far claiming they wanted to borrow me to investigate the SCP object they were studying. However, Dr. Bright was keeping me all to himself (herself?) at the moment. Apparently the hassle of dealing with that mad scientist outweighed the benefit of using me, for everyone kept their distance, refraining from placing any adamant requests.

Considering the fact I could have been deemed worthless and suffered a horrible fate such as getting neutralized or dissected, the results of being considered useful were overall favorable. It was the reason why I was able to go leisurely about my days without any sense of danger...for now.

"Yes, you are a very valuable and convenient entity. Consequentially, it is unlikely for you to be simply put to waste," Iris said, looking at me as if I were a loyal dog. I nodded my head while listening to her.

"Notice how you haven't been sent into photos concerning terribly dangerous SCP objects lately? In the unlikely event you died while in the photo-world, there is a possibility you wouldn't come back... This is evidence that no one wants to lose an entity as rare as you," Iris said. Listening to her through the translation collar, her style of speech was just as unusual and perplexing as ever, but I got the message. She was happy and relieved that the likelihood of me getting misused had decreased, which I found sort of sweet. She cared about what happened to me.

In all reality, not only was my first experiment with the Carnival of Horrors pretty extreme, I had some close run-ins with some mighty dangerous SCP objects in the initial testing phase. I felt certain I was going to die on more than one occasion. And I sustained minor injuries, was infected with diseases, and even placed under some sort of curse.

For example, the experiment regarding the SCP object SCP-517, Grammie Knows, still made me toss and turn at night with nightmares. Simply thinking of the sequence "SCP-076" or the name "Able" made my flesh crawl. In the end, I couldn't even get close...SCP-076 was a truly superior being, akin to an almighty god or demon. There was also—actually, there were enough examples to fill several books, so I decided to stop walking down memory lane for the time being and focus on the present.

Those initial experiments were brutal and perilous. But they hadn't been like that lately, due to the Foundation acknowledging my intrinsic value. That was one thing for which I was genuinely grateful.

Thank goodness I had powers that were beneficial to others! I vaguely knew of some SCP objects who were subjected to extremely inhumane living conditions, under the pretext of "observation" or "isolation." Compared to them, I was being treated exceptionally well.

"True, you don't seem to bring the injuries or diseases you pick up in the photo back with you to the real world. But that doesn't mean we know for sure that you'll resurrect if I pull your corpse out of the photo, and I don't want to test it to find out. It would be an irreversible mistake if it didn't work, and generally, people don't come back to life."

As Iris said, I couldn't bring anything back from the photo-world. It didn't matter if it was treasure I found in the photo, an SCP object, a plain ol' diary, or a stationary set. I couldn't even bring back the air or dirt! Dr. Bright was of the opinion that if I could, it would have been possible to mass produce these rare and invaluable SCP objects. I personally couldn't understand why they would want to mass produce these freaky anomalies that were so extremely difficult to keep under control.

Sure, there were some insanely useful ones, like SCP-500, also known as Panacea—as implied by the name, a bunch of pills that could cure any disease—but they were still incomprehensible SCP objects. I didn't really approve of increasing their numbers.

Unable to bring back my injuries, pain, or even my fatigue, I reverted to the state I was in when initially entering the photo (or so we'd surmised based on how not only my injuries, but also the wear and tear on my clothes vanished) the instant Iris pulled me out.

However, this was only a physical reset to my initial state. The one thing I could bring back were my experiences in the photo-world—my memories of what transpired. I didn't understand exactly how that worked (Dr. Bright was in the middle of figuring that one out), but I understood and accepted that this was the general premise behind my powers. I could enter photos, and only bring back my memories.

"How very poetic," Iris appraised my offhand comment. She whistled for some reason before laughing happily.

"Furthermore, those memories are unique to you and you alone, 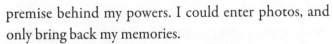. No matter what you do in the photo-world, it has no effect on the real world," she added.

Precisely. We proved as much through the course of countless experiments. Let's say, hypothetically speaking, I killed someone in the photo-world. Now if that person was alive in the real world, this didn't mean he would retroactively die or plop over dead. I'd spoken with people in the facility countless times in the photo-world, but none of them here in the real world had any recollection of ever speaking with me. As Iris said, the events in the photo-world were for me alone to remember. They were like dreams cut off from reality.

"In other words, you are not traveling against the flow of time. You are essentially experiencing simulations of past events," Iris pointed out.

Right. Just because photos displayed contents from the past didn't mean I was traveling through time when I entered one. No matter what I did in there, it would have no effect on the present—on reality. In other words, I couldn't prevent a tragedy that already occurred from taking place. My powers didn't extend that far. Of course, simply going to the past and observing events was extremely useful and beneficial for SCP object research.

"Shame you can't," Iris whispered to herself.

The crimson photo, pinned up in her room even now, flashed across my mind. Even if I could go back into the photo and heal the man dying in that blood-covered room with something like Panacea... Even if I could save his life in the photo-world, it wouldn't change reality out here. I never was told that man's name, but I knew he meant a great deal to Iris, and I couldn't save him. The dead remained deceased; history—the past—refused to change.

"Yeah, Dr. Bright theorizes that you're jumping to temporal parallel worlds and experiencing the events there. Upon leaving the photo, the parallel world vanishes... In which case, it truly would be like waking from a dream."

As if feeling that she'd come across unintentionally rude, Iris hastily continued, trying to gloss over her words. "Precisely because it's like a dream, we're unable to verify the validity of what you claim to perceive in the photos. That's the troublesome aspect of your ability. You could feed us a bag of lies and we would have no way of knowing one way or the other."

She was right, although I was honestly reporting the events as I saw them. I didn't know if the researchers took what I said to be true, and even if they did, it was all from my perspective. There were bound to be misunderstandings and unintentional lies mixed in. But I figured the researchers were pros at this sort of stuff. They could check for errors or falsehoods.

And so far, it was believed—determined—that the information I brought back was most likely accurate. As such, I—or rather, my powers—were put to effective use in the research facility. So long as I continued to prove a valuable asset, my peaceful life was secured.

"Indeed. I'm also glad you're guaranteed a peaceful life and things have finally settled down for you, but are you really okay with this? Don't you wish to return to your old life?" Iris asked, somewhat nervously.

I wasn't able to answer her. When I first wound up in this research facility, I was so freaked out and scared that I was dying to return to my old life—to the world I knew.

But honestly, that desire was growing faint as of late. It wasn't as if I had any pressing reason to return to my old world right away. If I went back, I'd probably just resume my monotonous bouncing back and forth between home and school...

When I thought about how my parents and that strange upperclassman were probably worried sick about me, I wanted to drop home and let them know I was okay. But the desire to stay with Iris—my new second family—outweighed that. And I honestly wasn't ready for these excitement-filled days interacting with various SCP objects to come to an end. I guess I already viewed life here at this research site as "normal." It didn't matter if everything was an illusion like the events experienced in those photos. I truly believed that I wanted to stay at least a little while longer.

"Now then," Iris said, after a short pause in the conversation. Walking ahead to lead the way, Iris suddenly looked back over her shoulder at me. "Today's tests will be held in the research cell down this hall."

There was a large, intimidating door in the direction she indicated with her chin. The metallic, gray door gave no indication as to what could be on the other side... On the wall next to it was a keycard reader and the simple text "SCP-914."

I cocked my head to one side, puzzled. No wonder our walk through these corridors dragged on longer than usual today. Apparently our destination wasn't Dr. Bright's lab, where we always conducted our experiments. Seeing as "SCP" was written next to those numbers, it was safe to say this research cell contained an SCP object. Were we going to use some sort of new, special method for this experiment?

"Actually, we're here to prepare for the experiment," Iris said lightly. "Dr. Bright supposedly has plans to move the research to the next phase, but in order to do so, he needs some things."

What was that all about? It could only spell trouble... Every once in a while, Dr. Bright would pop out with something that made me question their sanity, so I couldn't bring myself to fully trust the researcher. What type of experiment was that weirdo scheming to use me in?

"Beats me. But he said this experiment would prove extremely valuable to you. This just had to be one of the times he was excessively cryptic regarding the details... I'm not entirely certain, but I believe it is regarding the world you originally came from."

Hmmm... The world I originally came from? What was that supposed to mean? That wording sounded as if it meant I originally came from a world other than this one. I was suddenly filled with uncertainty. This was a covert research facility in the United States of America...supposedly. In which case, it was still on the same planet as the modern Japan I knew, even if it was hidden from the eyes of the public. Or was I wrong on that account? Was I truly in a strange and incomprehensible world other than my own? "Hmph! He'll only play you for a fool if you read too deeply into what he says," Iris grumbled in disgust.

"At any rate, the experiment requires quite a bit of preparation. Dr. Bright has work that demands his attention elsewhere today, so he won't be joining us. He said to get as much ready as we can while he's gone. Taking orders from that freak bothers me more than it should."

Hm, so Dr. Bright was busy elsewhere. I guess that was bound to happen. They were such a complete and total weirdo that it tended to slip my mind, but Dr. Bright was one of the most famous members of the SCP Foundation. I've heard they was quite the big shot! It wasn't surprising they didn't have time to focus solely on us.

"If you look at it another way, for Dr. Bright to take such interest in us and predominantly focus his research on us...it proves that we—or rather, you—are a highly valuable entity. I really do wonder... What *are* you?" Iris asked, as she heaved a heavy sigh.

In truth, no matter how much we gleaned about my abilities through countless tests, we still didn't have the answers to any of the fundamental questions. Why did I appear in this research facility? What was I? How did these powers work? Although the Foundation tended to lump us together as associated entities, what exactly was my relationship with Iris? The more I thought about it, the more confused I felt.

"Those are questions anyone who associates with SCP objects has. Speaking from my experience in the field, I think you're better off not thinking about it at a certain point. Dwelling on it too much is bad for your mental health. It is exceedingly common for researchers driven mad by obsessing over such thoughts to get walked off the site," she said, warning of horrifying possibilities. She proceeded down the corridor until coming to the gray door that was in our view for some time now.

This was where we were going to spend the day conducting tests—or to be more precise, where we would be doing the prep work for an experiment. Lifting up the cardkey dangling from her neck to verify ID, Iris opened the door.

"This is where SCP-914, The Clockworks, is contained," she said.

Clockworks? Unlike most of the labels that tended to describe SCP objects exactly as they were, this name didn't instantly evoke a mental image. What did "clockworks" mean in Japanese again? Was it some type of clock...?

"You'll understand when you see it," Iris said. She gave a charming wink before entering the room ahead of me.

I tried to hastily follow after her, but...

"Stop!" she suddenly shouted in a piercing voice and threw all of her weight into shoving me back. Although this looked serious, there was too much momentum behind my step to suddenly pull to a stop; I crashed into Iris. Seeing as she was smaller than me, I wound up pushing her down and falling on top of her. As she whimpered in pain, I opened my mouth to apologize— and was struck speechless. The room that contained The Clockworks was thrown into utter disarray.

The space was in chaos. The first thing that drew my attention was a massive, mysterious machine that dominated roughly half the rather spacious room (The floorspace was probably ten times that of the room Iris and I shared.). The construction was so bizarre, I couldn't begin to imagine what this machine was even used for.

Iris explained to me later that this giant contraption was none other than SCP-914, also known as The Clockworks.

SCP-914 was a large clockwork device—that was the origin of the name, and it had nothing to do with actual timekeeping. It weighed in at several tons and covered an area of 18 square meters, made from a mountain of interconnected belts, pulleys, gears, springs, and other clockwork parts. It was incredibly complex (or maybe just haphazardly thrown together), consisting of over eight million moving parts, most of which were arranged and configured in a way incomprehensible to the human mind. To my eyes, it looked more like an extremely difficult puzzle than a functional machine.

The majority of this grotesque contraption was made of copper and tin, with wood and cloth bits mixed in. The construction materials themselves were unspectacular, but the structure looked like a deranged artist poured his soul into creating an engineering masterpiece. Simply looking at it made my eyes whirl.

The main body of the machine was connected via tubes to two clean, encapsulated booths. Between the two booths was a control box referred to as the "Selection Panel."

Iris covered her mouth with both hands, groaning. Behind her, I stood in disbelief, feeling like I suddenly stepped into a near-future sci-fi film.

Seeing as the room didn't stink, I wondered what got into Iris. Worried, I followed her line of sight only to be struck speechless. The giant contraption—The

Clockworks—was surrounded by piles of junk strewn before it without any rhyme or reason. There were mountains of coins and screws, a toy model gun, and an oddly outdated smartphone. The majority of things were metallic, but there was also a handful of random golden stuffed animals.

It looked as if the warehouse to a factory that specialized in processing metal was hit by a massive earthquake, one that sent all of their wares tumbling to the ground. There was also liquid spilled on the messy floor. It was red. Blood! That was fresh blood, yet to dry.

Hidden behind the mountain of metal, I could only see a pair of feet. But whoever collapsed back there was the source of all that pooling blood. They didn't even budge. I sure hoped it wasn't a corpse!

I figured Iris had seen the body and was either so startled or filled with such involuntary disgust that it rendered her speechless. She was such a sweet girl; I bet she couldn't handle blood or violence. That was what I thought, but my speculation was a bit off the mark.

"Dr. Selkie!" Iris cried the unfamiliar name as she darted toward the pair of feet laying out on the floor.

Did Iris know the person laying over there? It was impressive she recognized them by their feet alone. Barely keeping up with this sudden turn of events, I pushed aside irrelevant details like that and instinctively raced after Iris.

Big as the room was, the mysterious feet were fairly close. We reached them pretty quickly. Peeking over Iris's shoulders, I looked over the person sprawled out on the floor.

The person laying in a pool of blood was a woman. It was hard to put an exact age to her, but I'd say she was still young. I couldn't tell a foreigner's age at a glance, so my best guess, no better than a rough estimate, was that she was probably older than Iris. In other words, this petite Caucasian woman was somewhere between her upper teens to early twenties.

There was a sense of maturity about her. Part of that could probably be attributed to the white lab coat, a uniform especially common among those who've earned the right to be called "doctor," but her facial features looked young. Childish, colorful clothes peeked out from under her lab coat. The material bore a print of small fluffy animals such as cute kittens. She wore thick, winter socks and super warm, fluffy slippers over them. And then there was the blood dripping from her mouth.

"Dr. Selkie! Are you awake? What in the world happened...?!" Iris grabbed the researcher (apparently named Dr. Selkie) by the shoulders and shook her, desperately calling out the young woman's name.

Even my untrained eyes could tell Dr. Selkie was in bad shape. Blood was streaming from her mouth. There weren't any glaring external injuries, but even now, there was an impressive amount of blood oozing out across the floor. I had no idea what happened, but simply leaving her here didn't look like a bright idea. If we left her as she was, it wouldn't take long before the researcher died of blood loss.

Iris slapped her cheeks to try and get ahold of herself. "███████! It could be dangerous in here, so please leave the room for now! This is beyond my knowhow, so I'm going to call the medical staff!"

She was right; this woman needed the medical staff, a crack team which essentially served as the research facility's in-house doctors. Seeing as neither Iris nor I had any medical knowledge, our being here wouldn't do her any good. I nodded my head in agreement and was just about to hurtle helter-skelter out of the room when...

"Not so fast," came a feeble voice.

Turning to look in surprise, I saw Iris was holding Dr. Selkie up by the shoulders. The researcher's eyes were just narrowly open. She croaked out an intimidating whisper. "Don't call for anyone... I'm begging—no, ordering you, by my authority as a researcher. Shut that door immediately, sever outside communication, and

y

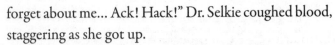

forget about me... Ack! Hack!" Dr. Selkie coughed blood, staggering as she got up.

Iris blanched. "You shouldn't be moving!"

The young researcher would hear none of it. "Shut up! If you won't follow my orders, I'll do it myself," she declared, her high-pitched voice still holding a youthful timbre. She pulled something that resembled a remote control out of the breast pocket of her lab coat. The moment she pressed one of the buttons on it, the door we came through slammed shut as if by magic. The room must have been made soundproof, for silence suddenly filled the air.

"Hmph. I've suffered minor internal damage, but this is hardly fatal," Dr. Selkie said as she examined herself, coughing multiple times as she rubbed her hands across her abdomen. "I guess I got off lucky. Though it actually might have been better if I died. What should I do...?" she groaned, tears brimming in her eyes as she grew visibly more depressed by the moment.

She finally turned to us as we looked upon her aghast and offered a faint smile. "...Do you two need an explanation?" she asked in a tired voice, to which we nodded several times.

"I don't believe I've met that boy before. I suppose introductions are in order first," Dr. Selkie said as she glared suspiciously at me. Not that it was a big deal or anything, but it felt strange hearing the rather youthful Dr. Selkie refer to me as "boy." Perhaps she was older than she looked. She waved her finger at me, shaking her head. She wasn't as bad off as I feared.

For the record, we'd already carried Dr. Selkie to a wall and helped her lean against it, as per her orders. Iris and I hunkered down beside Dr. Selkie as we listened. It didn't feel right to loom over her.

"Introductions can wait. Please tell us what happened," Iris said. She fretfully dabbed away the splatter of blood around Dr. Selkie's mouth with her handkerchief. In reality, Dr. Selkie was losing a great deal of blood. Her lab coat and cute outfit were so heavily dyed in gut-wrenching red that I could barely stand to look.

"What in the world happened, Dr. Selkie?"

"Of course... I'm sorry, you're right. I should prioritize that first. Sorry, but my head is a little foggy from all this blood loss...or...no, perhaps I was always this way... Selfish, childish, and emotional," Dr. Selkie rambled incoherently. Her consciousness was probably hazy at best. After all, it was obvious as the nose on my face that she was severely wounded. Her life was in danger if she

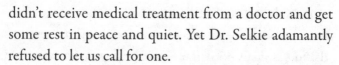

didn't receive medical treatment from a doctor and get some rest in peace and quiet. Yet Dr. Selkie adamantly refused to let us call for one.

"That was why, from the very beginning to the very end, I didn't get along with that man. He was constantly fair, ever mature, and always intellectual—Dr. Goldman." Dr. Selkie murmured, looking not quite right—as if she were possessed—as she glared at The Clockworks.

Dr. Goldman? I wondered who that was. I didn't recognize the name.

"Dr. Selkie and Dr. Goldman are highly renowned researchers in this facility. They both possess quite high clearances and primarily conduct research on SCP objects classified Euclid or Keter," Iris explained smoothly, on behalf of the barely conscious researcher. After seeing Dr. Selkie cough up blood so many times, Iris probably didn't want her to talk more than necessary.

"Although they appear to have polar opposite personalities, they get along extremely well. They've produced great results by teaming together on their research projects," Iris said, making a self-depreciating sneer flash across Dr. Selkie's face. However, she kept her silence, taking deep breaths instead.

It was obvious she was in pain. Iris looked at her apprehensively as she continued, "Always calm and collected, but not without his own unique sense of humor, Dr. Goldman takes a serious approach to research. Although she is sometimes compared to a runaway train, Dr. Selkie's wild ideas and reckless actions lead to astonishing experiments... Everyone talks about how they're this facility's greatest duo."

"Really? That's our reputation?" Dr. Selkie asked with a weak smile. "I could have sworn word had it we fought like cats and dogs."

"Well, there are eye-witness accounts that you two start fighting the moment you set eyes on each other. But I've always been jealous of your relationship. It's like you don't have to stand on ceremony—like you're close friends or family. It's wonderful to have someone like that here in this research facility. Perhaps you've noticed that the warmth of others is in short supply," Iris said without an ounce of sarcasm, probably expressing how she truly felt. She wasn't a terribly tactful girl. But her straightforward opinion hurt Dr. Selkie more than anything, making her twist her lips in silence.

Looking at her in concern, Iris summarized, "At any rate, these two researchers were scheduled to fill in for Dr. Bright, since he has business elsewhere, to oversee today's experiment—or rather, the tests to prepare for it. As such, there is nothing surprising about Dr. Selkie being here."

As if patting a child on the head to comfort her after falling down, Iris wiped off the blood splattered across Dr. Selkie's body with her handkerchief as she asked, "But what happened before we arrived? I don't understand that, but I'd like to know. It is surely the most important thing at hand. Could you tell us, Doctor?"

"Yes, I suppose I must." For a moment, Dr. Selkie caught her breath, as if overwhelmed by Iris's momentum, but then she dropped her head in resignation. Although she still seemed to be in pain, she sounded surprisingly lucid. Probably the brief rest had helped psychologically stabilize her. "In that case, will you hear me out? This was going to be the happiest day ever for me and that horribly wonderful Dr. Goldman. At least, that was what I was hoping."

Dr. Selkie told us what had happened as if making a confession. Even the way she spoke was childish, her thoughts bouncing every which way without rhyme or reason, making her rather hard to understand. Every now and then, Iris would provide clear and concise summaries, allowing me to just barely grasp what Dr. Selkie was trying to convey.

It was a strange story. It all began first thing this morning. For some time now, Dr. Selkie had been planning a certain magnificent and personal experiment (that was her bizarre way of describing it), so she was up earlier than usual to work on the preparations here, in this research cell dominated by the giant SCP-914.

"I practiced several dry runs of the experiment, and got so caught up in them that I completely forgot to eat breakfast. That was when my tummy began to get the rumblies. 'Goodness me, this isn't very elegant,' I said to myself, and started debating about heading over to the canteen," Dr. Selkie said. She was more of a talker than I first suspected; once she got going, there was no stopping her. Although her internal organs were damaged, that didn't seem to slow her down.

"But it'd be pretty stupid if I did that, you know? I'd have to make drastic changes in my plans if I went to go get food at that point. The schedule I spent all night devising for this experiment was so perfect and precise, there wasn't room for a single second delay."

"By experiment...do you mean the one we're supposed to participate in, or the preparations for it?" Iris asked.

"No, I told you this is unrelated... It's my...personal experiment," Dr. Selkie grumbled, embarrassed for some reason. "At any rate, while I was wondering what to do, that nasty Dr. Goldman suddenly popped up with a sandwich in hand. Acting as confident as ever, he said to me, 'My darling Selkie, aren't you hungry?'"

Having never met Dr. Goldman before, I couldn't really picture the man, but I got the impression he was quite the gentleman.

"He could really ruffle my feathers with that smug face of his. Acted like he knew everything about me... But he never noticed what really mattered. It wasn't like he knew and played dumb. I think he really was too oblivious to catch on," Dr. Selkie said, puffing up her cheeks in an immature display of annoyance before looking into the distance.

"He was aware that I have a tendency to get so absorbed in my experiments that I forget all about eating. Knowing we were supposed to use the highly valuable Clockworks in our tests with you today, he likely made a highly accurate prediction that I would be famished after dwelling over what experiments we should conduct."

"Isn't eating and drinking generally prohibited in research cells?"

"Yes, so please keep this between us. Every now and then, Dr. Goldman and I would sneak off to the corner for a quick bite to eat. See, we attended college together. So this was a little ritual carried over from those days.

Those brief moments meant the world to us," Dr. Selkie continued, looking somewhat heavy-hearted.

"Anyway, every single word out of Dr. Goldman's mouth grated on me like you wouldn't believe. To be fair, I guess there was nothing unusual about that... I was super annoyed at myself for being stupid and forgetting to eat and at him for patronizing me when he foresaw I'd do just that," Dr. Selkie said. Her mood was growing increasingly sour, as if the memory still irked her.

"I'm not the only one at fault here. I'll admit that I can be emotionally unstable, a little childish, and extremely temperamental, but Dr. Goldman would go out of his way to poke fun and tease me... It was like he poured oil on my fiery temper every time he opened his mouth. I'd get so mad, I'd blow up like a bomb," she explained, almost desperately. But eventually a look of sadness washed over her and she dropped her gaze.

"Dr. Goldman knew well and good how I'd react, but just had to go and play a prank on me anyway. After a lengthy fight, the hunger became too great, and I accepted the sandwich he offered me." Dr. Selkie smacked her lips, as if reliving the memories as she told us...

"The second I bit into it, I thought he tricked me again! My teeth hit something hard. A strange sound and pain rang through my head. Instinctively recognizing the object wasn't edible, I quickly spat out the sandwich," Dr. Selkie said, thrusting the hand held to her mouth out and flapping it in front of her.

The researcher's face grew serious as she continued, "That was when I noticed Dr. Goldman laughing so hard at me coughing up the sandwich that he was doubled over. I was red as a bull as I rounded on the idiot, demanding, 'You put something in the sandwich, didn't you? What was it? What were you thinking?'"

That was certainly uh, well, a childish prank. He had slipped something inside the sandwich he pretended to give out of kindness. Iris isn't too different. During my life with her, she's pranked me on more than one occasion. For instance, when we got into an argument over how to handle the laundry, she slipped some super spicy mustard into my food as a form of silent protest or punishment. When I ate the dish, I bounced around shouting about how my tongue was on fire. Feeling better after seeing that, Iris apologized for the prank and was willing to commence peace negotiations. It seemed like the sort of lighthearted prank you could only pull on someone you felt truly comfortable with.

"True, we played pranks like this on each other all the time. But today wasn't the day for it..." Dr. Selkie murmured. She crossed her arms and turned her head away in a pout.

"I was already hangry as it was, plus there was something super important I wanted to tell him… It felt like he was trampling all over my resolve and making light of my feelings. As you can imagine, I royally exploded at the man," she confessed with tears starting to form in her eyes.

"Of course, I realize I'm being extremely unfair. Dr. Goldman had no way of knowing what was going through my head. I'm sure he thought it was just another little prank like always… But it was the straw that broke the camel's back," Dr. Selkie whimpered, fighting back tears as she clutched the hem of her blood-soaked lab coat.

"When I realized the thing that I coughed up—the thing he stuck into the sandwich—was his beloved golden ring…I grew little devil horns. I snatched it up and threw it into The Clockworks' booth without a giving it a second thought. Then I wound the key to activate it."

"What were you thinking, Dr. Selkie?!" Iris exclaimed, making a full-body gesture to express her disbelief.

I still didn't know what exactly The Clockworks did, so I was having a hard time following the conversation. I was just getting the general picture that Dr. Selkie did something outrageous.

"Believe me, I know. I'm well aware of how foolish I am… But I wanted to teach Dr. Goldman a lesson. I wanted him to know what would happen if he didn't treat me right.

No, I probably just wanted to get back at him," Dr. Selkie groaned crestfallen like a little girl who just got scolded by her parents. "But my rash actions led to the worst possible outcome. I suspect Dr. Goldman was hoping to retrieve his gold ring before The Clockworks initiated its process and jumped into the booth after it."

"That course of action was highly problematic and careless in its own right," Iris said with a sigh, looking utterly flabbergasted. "I'm starting to see the gravity of the situation."

"Yes, well, unfortunately, the process initiated the moment he jumped in, refining everything in the booth. I raced to look inside, but Dr. Goldman was no longer there," Dr. Selkie said and buried her face in her hands. She began sniffling as she cried, "He vanished! No, he was 'refined' to the point I can't even recognize him anymore. Ah, this truly is a disaster."

SCP-914 was also known as The Clockworks. Ignorant of the nature of this SCP object, Iris offered me a brief explanation. According to her, The Clockworks was a device capable of altering or "refining" the state of an object.

I was struggling to imagine what exactly she meant by that, so we received permission from Dr. Selkie to conduct a simple test. That might seem awfully carefree with this Dr. Goldman guy missing (?) at the moment, but Dr. Selkie flew into a fit of tears after explaining what transpired. We needed to give her time to calm down anyway.

"Watch this, ███████," Iris said as she pulled out a ballpoint pen from somewhere and approached The Clockworks with it in hand.

"From our perspective, the booth to the right is the 'Intake' booth and the one to the left is the 'Output' booth. As you can see, both are connected to the main body of The Clockworks," Iris explained.

Intake? Output? I wondered what that meant, quietly listening to Iris's explanation. She gave me a satisfied smirk before continuing. "When using The Clockworks, first an object of some kind is put into the Intake booth. I'm going to use this pen for our test."

Iris casually approached the Intake booth, opened the door located in front, and somewhat cautiously tossed the pen inside. Then she simply shut the door. Once it was closed, a small bell suddenly went off.

The booth walls appeared to be made of thick metal, so we couldn't peer in from the outside to see what was going on.

"Okay, so as you can see, I've placed the ballpoint pen inside. I've already had you inspect the pen to see for yourself, but that was your typical, cheap disposable pen that you could get anywhere," she said.

This was starting to feel like a magic trick. As if reading my mind, or perhaps out of sheer coincidence, Iris channeled the style of a stage magician. "I've got nothing up my sleeve! ♪"

With a few steps, the two of us moved in front of the Output booth.

"Now we'll have to wait a bit. The process generally takes between five to ten minutes, during which time you must never, ever open the doors," she warned.

Eagerly waiting for it to finish, Iris turned back to face me and added, "The Clockworks uses this time to refine the object placed in the Intake booth. How it works is a mystery still being researched, but SCP-914's operators can arbitrarily manipulate what degree the object is refined."

Uh... What was that supposed to mean...? Refined? I hated how slow I was on the uptake, but Iris didn't seem to mind. In fact, she looked at me as if I were the cutest little thing. I knew she was older than me, but I couldn't help but get the feeling she was going overboard treating me like a kid... Despite feeling mildly offended, I was a good boy and listened to her explanation.

"There is a control panel here referred to as the 'Selection Panel,'" Iris said as she anxiously took another few steps, bringing her to the middle of the two booths in front of the main body. There was a panel there that definitely fit the bill.

A large knob was attached to it, holding a metallic sheen, as if made from copper. Turning the knob moved a small, adjoining arrow on top. Since it was currently in operation, Iris only pointed at the Selection Panel with her finger rather than outright touching it. "Can you see this? It says, 'Rough,' 'Coarse,' '1:1,' 'Fine,' and 'Very Fine.' Do you know what they mean?"

Well, after countless rounds of studying English (as a cover for goofing off) with The Coffee Machine, my English word bank was a bit richer... But the translation collar wrapped around my neck couldn't help me figure out written words, and there was one I didn't instantly recognize. What did "Coarse" mean?

"Well, you should be able to get the overall gist if you think of 'Rough' as the worst setting and 'Very Fine' as the best... That's all it means. By turning this knob to point the arrow at the various settings, you can increase or decrease the output quality," Iris explained.

Huh. Yeah, that made enough sense. So SCP-914 here was a device that modified stuff, and this Selection

Panel controlled the output refinement quality... With only five options, we were given a really broad range from "very bad" to "very good" to choose from.

The arrow was currently pointing at "Fine" (Come to think of it, I thought Iris had fiddled some with The Clockworks before activating it), so we should get something fairly decent. As such thoughts were running through my head, the bell sounded again, and Iris headed back toward the Output booth.

Bursting with excitement, she opened the booth door and pulled something out. A cylindrical, shining silver object came out of the Output booth.

"Hmmm. It would appear the cheap disposable pen was refined into a relatively valuable silver ballpoint pen. Go ahead and hold it. Isn't it nice and heavy? That's real silver," Iris said, offering the ballpoint pen, though it looked more like a fountain pen to me. Without thinking, I accepted it.

Sure enough, there was weight to it. I looked at it up close, but aside from the fact it was somewhat unusual to see a silver ballpoint pen, it seemed perfectly normal. I bet it would write just fine if it had ink.

"Hm, so this is the best 'Fine' has to offer. I bet it would still sell for a pretty penny. Of course, using The Clockworks to turn a profit is strictly prohibited," Iris said jokingly, as she walked toward the Intake booth and opened the door. Sure enough, there was no trace of the ballpoint pen she put in earlier.

"Now do you understand? As you just saw, The Clockworks alters the state of objects. Somehow or other, anything put inside the Intake booth is modified and transferred to the Output booth, where it reappears. No one understands exactly how it works, but this is essentially what the device does," Iris said. It was an ambiguous explanation, but SCP objects were illogical to begin with. It would be impossible for her to offer a perfectly coherent description. I fully realized that the best way of facing these things was either to use them with a vague understanding of what they did, or isolate them.

"Your collar—the translation collar—was also made using SCP-914's function," Iris said, pointing at my neck.

Oh, now that she mentioned it, I remembered her mentioning something to that effect before. I was pretty sure I'd heard her bring up The Clockworks in the past as well.

"Your collar was originally a dog collar," Iris said. "The kind that could be considered a sort of joke gift, while being marketed as the Holy Grail of dog lovers across the world, because it has the ability to translate a dog's emotions into words its owner could understand."

Oh, I could swear I've heard about those before. They measure the dog's perspiration to determine if it's hungry or tired and then translate that into words for humans to understand. They weren't terribly accurate, but they weren't a total sham either. But it wasn't like they were actually translating what the dogs said for humans to understand either...or so I heard.

"We put one of those in SCP-914's booth and wound the key with the arrow pointing at Very Fine. And it came out reborn as a terribly wonderful collar capable of translating any language," Iris explained.

Ah-ha! Now it all made sense. I thought this translation collar seemed like some sort of incredible sci-fi device beyond the scope of modern science. In fact, it was only a product of coincidence, born from a collar through the phenomenal SCP object known as The Clockworks.

"Right. Even if you repeat the exact same procedures, The Clockworks won't necessarily give you the same results. And since you have to fill out a pile of complicated forms every time you use it, mass producing that translation collar would prove difficult. As such, be very careful not to break it," Iris warned.

Well, yeah. That went without saying. I was still a far cry from proficient in English, so I'd hardly be able to communicate with Iris without it. Basic daily life would become a struggle.

When I found myself fingering the collar, Iris said in an attempt to cheer me up, "But it'd be inconvenient if you didn't have the translation collar. As such, we need to make a spare, along with a variety of other useful goods for future experiments. That is the purpose of today's tests—or rather, the prep work for the upcoming experiments."

Oh, now everything was starting to fall into place. The purpose of coming to this room dominated by The Clockworks today was to make things as helpful as this translation collar, if not more so. I could certainly use some handy gadgets. Although I could enter a photo at will, my body was still that of a normal senior high boy. I couldn't put up much of a fight against any dangerous anomalies. I was powerless. The logical response was to try equipping me with gear that either heightened my physical capabilities or improved my investigative prowess.

I'd personally appreciate gaining a means to protect myself or expand what I could do. In all of the tests so far, I simply wandered aimlessly, feeling like a miserable nervous wreck more often than not... I would love to have something to set my mind at ease.

"I know. I consider it foolish to send you into the photos completely unarmed. I'm beside myself with fear each time you go." Iris looked down, somewhat disgruntled.

Her eyes were on Dr. Selkie, who was still off in the corner of the room crying with her head buried in her hands. Combined with the blood she lost earlier, she was wailing so hard I was afraid all of the liquids were going to drain out of her body.

"Well, let's put that aside for now. We should focus on the issue at hand: The researchers who were supposed to direct and supervise the process to create those handy items are currently in a nasty bind."

Yeah, I wondered what we should do... After hearing the explanation for how The Clockworks functioned, I finally realized the severity of the situation. This Dr. Goldman guy ran after the gold ring Dr. Selkie threw in a hissy fit, following it into the Intake booth. And even after The Clockworks finished the refining process, he wasn't anywhere to be seen in the Output booth... supposedly.

Where in the world did Dr. Goldman disappear to? I assumed he was probably modified to some shape or form... But if this contraption was so incomprehensible that even expert researchers couldn't predict how things would come out, I couldn't even begin to imagine his fate.

The idea of a missing body reminded me of some good old mystery novels. But seeing as a bizarre SCP object lay at the root of the mystery, I doubted any amount of clever deduction could crack this case.

"Kiddies, it's great you two get along and all...but could you lend me a hand?" Dr. Selkie called to us after getting all that crying out of her system.

Iris and I nodded to each other and walked over to the youthful researcher. Crying so much left Dr. Selkie's eyes puffy. Her hair and clothes clung to her skin in patches due to the dried blood and tears. She looked like a train wreck, but her eyes still shone with a piercing light.

Her own careless actions led to the loss of her precious partner (If Dr. Selkie heard that description, she would probably have a cow... But when she told us about Dr. Goldman, her words were filled with affection.). I wouldn't blame her if she flew into a hysterical panic.

Either she lacked the strength to go into a frenzy or she was a stronger woman than her childish appearance suggested. Her breathing pained, Dr. Selkie said, "Notice all of the stuff scattered throughout the room? I realize it'll be rough, but I'd appreciate it if you gathered it up.

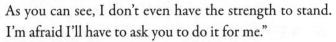

SCP FOUNDATION

As you can see, I don't even have the strength to stand. I'm afraid I'll have to ask you to do it for me."

I'd forgotten about all the things arbitrarily strewn across the room until she mentioned them. There was no correlation between the primarily metallic piles of random stuff... What was the deal with all of it, anyway?

"Well, I must have completely lost my head after Dr. Goldman vanished. I took what appeared in the Output booth and put it back in the Intake booth, repeating the process over and over again," Dr. Selkie said, forcing herself to answer our question.

"I thought that if I operated it just right, I could reverse-refine the materials back to Dr. Goldman. Yes, yes, I know good and well that the refinement process is usually irreversible. Even if you don't like the end results, there is no going back," she said, downcast, but I could fully understand the motive and sentiment that drove her to such drastic measures.

Dr. Goldman vanished. He was probably modified by The Clockworks... In which case, there was a sliver of hope reversing the process and modifying the materials over again might bring him back to his original state.

"But you can see how that ended. No matter what setting I put the Selection Panel on, it only betrayed my expectations with all that junk. Once it even ignored the law of conservation of mass to produce a massive pile of gold. It was a nightmare hauling all of that out of the booth."

Ah, so throughout the course of repetitively winding up The Clockworks and refining the materials, she created this massive mess. It was a testament to all of the times she wound the key and waited with bated breath for five to ten minutes... Each time she opened the Output door, filled with hope that it finally worked, only to be met with bitter disappointment. She repeated that process over and over again...

Growing utterly exhausted, Dr. Selkie must have fallen into despair. If it were me, I would have curled into a ball out of frustration, but she didn't give up. And evidently, she did the unthinkable.

"After repeating that for a good while, I came to the conclusion that normal methods wouldn't cut it. No matter how much I refined these things, Dr. Goldman wasn't coming back..." Dr. Selkie whispered, glaring spitefully at the junk scattered everywhere. "As such, I put myself in the Intake booth."

"...That was suicide. Biological testing with The Clockworks was discontinued. It usually ended in tragic results," Iris said, the blood draining from her face. "Did you feel an impulse to punish yourself due to the guilt

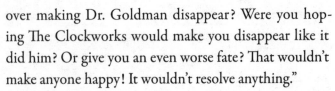

over making Dr. Goldman disappear? Were you hoping The Clockworks would make you disappear like it did him? Or give you an even worse fate? That wouldn't make anyone happy! It wouldn't resolve anything."

"Yes, of course I know that," Dr. Selkie replied. She suddenly came across mature as she rubbed her abdomen. "I set the Selection Panel's arrow on Very Fine before I stepped into the Intake booth. Do you know what that means?"

She waited for our reactions, pausing briefly like a school teacher waiting on students to answer a difficult question posed to the class, before continuing, "I tried to make it refine me into a much, much better me. I was hoping that if it gave me a brilliant mind, I might be able to find a way to bring Dr. Goldman back... That was my ray of hope."

I...I understood how she felt, but that was insane. There was no way to predict the results rendered through SCP-914's refinement process. It was an unstable, irrational contraption that mankind could never hope to fully control.

Yet that was the method Dr. Selkie chose. Did she feel that responsible for Dr. Goldman's disappearance? I didn't know if there were greater emotions—a deeper meaning—that drove her to such lengths. Something about her actions seemed very noble to me. Dr. Selkie acted boldly to save another despite the danger to herself. Such self-sacrifice was commonplace in manga and movies, but I didn't know there were people capable of that in real life... It was rather touching.

Unfortunately, Dr. Selkie's perilous actions went unrewarded. They failed to bring about the desired results.

"It ended with a horrible flop. Rather than give me the brilliant mind I wanted, The Clockworks toyed with my insides and called it a day. I won't know exactly what it changed until I undergo a proper exam," Dr. Selkie said with a dry smile as she gripped her abdomen. "As far as I can tell from my self-examination, it seems like the thing just damaged some of my organs. I should consider myself lucky it didn't instantly kill me..."

Coughing up more blood, she began to tremble, as if she were suddenly freezing. "No, I suppose you could say I got off quite lucky, seeing as I could have been turned into a ludicrous monstrosity. Certainly that would be consistent with the results that made us discontinue biological testing... But now I'm essentially up the creek without a paddle."

Her face suddenly went frighteningly blank as she stared at us. "Listen, after you gather the things spread across the room, I want you to temporarily take them out of here. They are what Dr. Goldman turned into. So long as we have these items, it might be possible to revert him. No matter how small, the possibility is still there," she said, resolute.

Hearing Dr. Selkie reminded me of the lady soldier I encountered in that terrifying Carnival of Horrors. She wore the proud expression of a determined adult.

"Once you're done, I'll go back into SCP-914's booth, even if I have to crawl to get there. I'm betting all my chips on the improbable... I might die this time, or face a fate worse than death, but I'm betting everything on the hope that this time I will receive a wonderful brain capable of resolving this."

With a gentle smile, she looked us square in the eyes and continued. "The Clockworks is a strange and mysterious SCP object in its own right. I don't know how this will end, but chances are it won't end well. So before I change, please run as far from here as you can."

At the end, Dr. Selkie gave Iris and I each a gentle pat on the head. Perhaps due to severe dehydration and blood loss, her fingertips felt cold as ice. But strange as it might seem, there was still warmth to her touch. It was the warmth of her love and affection. I bet she put her heart into that pat...

"And then I want you to pass on everything you've seen and heard here to the Foundation's higher-ups. Submit it as a single report compiled on the events concerning The Clockworks. That will pave the way for the future," she instructed.

She sounded as if she were praying as she said, "No matter how great the sorrow or pain, no matter the accident or tragedy, we can confront it if we have the knowledge. Why, that is how we humans have isolated the threats posed by SCP objects so far, all to protect our peaceful daily lives."

Having confronted these strange and bizarre SCP objects unknown to the masses, Dr. Selkie proclaimed proudly, "This case is no different. At the very least, I hope you put my failure to good use. Otherwise I won't be able to pass on. My soul won't be able to rest in peace."

"Dr. Selkie," Iris called to her, a serious expression on her face.

Seeing Iris grow tense, Dr. Selkie jumped to the conclusion the younger girl was filled with pity for her, or stiff with terror over the perilous situation, and so she offered a brave smile as she said, "Don't worry; I don't intend to die. The odds aren't very favorable, but I'm

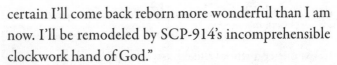

certain I'll come back reborn more wonderful than I am now. I'll be remodeled by SCP-914's incomprehensible clockwork hand of God."

"No, uh, Dr. Selkie... I don't think you need to go to such drastic measures."

"...Why not?" Dr. Selkie asked dubiously, feeling she was no longer on the same page as the dazed Iris. Noting the other girl's eyes were focused elsewhere, Dr. Selkie followed her gaze. Her whole body went taut as if struck by lightning.

"Wh-Wha... Wh-Wh-What?!" Dr. Selkie jumped to her feet as if she completely forgot all about her damaged internal organs.

Swinging her arm up and down countless times like a little girl, she shouted, "You! Why are you alive, Dr. Goldman?!"

At the receiving end of her angry glare... Someone suddenly popped his face out from the shadows of the massive SCP-914's main body. He was a tall man I had never seen before. He wore a pure white lab coat that perfectly matched Dr. Selkie's. His facial features were extremely well defined and his fingers were long. His beautiful blond hair seemed to emit an inner light.

This man—probably the very same Dr. Goldman we'd so long discussed—quietly looked around, as if disoriented. Then, in calm contrast to the practically hysterical Dr. Selkie, he winked. "Philosophy? That was never one of your strengths, my darling Selkie."

"O-Of all the...! Damn you, Dr. Goldman!" Dr. Selkie cried.

We assumed Dr. Goldman was refined to oblivion by The Clockworks, but now he'd reappeared as if nothing ever happened. Dr. Selkie was struggling to accept the reality he was alive; her mouth flapped open and shut as her voice issued sounds that refused to resolve into words. Tears streamed down her cheeks. Relief gradually washed over her face, which turned to joy...

"You *jerk!* I can't believe you! How far must you push my buttons before you're satisfied? I swear, I will never, ever forgive you for this so long as I live!" Dr. Selkie shouted, pouring such strong emotion into her words that it came across like a marriage proposal.

Then she ran straight toward Dr. Goldman. On the verge of death, her innards a scrambled mess, I wondered where she found the strength to run. Was a flood of endorphins making her oblivious to the pain? Or was this the power of love? The only reason that bit about love popped into my head was due to what Dr. Selkie did next.

Overcome with emotion, Dr. Selkie flung herself onto Dr. Goldman in an ecstatic embrace. It was a passionate hug. Feeling like we weren't meant to see this, I reached my hands out to cover Iris's eyes. But Iris was doing the exact same thing, and my hands met hers midway in the air. We slipped our fingers together without thinking, falling into a funny position as if we were dancing a waltz or something. The wild turn of events left us too stunned and confused to realize how awkward that was and pull our hands apart.

"There, there," Dr. Goldman cooed. He lovingly wrapped his arms around Dr. Selkie while she cried like a baby. He gently laid his cheek on the top of her head as if they were tight-knit lovers. Actually, that could very well be the case.

The two researchers had a long relationship extending all the way back to their college days. After all the years they've spent working so closely, perhaps a special sort of bond formed between them. Whether it was romantic or not, I lacked the experience in such things to say for certain. But I vaguely felt jealous of the two.

...This was awesome. It was like they got their fairytale happy ending. Not that I had any idea what the heck was going on.

"Now if you'll allow me to explain what happened! This was payback for the way you cruelly threw my beloved ring into SCP-914's booth," Dr. Goldman said in a resounding voice, then laughed merrily. "It was to be an innocent, little prank. Upon giving the appearance of following the ring into the Intake booth, I immediately concealed myself in the shadows of SCP-914's main body. I'm proud to say that glorious performance would put any magician to shame."

"......" Dr. Selkie didn't respond. She was aghast. It seemed less like she couldn't understand what Dr. Goldman was saying, and more like she didn't want to understand.

I couldn't see her very well from where I was standing, but I could sense intense emotions raging throughout her entire tiny body. She was like a volcano about to erupt.

"I was hoping you would realize the egregious mistake you made, grow flustered, and ultimately regret the error of your ways. You have a tendency to be somewhat impulsive and reckless. While I find both traits endearing, I hoped some introspection would help you grow as a person," Dr. Goldman continued.

"......"

"But you were so much fun to watch, I missed my chance to come out. I actually planned to pop out shouting, 'Surprise!' much sooner."

"......"

"While I was watching you fiddle around, things suddenly took a drastic turn for the worse... You threw yourself into the Intake booth. Don't do anything dangerous like that ever again, my darling Selkie. It's truly a blessing you're still alive."

"But," Dr. Selkie whispered in a forced voice, finally breaking her silence, "you vanished...! I had to do something! My rash actions brought about that accident, and there's no one in the facility I can turn to! I-I had to figure something out myself! That's why I—Oh, forget it!"

Dr. Selkie pushed Dr. Goldman away and stomped her foot. "I can't believe it! I risked my life to save you! I was worried sick! And you were off in some corner laughing at me the whole time?! Unbelievable! You're the worst! I hate your guts!" Dr. Selkie's voice cracked as she shouted, unable to restrain herself against the tide of anger, embarrassment, and a surge of other emotions.

I didn't blame her. That was definitely a bit cruel of him. He took the prank too far. But something about his story didn't add up.

Before I could determine why I thought something felt off, the gears in my head froze as Dr. Selkie began to make the most incredible proclamation. "I came here today with a specific purpose in mind. I wanted to move our relationship to the next level... I carefully practiced for the big proposal to ensure it was perfect down to the most minute detail, from the speech to the flick of my wrist," Dr. Selkie wailed, her head lowered. She wiped the stream of her tears with the back of her hand.

"Here I was going to discuss something very important with you, and you had to pull that stupid prank... It made me so outraged, I lost my temper and threw your precious ring. But after this, I'm glad I didn't tell you any of the things I had planned," she sobbed.

With a loud crack, Dr. Selkie slapped Dr. Goldman across the cheek, spat in his face, turned on her heels, and ran toward the closed door. She didn't turn back, face twisted in pain. She howled: "Stupid! A scoundrel like you should spend his whole life unloved and alone! I hope you die in some ditch without leaving any footprint on the world! Jerkface! I'll have you know, I—" The rest of her words were lost in sobs.

Opening the door, Dr. Selkie ran out of the room. We could hear the sound of her feet hitting the floor grow distant. Silence began to waft through the space dominated by The Clockworks.

"......"

Left behind, neither Iris nor I were able to say anything as we simply stared like fools down the direction

Dr. Selkie ran. Honestly, what could more-or-less uninvolved bystanders such as ourselves do when caught in the middle of a fight like this?

But Dr. Goldman was still frozen stiff on the floor where he fell from the slap, so I turned toward him out of concern. I hoped he was all right. If everything he said was true, he really was as big of a scumbag as Dr. Selkie claimed... While there was no room in my heart for sympathy, I couldn't shake the feeling that something was amiss. The whole time he played the villain, his eyes were filled with sorrow...

"Ha ha ha! What a riot! I have a feeling this will go down as the funniest story of my life," Dr. Goldman suddenly exclaimed with a bark of laughter, making me jump.

He slowly sat up and elegantly brushed the dust off his lab coat. He appeared to be wearing a fine suit under the coat. He straightened his necktie to perfection, the image of a sophisticated gentleman. Yet in contrast to his refined mannerisms, the look on his face was as much a mess as his hair.

"We may seem like polar opposites, but we're kindred souls where it counts, my darling Selkie. I, too, intended to tell you something important today. But I was too embarrassed to straight up tell you how I love you when we always bicker like an old married couple," he said.

Suddenly jumping to his feet, Dr. Goldman simply stood in a frozen daze like an abandoned scarecrow.

"So I decided to tease you a little with an innocent prank. I slipped your wedding ring into the sandwich... Would you get angry like always upon finding it? I love that fiery temper of yours. I was going to say that, hug you, and take our relationship a little further..." he said as if talking to himself, but loud enough I could hear every word.

Well, they certainly were made for each other. They just so happened to come here today with the exact same purpose in mind. But minor misunderstandings and accidents prevented their dreams from coming true. The gears slipped off track, failing to mesh...

No, something still felt off. It wasn't adding up. If Dr. Goldman genuinely loved Dr. Selkie, there was no way he would have acted the way he portrayed himself in that explanation. It was hard to believe he pretended to enter the Intake booth and watched everything unfold from the shadows... Could he really play such a cruel prank on Dr. Selkie and then watch her panic the whole time?

That was actually unbelievably mean. If he cared for Dr. Selkie, he'd rush to show her he was okay and put her mind at ease. At the very least, he would have tried to stop her from entering the Intake booth, by force if necessary.

Would he pop up claiming she was so much fun to watch, that he missed his cue because he was too busy laughing? And after being so heartless, would he have the nerve to mope like a character from some tragedy now that it was all over? I'd question his sanity if all of that was true!

"Oh, you two... That's right. I was supposed to supervise your work today," Dr. Goldman said. As if finally noticing us, he flashed Iris and I a bright smile.

Neither of us were able to respond. Iris and I turned toward each other at a loss of what to do.

"I'm terribly sorry, but I'd appreciate if that could wait a bit. We need to clean this room first and fore—" I cut Dr. Goldman off with a shriek when I turned to look the researcher in the face. I couldn't believe my eyes.

Dr. Goldman had a handsome face, but his cheek was peeling off! The impact of Dr. Selkie's slap was making chunks crumble from his face. It was reminiscent of paint slowly peeling away from a rickety old building. Normally muscle peaked out from under flayed skin. Dark-red muscle. But for some reason, his cheek was shining—shining golden. Was a layer of his flesh replaced with gold...?

"Oops. You'll have to pardon me. Please pretend you didn't see that," Dr. Goldman said with a charming wink as he covered his cheek with one hand.

"I'm afraid Selkie would blame herself. She had no way of knowing The Clockworks would refine me into nothing more than gold retaining Dr. Goldman's personality when I entered the Intake booth with that gold ring.

"It's most fascinating. Much like in the old movie, *The Fly*, I've merged with the gold ring that was inside the Intake booth at the same time as me to create a hybrid. I've been reborn as organic gold capable of altering my own form at will," he said and regrew the skin that peeled from his cheeks right before my eyes. It regained normal flesh tones, turning back to Dr. Goldman's usual face. The flakes of flesh that peeled off turned into gold dust that danced around him.

"Although my psyche belongs to Dr. Goldman, I was fundamentally reborn. The lucky man who loved Selkie and was probably loved by her in return—*that* Dr. Goldman—has already died. As I am now, in this form, I cannot return her love," he explained.

So he intentionally said all of those cruel things to push her away. She leapt toward sacrificing herself as atonement without a moment's hesitation, so he did it to ensure she wouldn't do anything else rash.

But this was love, too. It was a very human emotion filled with devotion and consideration. Dr. Goldman was a man who knew love. But that was precisely what made this such a tragedy.

If Dr. Selkie knew it was her fault Dr. Goldman changed, she would be overcome with regret. This time she really might leap into SCP-914's booth again to change him back. Knowing how she would react, Dr. Goldman told that gentle lie and intentionally tried to make her hate him. It was all done out of love. Still lacking life experience, it was hard for a simple high school kid such as myself to comprehend such deep affection.

"Now, now! Don't look so serious. I can't stand when things get tense. I'll have you know, the scientist in me is somewhat enjoying the situation," Dr. Goldman said. He rubbed his finger along his body and barked an indomitable laugh. "The results for this test are most fascinating. This is what makes researching SCP objects so alluring."

It sounded to me like he was putting on a show for us, but there was nothing I could say. It wasn't my place as an ignorant kid to speak against him, not if this was what a mature adult had decided was best after careful consideration. I couldn't explain how or why I thought it wasn't right. So at the very least, I wanted to remember how he truly felt. I didn't want to forget about his love, which shone as majestically as his golden body.

"Now then, let's get busy cleaning up. Of course, you're willing to help, aren't you? I'm eager to finish our tasks so I can gently pacify Selkie and reconcile with her. So let's clean this up in a jiffy. The possibility of being united with her has greatly decreased, but even so, I still want to be with her," Dr. Goldman said with a somewhat forced smile. We both nodded in understanding.

I finally noticed I was still holding Iris's hands, but somehow it felt right to keep holding them anyway... For a while, I couldn't budge. I stared at what became of a man who knew what it was to love someone—or perhaps I should say, at the nonhuman organism that was filled with a love greater than any other.

In the back of the room, the countless springs and gears that created The Clockworks made a sound like an innocent baby laughing.

SCP FOUNDATION
IRIS THROUGH THE LOOKING GLASS

SCP-131
[THE "EYE PODS"]

SCP-105

Special Containment Procedures: SCP-105 is implanted with a tracking device and is currently housed at Site-17. SCP-105 is currently allowed Class 3 (restricted socialization privileges with approved site personnel, granted based on continued good behavior and cooperation with Foundation personnel... →For details, refer to the section for SCP-105

WHO ARE YOU?

Confidential

WARNING

THE FOUNDATION DATABASE IS CLASSIFIED
ACCESS BY UNAUTHORIZED PERSONNEL IS STRICTLY PROHIBITED
PERPETRATORS WILL BE TRACKED, LOCATED, AND DETAINED

 Content relating to the SCP Foundation, including the SCP Foundation logo, is licensed under Creative Commons Attribution-Sharealike 3.0 and all concepts originate from http://www.scp-wiki.net and its authors. SCP Foundation: Iris Through the Looking Glass, being derived from this content, is also released under Creative Commons Attribution-Sharealike 3.0. To view a copy of the license, please visit https://creativecommons.org/licenses/by-sa/3.0/ or contact Creative Commons, PO Box 1866, Mountain View, CA 94042, USA.

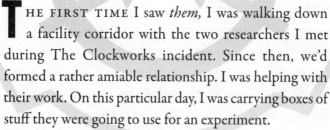

THE FIRST TIME I saw *them,* I was walking down a facility corridor with the two researchers I met during The Clockworks incident. Since then, we'd formed a rather amiable relationship. I was helping with their work. On this particular day, I was carrying boxes of stuff they were going to use for an experiment.

Seeing as the SCP Foundation was a secret organization, they were always understaffed. That was especially true regarding work with the most valuable SCP objects, which could only be handled by personnel with high-level clearance. Merely divulging information to lower-ranked personnel was prohibited, making it difficult to find assistants for even simple tests.

They could always resort to using expendable Class D personnel or recruit random handymen and apply amnestics upon completion, but the preparations and cleanup were a hassle. While I had a certain degree of basic knowledge and a bit of authority as Iris's accessory, I wasn't so important that it would be a terrible loss if something did happen to me. All told, this put me in a rather convenient position.

It wasn't as if Dr. Bright implemented experiments using me every day. With more time than I knew what to do with, I actively sought out such odd jobs as a means to kill time. I wasn't sure if they took a liking to me or if they simply viewed me as a handy helper, but these two researchers in particular started calling on me rather casually to go help with their experiments.

"I can't help but think when I see Young Girl that God put her on this world as an ironic testament to the violent nature of foolhardy men." Dressed in soft, white clothing again today, Dr. Selkie made that scathing remark and sharply clicked her tongue. "Tsk, tsk, tsk!" More often than not, that tongue clicking was a warning sign she was in a bad mood. But as far as I could tell, she was almost always in a huff about something or other.

Donned in gold from head to toe (looking closely, I was impressed to find even his matching lab coat held a hint of gold), Dr. Goldman gazed lovingly at Dr. Selkie. He offered her a pleasant smile that revealed his shining white teeth. "Your theory is flawed, my darling Selkie. It's not just men—women are affected by Young Girl as well. And when you say 'God,' to which religion or mythology are you referring?"

"Jeez, it's not like you're three years old! Can't you comprehend abstract expressions?" Dr. Selkie snapped.

"May I consider that a discriminatory remark against three-year-olds or immature children?" Dr. Goldman quipped.

"You're so quick to change the subject! Take my frumpy puppy death glare! Why do you turn tail and run the second someone finds fault with you?"

"Maybe because you don't simply point out my flaws, you dig into them with a knife. Now, in short, you're trying to say men are insufferably violent and foolish creatures. As a man, surely that means I am no different. Correct?"

"Don't tie it into a neat package with that 'in short' crap! You're getting under my skin! Oh, you drive me batty!" she howled.

The two researchers were having fun (I only just recently realized this, but their foulmouthed banter was actually a form of expressing their affection) chatting like usual. They soon realized I was straggling fairly far behind and turned back in unison to face me.

"Dear, aren't we walking a bit too fast?" Dr. Selkie asked.

"I believe so. You're falling awfully far behind, ███████. Seeing as my masculinity is under fire at the moment, I would rather avoid emphasizing my brute strength—a symbol of manliness—by taking half of those boxes off your hands," Dr. Goldman said smoothly.

"Unbelievable! You always have an excuse for everything!"

I hobbled along as the quarrelsome duo looked back at me. I was carrying a bunch of boxes of something or other at their request today. There were a total of six. None were all that heavy on their own, but they were a nightmare to carry when stacked. It wouldn't be so bad if I could use some sort of cart, but I was stuck carrying them in my arms.

As a normal high school boy without any weight training, this was a pretty exhausting task. Not only were they getting heavy, they were so bulky that it was outright hard to walk—I could barely see around the stack.

The rule of thumb regarding anything related to SCP objects was "see no evil, hear no evil, speak no evil." While I hadn't asked about their contents, I couldn't help but wonder: What was inside?

"Nothing much. It's not like we've got anything creepy stuffed in there," Dr. Selkie said as if the question was written on my face. Unable to bear watching me struggle any longer, she stretched to grab the box on top of the stack with both arms as she said, "They're full of toys, picture books, and—what else was it again?—to give Young Girl."

"Four of the six boxes are full of candy and snacks," Dr. Goldman answered. Grabbing two of the boxes, he said, "Look," as he broke one open to reveal the contents.

Sure enough, it was stuffed with the brightly colored wrappers typical of foreign candies. There were hard candies, gummies, biscuits, and a variety of chocolates... It was loaded with the sort of candy that most kids would flip out over.

"Sweets are good for when you're tired. Here, you can have one," Dr. Goldman said.

Smiling pleasantly as usual, Dr. Goldman peeled off the silver wrapper of a chocolate bar he snatched from the box before unceremoniously stuffing it in my mouth. My mouth was filled with the sweet flavor. With a disapproving glare, Dr. Selkie once again clicked her teeth, "Tsk! Tsk! Tsk!"

"Is it wise to give him a piece on a whim, Dear?" she asked.

"Everyone is so scared of Young Girl right now, they're increasing her treats in hopes of keeping her happy... One less is no big deal. Don't worry, it's fine," Dr. Goldman assured her.

This had been bugging me for a while now, so I threw my question at Dr. Goldman while he was trying to assuage Dr. Selkie. I wanted to know who exactly this "Young Girl" the two researchers kept mentioning was... It was an innocent question, but their expressions instantly turned grave.

"Even among the SCP objects, it's an extremely dangerous monster," said Dr. Selkie.

"You must never go anywhere near it," answered Dr. Goldman.

It was unusual for the two chatterboxes to come out so harsh and concise. I wondered what the deal was with this Young Girl... But when it came to SCP objects, it was quite literally best to let sleeping *gods* lie, so I didn't press any further.

"Oops!" Due to grabbing the boxes and opening one while walking, a piece of candy slipped out and fell to the ground. It bounced across the floor. And just our luck, the candy—a piece of chewing gum, I thought— slipped right under one of the vending machines scattered throughout the corridors.

"Oh, jeez," Dr. Selkie snapped. "Why must you be such a klutz, dear?"

"Why must you act like I did something wrong?" Dr. Goldman retorted.

I told the constantly bickering couple something along the lines that I would go get it. I put down the cardboard boxes and made my way over to the vending machine.

After carrying the heavy burden for so long, my back and arms were sore and tired. Grunting like an old man, I dropped down to peek under the vending machine. And that's when I found them. No, perhaps it was the other way around and *they* found *me*.

The first thing I saw were eyes. In the sliver of darkness born in the small space below the vending machine, there were two gleaming, giant eyeballs. Certain something creepy was lurking under there, I instinctively screamed and scooted away. Noticing how I was freaking out, the two researchers looked at me with eyes wide in surprise.

"What's the matter?" Dr. Goldman asked as he put the boxes down on the spot and quickly raced toward me out of concern. He thrust his hand toward the slightly golden lab coat's inner breast pocket to pull out a handgun of sorts. Due to the dangerous nature of their work, quite a few researchers bore arms on a regular basis. Still carrying the box, Dr. Selkie was timidly inching toward me.

"Is everything okay? Do you see cause for me to call security…?" Dr. Selkie asked.

"No need," Dr. Goldman replied with a deep sigh of relief upon squatting next to me—I was too scared to stand. He took a peek under the vending machine for himself. "There's nothing dangerous. The Eye Pods here gave him a fright."

The Eye Pods…?

"Hey, come here. Come on out," Dr. Goldman coaxed as if calling cats.

He placed a biscuit from one of the boxes on the palm of his hand and waved it in front of the vending machine. As he did this, I could hear the sound of a small wheel squeaking, and something slipped out from behind the vending machine. Possibly as a safety provision for earthquakes, the vending machine wasn't pressed flat against the building wall, leaving a narrow space between it and the paint. The thing must have slipped through that narrow crack, just like a cat!

It was a strange creature unlike anything I had ever seen before. The thing was roughly thirty centimeters in height, making it about as tall as a human toddler. It didn't resemble any other creature that existed on the face of the planet. Overall elliptical, the top of its body gently came to a point. In other words, it was tear-shaped—or you could say it was shaped like an almond. It was a dull orange (I didn't learn until later, but apparently that color was called "burnt orange"). What appeared to be a massive blue eyeball was located smack in the center of its body.

I wasn't sure how, but this strange creature was able to move on its own. Upon closer observation, I found a wheel-like protrusion at the base of this mysterious creature, which was how it slid across the floor.

What the heck…? I've seen a bunch of strange things since I first started living in this research facility, but these weird things never ceased to amaze me.

"It's SCP-131-A, one of the 'Eye Pods,'" Dr. Selkie explained with a smile as she came closer. She'd dropped her guard once she deciding there was no imminent danger. "Considered to be biomechanical creatures, they are deemed safe to be left unattended. Much like Builder Bear and Josie the Half-Cat, they are allowed to freely roam this site… I wonder why we have so many running loose here."

"I imagine the Foundation is intentionally allowing multiple Safe SCP objects to wander around in order to observe how they interact," Dr. Goldman responded.

I hesitantly interrupted the two researchers as they fell into another scientific-sounding conversation. Uh, it looked like another one of those so-called "Eye Pods" was under the vending machine. It was staring at me with its one big blue eye for some time now. Staring as if it needed help...

"Really?" Dr. Selkie bent over to check under the vending machine and clapped her hands to her mouth. "Good Heavens! Is the poor thing stuck?"

As if to agree, "Yes! This is horrible!" the burnt orange Eye Pod noisily squeaked its wheel as it spun excessively around us. With a shrug, Dr. Goldman thrust his hands beneath the vending machine. He motioned me to help with a flick of his eyes, so I went over to give him an assist.

"For the record, we have only verified the existence of SCP-131-A and SCP-131-B. They aren't all that bright, so they get themselves caught in messes like this rather frequently," Dr. Goldman explained.

"They've even managed to get stuck in air vents," Dr. Selkie added.

The air vents...? As in the ducts behind the ventilation fan near the corridor ceiling? What I wanted to know was how the heck they got there to begin with.

"Beats me. They can climb sheer surfaces, so I suspect they accidentally *fell* in while running along the wall or ceiling," Dr. Selkie said.

They really weren't the sharpest tools in the shed. I found that adorable, honestly. My heart melted for the little guys.

But moving right along! It took a bit of time, but with Dr. Goldman's help, I was able to pull the other Eye Pod out from under the vending machine. It got itself jammed in there nice and good, and it took a great deal of strength and perseverance to save it. But it was well worth the effort. We successfully managed to rescue the other Eye Pod, which looked almost exactly the same as the one that popped out from behind the vending machine, albeit a bit dusty. The variation in color was the only true discrepancy, with this one a being dull yellow (supposedly called "mustard yellow").

Rejoicing over their reunion, the two Eye Pods squeaked their wheels as they spun in place in a strange display of affection (I think?).

"I'm so happy for them. They must be relieved," Dr. Selkie said, a surprisingly gentle expression on her face as she watched them.

As if in a show of gratitude, the two Eye Pods raced around us and rubbed up against our legs. However, their relief was short-lived. The Eye Pod that was trapped under the vending machine slipped on a dust bunny stuck to its wheel, tripping spectacularly. Racing directly behind it, the other tripped over the first and flipped over like something out of a hilarious slap-stick routine.

They really were stupid... But funny, too. We broke into peals of laughter as we watched their comical yet en-dearing antics for a while. Here at the SCP Foundation's research site, this was one of the rare moments that was genuinely jovial and peaceful.

From that day on, I occasionally spotted those mysterious and adorable creatures, the "Eye Pods." Those little guys (they appeared genderless, but I decided to call them that anyway) truly were harmless by all accounts, and allowed to freely roam the research site on a daily basis. From what I gathered, the on-site personnel treated them along the lines of stray cats. I myself would pet them whenever I came across them.

For the record, these little buddies didn't require food or sleep. They didn't even leave droppings! Not only were they free of all the headaches involved with feeding a pet and taking it out on walks, they were friggin' adorable.

I guess they didn't have breaks despite moving at pretty fast speeds, for sometimes they would crash into walls and flip over... After helping them back up and having fun holding them, they eventually took a liking to me.

The Eye Pods were constantly trailing behind me as of late. It wasn't like they were underfoot, and many of my days were filled with nothing to do, so I often spent my time playing with them. For instance, I would use a rubber ball to play fetch, like if they were puppies or something (For the record, they would trip and tumble over the ball. They never got so much as a scratch, so evidently they were super tough). That was how they came to enrich my life as some sort of beloved pet...

Then one day, these guys actually came into my room. Always tagging along at my heels, they simply rolled right in. It didn't seem right to kick them out, and there was still time before bed, so I decided to play with them.

There was a rope laying around, so we played tug-of-war. I tied a loop at one end of the rope, wrapped it around one of the Eye Pods, and began the endless game of tug-of-war. It was so much fun feeling it resist my tugs and pull at me in turn, that I got totally immersed in the game and lost track of time. It was just an innocent game.

For the record, this was around when Iris offered to let me have half of the room as my own personal space. She brought in a bunch of stuff, like a bed for me to sleep on along with a locker to store my personal possessions.

Interior decoration didn't mean anything to me, so we kept the wallpaper and carpet as they were.

It felt as if I'd upgraded from freeloader to roommate. I still felt it wasn't right for a mature young man to sleep in the same room as a mature young woman, but apparently I was viewed as nothing more than an accessory to Iris. We even received official orders to coexist in the same room for observation purposes.

Honestly, the idea of living alone in a foreign country I didn't know anything about made me uneasy. Iris didn't show any indication she minded my being here, so I accepted her kind offer and complied with the arrangement. We had the occasional, minor mishap that were inevitable in co-ed life, but overall, Iris and I got along just fine as roommates. At least, we did until this day.

"......"

Iris didn't come back until late that evening. She occasionally had late days like this. Unlike how I was regarded as little better than a guinea pig, she operated as a researcher (Elements of her job were top secret, so she couldn't tell me about it. I didn't know any of the details concerning what she did.). It left her working like a beaver.

Unusual for the typically bubbly and chipper Iris, a raincloud was hanging over her head this day. I wondered if she made a mistake at work, or if something bad happened. Growing concerned, I called out to her after she silently entered the room. I welcomed her back... And then I asked what happened. Was she feeling okay? Did something happen?

"Yes, there is a somewhat...sticky situation," Iris said, her face slightly softening with relief upon seeing me, only to darken with a frown. "What the heck? What do you think you're doing?"

I honestly told her how I was playing with the Eye Pods.

"Please don't let those things in our room... You do realize that just because they're Object Class: Safe doesn't mean they aren't SCP objects, right?" Pressing a finger against her forehead, Iris spat with disgust, "Jeez, don't tell me you're wanting to keep them here!" The thought never occurred to me, but it sounded like a wonderful idea. So I basically asked if we could keep them. At this point in time, I was pretty infatuated with the fun and adorable Eye Pods. They bonded to me as quickly as if they were cats, begging for attention in the most adorable of ways. The idea of a future that featured them constantly scooting about our room sounded pretty exciting to me.

"Forget it," Iris said, arms crossed, a baleful expression on her face. "As the owner of this room, I won't allow it.

Go dump them outside," she said bluntly. So harsh! It was like she was scolding a little kid.

Growing a little bent out of shape, I brought up a variety of points in hopes to win her over. There were mental benefits to having them in our room. We already made the rule that I could do whatever I wanted in my half of the room. And not to mention, humans had the right to pursue happiness...

"When I say, 'No,' I mean it," Iris said adamantly, refusing to budge.

Ultimately she resorted to force. Marching straight toward me, she snatched up the Eye Pod I was playing tug-of-war with in both arms. Then she roughly tore the rope off the little guy, made a beeline for the door, swung it open, and literally dropped it out into the corridor. Quickly slamming the door shut, she snatched up the other Eye Pod that tried to flee from her when it sensed danger and dumped it outside in much the same manner.

She quickly shut and locked the door, effectively kicking them out. Upset by how outrageously unfair she was acting, I gave Iris a piece of my mind. I felt grateful toward Iris, yes, and she generally treated me nice up till this point. I respected—even loved—this straight-forward and kindhearted girl as a person, but the heavy-handed approach she took ticked me off.

"No matter what you say, this is the way it is," Iris insisted, refusing to hear reason. Not bothering to change into her pajamas, she flopped onto her bed. "This discussion is over. I'm going to bed and you should go to sleep soon yourself," she snapped.

Grabbing the remote by her pillow, Iris turned the lights off and refused to say another word. Outside our room came the sad sound of the Eye Pods continually bonking against our door as if to say they didn't understand why they were kicked out.

From that day on, Iris and I pretty much stopped talking to each other. No morning salutations for us upon waking in the morning! Every morning we ate breakfast together without fail, but now our breakfasts were silent as we stuffed the cereal into our mouths, refusing to so much as look the other in the eye.

Despite our rocky relationship, for some odd reason, Iris pushed off her usual obligations to constantly hang over my shoulder. She was in a rotten mood the whole time, barring any hope of working things out with her silent brooding.

Whenever Iris saw the Eye Pods, which would affectionately race toward me if I entered their line of sight, she would chase them away with threatening behavior such as stomping her feet or yelling at them. When I asked what would possess her to do such a thing, she refused to tell me. I was getting the royal silent treatment.

As she grated on my nerves more and more, our relationship grew increasingly strained. The air between us was constantly heavy. Clueless how to repair our failing relationship, things grew so brutal even the high-handed Dr. Bright asked, "What's wrong? Are you okay?" out of concern.

The mere memory of these never-ending bleak days was enough to make me feel depressed... After roughly two weeks passed, my long fight with Iris suddenly came to an end.

Iris and I returned to our room at the same time that day. Dr. Bright had discontinued all testing until such time as our relationship returned to normal. If ordered to continue the tests while our relationship was still unstable, there was no telling what sort of accidents could ensue. That was the official excuse Dr. Bright offered, but I bet they simply didn't want to get caught in the awkward atmosphere we created. Our Dr. Bright was the type of person to alter the schedule for important tests over such trivial personal whims.

As a result, I spent day in and day out in a mindless daze... At times like this, the hands on the clock seemed to move at an agonizing crawl. It felt like this was one of those "times that try men's souls." Even though I wasn't really doing anything, I felt completely drained.

Iris was in no better shape than I; it wasn't unusual to find faint rings hanging under the usually energetic girl's eyes. But our relationship was so chilly that I couldn't even bring myself to show concern.

Darn, I hoped we wouldn't stay like this forever... Now that I had lost Iris and the Eye Pods—the two things that set my heart at ease—harsh reality suddenly came crashing down upon my shoulders all at once.

What was going to become of me? Would I have to spend the rest of my life in this shady research facility? What was my family doing? If I continued to skip school, would I be forced to withdraw? Even if I wasn't kicked out, wasn't it just a matter of time before one of these dangerous SCP objects took my life, anyway? The more I thought about it, the darker my prospects seemed. I couldn't help but drop my head despondently.

I wanted to recover my peaceful life. If I couldn't have that, I wanted something to lighten my heart, even if only a little. I was reaching my limit—on the verge of bursting into an unwarranted fit of tears.

"Gah...! I can't take it anymore," Iris suddenly groaned.

Turning toward Iris out of curiosity, I saw she was sprawled across her bed on her stomach, kicking her feet wildly. It looked like she was practicing the flutter kick.

"It should be fine now. Yeah, this has extended well beyond the prescribed timeframe. I've personally determined the problem has been resolved," she whispered nonsensically to herself before lifting her head up.

Realizing I was watching her, Iris broke into a broad grin and apologized, "I'm so sorry!"

Uh, what...?

Sitting on her knees atop her bed, Iris's face turned bright red as she trembled in anger. "First, hear me out! The inhumane way that I, Iris Thompson, have treated you these past two weeks was under orders by Dr. Bright and by no means of my own accord!" she cried.

I wouldn't go so far as to call it "inhumane..." But hold up! What was going on here?

"That's what I'm telling you!" Iris fervently insisted, pounding the bed several times like a child throwing a tantrum. "I stopped greeting you first thing in the morning, holding decent conversations with you, and overall ignored you! I threw out the Eye Pods when I knew you're fond of them! But I didn't do any of those things because I wanted to!"

Iris practically tumbled off her bed and walked up to me. While I stared at her dumbstruck, she grabbed my hand and held it tight. It was a painful, bone-crushing grip.

"Please believe me! I care for you greatly!" she insisted.

Simply hearing that was enough to make me forgive and forget all that transpired. As I felt the warmth of her body, I strived to fully understand the weight of her words.

"I realize you might find this strange since we haven't even known each other for a full year yet, but you're my family! You don't mind if I think of you as family, do you?" Tears welled in her eyes as she looked at me straight on. "I no longer have a real family. I was torn from them when I was identified as an SCP object, and I can never reach out to them again. But you and I are like two peas in a pod. We stay in the same room and dine at the same table—we're family!"

Family. They were part of my distant normal life now... I guess the same was true of Iris as well. Branded an anomalous entity—an SCP object—the normal, peaceful life she enjoyed was ripped away from her.

"The two of us are bound together by the name SCP-105! The concept of 'SCP' that stole everything from me now serves as a bond between us! And that honestly, really makes me happy...!" Unable to hold it back any longer, Iris began sobbing.

It took a hefty amount of time offering Iris words of comfort and reassuring physical contact such as holding her hands to get her to stop crying. But through it all, I finally came to understand the situation. This was what I gleaned between sobs...

The Foundation restricted growing too attached to SCP-131, also known as the "Eye Pods." There were a variety of reasons for this, which included an SCP object I still didn't have any dealings with (she mentioned something about an SCP-173...) that went right over my head. Oblivious of the Foundation's regulation, I displayed strong affection for the Eye Pods. In order to contend with this problem, Iris acted under Dr. Bright's orders and followed the semi-standardized protocol on how to terminate amiable relationships with the little guys.

The protocol was essentially ensuring the Eye Pods absolutely never got near me. With temperament akin to domestic cats, they were quick to bond with people who treated them well or played with them, but would lose all interest in the bonded individual if ignored for roughly two weeks.

Come to think of it, I didn't so much as hear the unique sound of their wheels once since I woke this morning, let alone catch sight of them. I guess they lost interest in me...probably.

They moved at rather high speeds—from what I heard, they averaged anywhere from five to thirty meters a second, but could go even faster—so Iris was constantly on high alert to ensure they never got anywhere near me. That took so much focus, she was evidently too preoccupied to chat. All the questions weighing on me melted away.

"That was part of it. At the time, I was also trying to squeeze in any paperwork—whatever I could complete over my PDA—so I simply didn't have time to talk," Iris said, looking dejected. She was such an earnest girl, she probably tried to stay on top of her work as best she could rather than taking time off from her usual duties.

"Plus, I was basically ordered to ignore you as much as possible. I'm not really sure why, but that is what Dr. Bright instructed. That's right, this is all Dr. Bright's fault," she spat.

I felt that was too harsh—not that I blamed Iris for dissing that depraved researcher. In fact, I had a hunch I knew where Dr. Bright's true intentions lay. This was a threat. If I didn't learn my lesson after enduring this hell and still sought to befriend the Eye Pods for temporary solace again, Dr. Bright would enact this protocol to tear me from them once more. They would throw us into another war of frigid silence. They was warning me never to befriend the Eye Pods again if I didn't want that to happen... That was the nature of the threat. No, it was more like punishment.

I didn't feel alive these past two weeks. Simply being unable to chat with Iris made my heart gradually fall into decay. I never wanted to go through that again.

I felt like a prisoner who'd committed some sort of crime, received his sentence, and was thrown into the slammer... I was to reflect and mend my ways, resolving never to act in defiance of the rules again. That was the nature of this threat, punishment, and mandate.

Henceforth, I would adhere to the rule I learned though this incident. As I promised that to myself, Iris gave me a strained smile and said, "It's okay, ████. I realize it is truly sad and upsetting to push away something that likes you... I felt the exact same way these past two weeks."

Huh? By any chance, did Iris think of me as some pet along the lines of an indoor dog...? Even if it wasn't intentional, that was how it sounded.

"I will bury the space—the hole—in your heart that you used the Eye Pods to fill," Iris said as she drew her face close to mine, her proclamation making my heart go pitter-patter.

She pulled a rope out from somewhere. I recognized that rope! It was the one I used when playing with the Eye Pods.

"Here, you take that end. I'll hold this end," Iris said happily, back to her usual chipper self. Wrapping her fingers around the rope, her eyes sparkled adorably.

"We tug over the rope, right? And that's supposed to be fun? I don't really get it myself, but I'll do my best!" she declared and began yanking at the rope... The sight of that alone was enough to blow the dissatisfaction and depression accumulated in me to smithereens.

SCP-105

Special Containment Procedures: SCP-105 is implanted with a tracking device and is currently housed at Site-17. SCP-105 is currently allowed Class 3 (restricted) socialization privileges with approved site personnel, granted based on continued good behavior and cooperation with Foundation personnel... →For details, refer to the section for SCP-105

SCP-529
[JOSIE THE HALF-CAT]

WHO ARE YOU?

Confidential

THE FOUNDATION DATABASE IS CLASSIFIED
ACCESS BY UNAUTHORIZED PERSONNEL IS STRICTLY PROHIBITED
PERPETRATORS WILL BE TRACKED, LOCATED, AND DETAINED

Content relating to the SCP Foundation, including the SCP Foundation logo, is licensed under Creative Commons Attribution-Sharealike 3.0
and all concepts originate from http://www.scp-wiki.net and its authors. SCP Foundation: Iris Through the Looking Glass, being derived
from this content, is also released under Creative Commons Attribution-Sharealike 3.0. To view a copy of the license, please visit
https://creativecommons.org/licenses/by-sa/3.0/ or contact Creative Commons, PO Box 1866, Mountain View, CA 94042, USA.

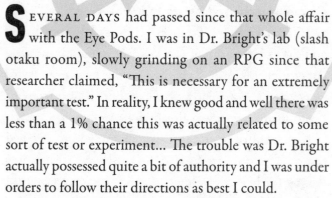

SEVERAL DAYS had passed since that whole affair with the Eye Pods. I was in Dr. Bright's lab (slash otaku room), slowly grinding on an RPG since that researcher claimed, "This is necessary for an extremely important test." In reality, I knew good and well there was less than a 1% chance this was actually related to some sort of test or experiment... The trouble was Dr. Bright actually possessed quite a bit of authority and I was under orders to follow their directions as best I could.

Besides, it wasn't like I had anything that demanded my immediate attention. Since I was no longer allowed to relax by playing with the Eye Pods, I was feeling pretty down in the dumps. By endlessly repeating the same monotonous task, I was attempting to bury my sense of loss and loneliness.

If I sat doing nothing, my mind would only hurtle toward depressing thoughts. But that having been said, I wasn't up to anything mentally challenging in my current state. As such, I had to admit, this was currently the perfect way for me to kill time. As I methodically continued an endless level grind—one that somehow seemed reminiscent of meditation, something that could accidentally lead to enlightenment—the door suddenly swung open.

"Hello! ██████, would you like to join me for lunch?" Iris asked, peeking her head into the room. There was an adorable lunchbox dangling from one hand.

I had been holed up in Dr. Bright's lab since bright and early that morning. That made it sound like we were conducting highbrow experiments, but I was just playing video games. Apparently, time had slipped away from me. I couldn't believe it was already time for lunch.

I glanced over at the clock in the room to check the time before turning back toward Iris and nodding. Asking for her to give me a second, I hastily saved the game, found a reasonable enough home for the controller, and rushed over to her.

Iris seemed in high spirits, wearing a bright grin. "Sorry for suddenly dropping by. Were you in the middle of an important task?"

I told her it was by no means important.

"Really? Glad to hear it! When I asked some of the other personnel, they said I could find you here, ███. So what were you up to?" she asked.

I told her I was saving the world.

"...What do you mean?" Despite asking that with a puzzled tilt of her head, she snatched my hand, unable to wait a moment longer—truly happy and hyper today—and began tugging me along.

"There is something I'd like to show you. Please come with me," she said, thrusting her thumb to point the way in a gesture not typically done by Japanese.

We walked for a good while, Iris pulling me by the hand all the while. Along the way, we got on the elevator to the ground floor. It was surprisingly easy to forget, but the area where we generally went about our business was part of a primarily underground research facility. We didn't have much business with the surface (not that there was much there to begin with). And since we were still considered an SCP object and *its* accessory, an alarm would have on-site security rushing to secure us if we stayed out too long. As such, the amount of time we could spend outside was fairly limited...

"This way! Over here!" Iris said, walking with such a spry step she practically bounced. She led me toward a certain area.

It was located in a courtyard, probably in the center of the ground-floor building. I only said "probably" because the research site's blueprints and floor plans weren't made public in order to maintain confidentiality. It didn't help that the place was freaking huge, preventing me from forming any sense of direction.

Iris simply referred to this as the "courtyard." It was essentially a glass-encased greenhouse, where a variety of flowers bloomed with no regard for the season. There was everything from unwieldly tropical plants to some bored personnel's efforts to grow the semblance of a vegetable garden.

It was a rare plot of abundant greenery in the otherwise drab gray and metallic research site. But the stifling humidity characteristic of greenhouses made it a less-than-ideal location to kick back and relax. There were a bunch of bugs flying around, and mud was getting all over me after hardly walking a few feet... Raised in a city pretty close to Tokyo, I lacked that drive to "return to nature."

"I'll never get over how great the air is here," Iris exclaimed.

Unlike me, it was apparently in her nature to love the great outdoors. She happily took in a great, deep breath. She seemed to enjoy looking at the flowers and pantomimed taking pictures. Not only was Iris prohibited from carrying around her beloved Polaroid camera, she wasn't even allowed to have a normal camera or photos, so she couldn't actually take any pictures. I felt a bit bad for her, but there was nothing I could do about it. Iris waved me over once she had taken enough photos of stuff with the imaginary camera made from both her hands' pointer finger and thumb.

"I made sandwiches," she said, sitting on a bench in the courtyard and placing the lunchbox that she brought on her lap. For some reason, she was looking about the area with restless excitement.

...Was she searching for something?

"Yes, Josie the Half-Cat has been spotted here lately. Really, that kitty should be underground, but it must have slipped out sometime," she said.

I could swear I had heard that name before. After thinking for a minute, it hit me. During the string of events concerning the Eye Pods, Dr. Selkie mentioned that name.

"Ahh, the Eye Pods. The rule is there for a reason, but you really have been down ever since you were prohibited from playing with them," Iris observed.

She popped open the lunchbox, grabbed one of the sandwiches, and took a big bite out of it. Then she handed one of the plastic-wrapped sandwiches to me. Gratefully accepting it, I sat down next to Iris to join her for lunch.

"So I decided to introduce you to a new cute friend. There are reasons why you can't interact with the Eye Pods, but there's no reason why you can't befriend something else."

Iris... She could tell I was down and went out of her way to cheer me up. I was honestly happy. Grateful. It gave me the warm fuzzies. Iris's kindness alone was enough to unravel the knot of loneliness that was growing in my heart. Overwhelmed with happiness, I chomped into my sandwich. She went heavy on the mustard (a good portion of the people here went surprisingly heavy on condiments and spices), but it was still good.

"I've been a bit lonesome of late myself. I haven't been informed of the details, but Bill—Builder Bear—has gone missing," she confessed.

Oh, that moving teddy bear... I knew Iris was pretty infatuated with that thing... So it was missing, huh? What could have happened to it?

"I don't know. The site director—the whole Foundation, for that matter—doesn't seem to know.

It's currently under investigation. But things don't look good... I've heard a task force from another facility has been mobilized to handle the situation."

A task force... Like the soldiers I maneuvered with back in the Carnival of Horrors, or to be more precise, inside a photo of SCP-823. Those soldiers boasted they could neutralize a small town! I felt throwing such strong forces at a moving stuffed animal was overkill.

"Agreed. I suppose they are being extra careful since it's always possible the situation will develop in the most unlikely of ways when SCP objects are involved." Iris sighed heavily, probably beside herself with worry for Builder Bear.

Nevertheless, Iris was an overall cheerful, optimistic girl. Rather than fret over the various possibilities, she focused on the fun things in life as she put on a smile, once again looking around us.

"That having been said, in order to avoid losing my mind for want of something cute to cuddle while I wait for the issue concerning Builder Bear to resolve...I'd like to get closer with Josie the Half-Cat."

I could see where Iris was coming from... But what type of creature was this "Josie the Half-Cat?" Dr. Selkie put it on the same level as Builder Bear and the Eye Pods, so I assumed it was an SCP object.

"That's right. It's SCP-529, Josie the Half-Cat. It's an overall extremely harmless cat that is absolutely adorable with gray tabby markings. But as the name implies, it is only half a cat," Iris said with a grin.

I didn't quite follow. I outright suspected the translation collar around my neck had failed to properly translate what she said. Uh, what did she mean by "only half a cat…?"

"It's hard to explain. It'll be quicker if you see for yourself. Josie the Half-Cat loves cheese, so let's use that as bait," Iris suggested.

She pulled the slice of cheese from her partially eaten sandwich and flapped it between pinched fingers as she called out, "Hey, Josie! Cute little Josie the Half-Cat!"

Mere seconds after Iris's voice echoed throughout the greenhouse, a sound came from beside the bench we were sitting on. A bush with a bunch of red berries rustled as a cat popped its tiny head out.

This was probably the aforementioned Josie the Half-Cat. With a clever countenance, this was quite a handsome little fella (I didn't learn until later that Josie was female, so "handsome little fella" probably wasn't the most accurate description). Its gray coat was regal and dignified, boasting pattern-like swirls. There was an intelligent gleam in its eyes. From the look of it, this was just a typical cat. It was hard to believe this was a mysterious SCP object.

"Oops. I should eat this now that we've managed to lure the little dear out," Iris said.

Practicing less than great table manners, Iris tossed the piece of cheese pinched between her fingers into the air and caught it with her mouth like a frog. That took skill... But I was under the impression she was going to give the cheese to Josie, so I was a bit surprised she ate it at all.

"There are hardly any rules or regulations concerning Josie the Half-Cat... But there is one restriction: Staff are not permitted to feed cheese to her," Iris said.

Why not? Seeing as we used cheese to lure her out, I bet she loved the stuff. Don't tell me she'd turn violent if she ate it and go on a killing rampage!

"No, nothing of the sort," Iris said, her face a bit taut as if disturbed by the idea.

She explained, "It's just, if she's unsatisfied with the scanty amount of cheese you give her, it makes her terribly distressed. She gets so sad, it's really very...pathetic. So it was made against the rules. Not that it stops me from sneaking her some every now and then." Upon making her confession, Iris stuck out her tongue naughtily. Jeez, everything about her was so cute!

While I was busy relaxing with Iris, Josie the Half-Cat stealthily walked up to us without me even noticing. I guess it was true that cats walk silently. As I was musing over that, I looked back down at Josie now that she stepped all of the way out of the bush...and was shocked speechless! Wow, she really was only half a cat... That was the only thought I could come up with.

It looked like Josie the Half-Cat was sliced in two. Everything from the tip of her tail to her mid-abdomen— the end of her ribcage to be precise—was missing. Nevertheless, she was walking just like usual. Weird, to say the least. So weird, I blinked several times, unable to believe my own eyes.

"As you can see," Iris said with a giggle, finding my surprise humorous, "Josie the Half-Cat lives up to her name; she's a cat missing half her body. It's not as though it's outside the visible spectrum for humans. The hindquarters simply do not exist."

That made no sense. Oh, but that must have been precisely what made her an SCP object. If I thought about it logically, simply surviving without half a body would be hard in its own right. From the looks of it, Josie was missing nearly all of her major internal organs! But, completely unperturbed by this, she seemed perfectly healthy.

"Oh, whoa!"

I had no idea what was going through Josie's mind as she crouched down only to suddenly lunge up at Iris. Then she climbed up Iris's chest and began licking the young lady on the lips!

"Ah! Hey! Wh-What's gotten into you, Josie? You're such an attention hog!" Iris cried happily, cuddling the cat.

I bet Josie was just licking off some remnants of the cheese that disappeared into Iris's mouth a second ago... But the way it looked like they were kissing made me feel uncomfortable, like I was watching something inappropriate. I averted my eyes.

"Tee-hee! Isn't she something else? This is our mysterious Josie the Half-Cat!" Iris boasted, beaming happily, evidently under the impression the bizarre cat was fond of her personally. Well, I suppose there wasn't any need to point out the truth if she was happy.

But even looking at the thing up close, this was one weird cat. It really didn't have any hindquarters. Yet it was able to walk and jump normally without falling off balance.

Curious what it looked like at the cross section—the part where its torso was severed—I took a peek...only to discover that part of the body was blacked out. I was afraid I'd see the cat's innards, so this was actually a bit of a relief.

"If you're curious, why don't you touch her?" Iris suggested. She held Josie securely in her arms, pointing the black cross section toward me.

Wait! Was it okay to stick my hand in there? From the looks of it, the blackened part seemed less like a flat surface and more like a hole. If I stuck my hand in, I was afraid it'd pull me in somewhere.

Iris looked at me with such anticipation that in spite of my fears, I hesitantly put my hand against the black part of Josie the Half-Cat.

At first, I couldn't feel anything. My fingers were absorbed by the black hole in Josie, eventually meeting gentle resistance. It was a strange sensation unlike anything I had ever experienced before. It was like I was touching a hole, something which normally only existed as an abstract concept.

"Please be gentle," Iris said.

She was still holding Josie, which made me feel like I was actually touching her instead. I suddenly started to feel horribly nervous. But Josie seemed to take pleasure in me petting her (it was less like petting and more like being absorbed) in there, and began to purr contentedly.

I started to ease up a bit, a sense of peace washing over me. Albeit a bit unusual, Josie was still a beautiful and charming cat. I felt extremely fortunate to be able to pet her to my heart's content.

"Ah!"

But apparently I went a bit overboard petting her, for Josie hissed angrily. A second later, she snatched up one of the sandwiches from the lunchbox and took off like a flash of lightning.

"Poop... She got away. I wanted to touch her hole, too!" Iris pouted in disappointment. But then she burst into a dazzling smile, happy she at least got to hold Josie.

"Hee hee! There are plenty of dangerous things or creatures you can't interact with for various reasons...but there are also cute, harmless anomalies like Josie. I hope you get a chance to reach out and interact with the different entities around here without holding any prejudice toward them as SCP objects." It was like she was teaching a moral lesson or doing a PSA. While talking, she evenly split the remaining sandwiches with me. There was one extra, so we broke it in half and shared. After stuffing our respective halves into our mouths, we broke into broad grins.

"It's nice to split things in half sometimes," Iris said. Her smug expression just screamed pride over saying something cool. How adorable!

SCP-348
[A GIFT FROM DAD]

WHO ARE YOU?

SCP-105

Special Containment Procedures: SCP-105 is implanted with a tracking device and is currently housed at Site-17. SCP-105 is currently allowed Class 3 (restricted) socialization privileges with approved site personnel, granted based on continued good behavior and cooperation with Foundation personnel.... →For details, refer to the section for SCP-105

IRIS THROUGH THE LOOKING GLASS

WARNING

THE FOUNDATION DATABASE IS CLASSIFIED
ACCESS BY UNAUTHORIZED PERSONNEL IS STRICTLY PROHIBITED
PERPETRATORS WILL BE TRACKED, LOCATED, AND DETAINED

Content relating to the SCP Foundation, including the SCP Foundation logo, is licensed under Creative Commons Attribution-Sharealike 3.0 and all concepts originate from http://www.scp-wiki.net and its authors. SCP Foundation: Iris Through the Looking Glass, being derived from this content, is also released under Creative Commons Attribution-Sharealike 3.0. To view a copy of the license, please visit https://creativecommons.org/licenses/by-sa/3.0/ or contact Creative Commons, PO Box 1866, Mountain View, CA 94042, USA.

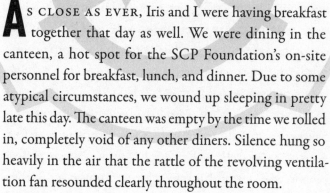

As **CLOSE AS EVER**, Iris and I were having breakfast together that day as well. We were dining in the canteen, a hot spot for the SCP Foundation's on-site personnel for breakfast, lunch, and dinner. Due to some atypical circumstances, we wound up sleeping in pretty late this day. The canteen was empty by the time we rolled in, completely void of any other diners. Silence hung so heavily in the air that the rattle of the revolving ventilation fan resounded clearly throughout the room.

"......"

Iris and I had been drawn into the upheaval concerning that horrifying Builder Bear until late the previous night. I have no doubt there will come a day I have a chance to recount that episode, although I'd personally prefer it stayed buried in my memories. It left us mentally and physically exhausted. It was obvious Iris took it particularly hard, since she used to dote on that strange, moving stuffed animal. For every nibble of toast, she sighed three times.

I didn't have much of an appetite myself. It took all I had to slowly—*slowly*—sip at the piping hot, extra-strong coffee I'd brewed in hopes of fending off drowsiness. My actual breakfast of toast, a salad, bacon, and eggs remained untouched.

"You should force yourself to eat, 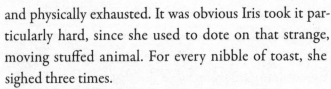," Iris said in her typical mom-or-big-sister tone. "Dr. Bright is scheduled to return today from wherever he took off to under the pretext of work again. He'll probably want to resume testing with us immediately upon arrival, so you need to eat up and get lots of nutrients," she said.

I knew that. With a nod, I mechanically stuffed a cherry tomato into my mouth. It was surprising how that eccentric researcher—Dr. Bright—was constantly popping in and out of this research site. Rumor had it they visited research facilities around the globe. They seemed to truly be an elite researcher run ragged by their schedule. Dr. Bright had been gone a while, but supposedly they would return today.

Honestly, I mildly dreaded dealing with them. Neither Iris nor I were emotionally capable of dealing with their outlandish comments politely. They claimed the position of head researcher presiding over us as SCP objects, so if that weirdo said they wanted to use us for a test, we had to suck it up and comply.

At least we reaped some benefits from Dr. Bright becoming our supervisor and guardian. We hardly ever had anyone give us a hard time. It was almost as if no one wanted to get involved with Dr. Bright if they could help it.

There were times Dr. Bright's presence came in handy, but they were fairly annoying and troublesome when around. We basically viewed them along the lines of an irritating parent. Iris and I were half-heartedly discussing our thoughts on the mad scientist when...

"Hey there! I'm home, kids! Did you miss me? It's Daddy! ☆"

I could have sworn a grenade went off. Iris and I grudgingly turned toward the sound of the voice. As extravagant as ever, Dr. Bright was standing in the entrance of the canteen. I wasn't sure if this was their favorite host, but lately they always used that mature, female beauty. Dr. Bright was in a crimson dress with a pure white lab coat. For some unknown reason, a massive number of paper bags dangled from both hands. For the finishing touch, a cheap lei hung from their neck. What in the world...? Did Dr. Bright go to Hawaii or something...? Lacking the energy today to balk over their antics, we simply gave unamused glares.

"My, my! Not much of a reaction! You're going to make me sad! Of course, I heard all about the fascinating phenomena—er, I mean, unfortunate incident that you got mixed up in during my absence. Don't let the past weigh you down forever! Turn your eyes toward the future! Push forward toward a bright tomorrow! C'mon, don't break your promise to Daddy! ♪" Dr. Bright shouted gratuitously infuriating crap as they zoomed toward us at an amazing speed. They wasted energy trying to give Iris a return-home hug only for the younger girl to dodge it. Then Dr. Bright lunged at Iris and kissed the ground when the younger girl dodged again. Why did this weirdo always have to be so rowdy?

But thanks to Dr. Bright's abnormally cheerful personality, the heavy, funereal atmosphere hanging over us dissipated as if it was never there. I was willing to give them that. As the rather rude thought of how even this freak could make themselves useful ran through my head, Iris spat, a finger pressed to the middle of her brow. "There are several issues I would like to raise, Dr. Bright. But first, you are not our father. Haven't I told you countless times it's unpleasant hearing you imply that we are related? Furthermore, wouldn't you be our mother in that form, not our father?"

"Ah ha ha! You're surprisingly nitpicky, Riss! If you're too uptight, you'll get wrinkles before your time."

"Don't shorten my name. Even if intended as an expression of affection, hearing it from you is infuriating."

"That's not a problem! Love and hate are two sides of the same coin! Just think, the disgust swirling around in your chest could be the buds of romance!"

"There is a 0% possibility of that. In fact, there is no need to discuss it further," Iris snapped.

"I'm not surprised! After all, my sweetie Riss is too busy enjoying co-ed life with a boy nearly the same age, like something out of the pages of an old romcom manga. Your maiden's heart is preoccupied with that!"

"......" Iris fell silent for a while. Either Dr. Bright's last jeer threw her off-kilter, or she finally remembered a fundamental law of being left alone: don't feed the trolls.

After moistening their mouth with some coffee, Dr. Bright began going over the contents of the paper bags—evidently souvenirs—without any prompting on our part. For the record, they were silly odds and ends from around the world, including an Akabeko cow from Japan, of all things. As the researcher commenced show-and-tell time, Iris gave them a death glare.

"I'm sorry, Dr. Bright, but you're such an eyesore, please die... I mean, did you need us for something?

SCP FOUNDATION

You didn't have to come out of your way to barge in on us while we're eating breakfast. If you called for us, we would have gone to your lab later." Iris tilted her head in curiosity even as she accidently let a rather terrifying comment slip out. Apparently, she really didn't have the patience to deal with Dr. Bright today, and was sharper than usual. "Did you have something urgent to tell us?"

"Well, I wouldn't say it's urgent, but it *is* extremely important," Dr. Bright answered. Instead of taking offense at Iris's questionable attitude, Dr. Bright seemed bemused as they gazed at her, and helped themself to a seat next to us. As if famished, they began to plow into the salads we had barely even touched. I swear, this person was too much.

"Num, yum! Dang, everyone gathered together at the table truly is wonderful! This is what life is all about! It is sheer bliss. And I actually mean that pretty seriously!" Dr. Bright released a satisfied belch and roughly pushed the dishes off to the side, making room for one of the paper bags they'd been holding.

"But unlike me, your lives are limited. Let's make the most of your time. I'd like to take advantage of the fact we're gathered around the table to conduct a little experiment. Is that all right with you?"

"If I said it wasn't, you'd still drag us into it, wouldn't you?" Iris said in defeat, too tired to put up a fight.

And with that, we began a somewhat spontaneous experiment led by Dr. Bright. Not knowing the nature or purpose of the experiment made me nervous, but honestly, it wasn't like I had a reason to dig my heels in and refuse to participate. I didn't have that kind of energy, either. Both of us were truly dead on our feet today.

With unconcealed excitement, Dr. Bright shuffled through the paper bag on the table. They pulled out some sort of dishware—a ceramic bowl—to show off to us.

"Okay, kiddies, check this out! I received permission from a certain site to bring this here! I didn't steal it! I actually filled out the paperwork to transfer it for once!" Dr. Bright sounded so suspicious, I couldn't help but suspect otherwise.

At any rate, it appeared to be a perfectly ordinary, unspectacular bowl. There was a pattern of light blue flowers on the exterior along with what appeared to be Chinese characters, although I couldn't read what they said.

"By any chance," Iris said with her eyes round in surprise, evidently recognizing the bowl, "is that A Gift from Dad?"

"Goodness! You already know about it, Iris?"

"Just the rumors. Isn't it so beneficial to mankind that it's held in the same light as the Panacea?" Iris asked.

"You have the right of it. And unlike the highly limited Panacea, it can be reused indefinitely, so there's no need to be frugal with it. Sadly, it isn't terribly effective unless you're young, so it's nothing more than a nifty bowl to me," Dr. Bright said.

Iris noticed I was floundering, unable to follow the conversation held by these two SCP object experts. She was kind enough to fill me in. "Ah, you don't know about it, do you, ████? As I recall, this is SCP-348...I think. It's also known as A Gift from Dad. Object Class: Safe. As I just said a moment ago, it is considered an extremely useful item. I've never personally used it, but that's what I've heard."

Object Class: Safe, huh? One of the frustrating things with SCP objects was that even a Safe designation didn't necessarily mean you could let your guard down. Up until just recently, the Builder Bear that threw us into the pit of Hell last night was also designated "Safe." Whatever. I should put that accursed stuffed bear out of my head for the time being.

A "?" practically appeared over Iris's head as she watched me shake my head to shoo away unnecessary thoughts. Despite being puzzled, she was kind enough to further elaborate. "A Gift from Dad is quite similar to the first SCP object I showed you, The Never-Ending Pizza Box, ████."

Man, that took me back. The box that could produce an infinite number of pizzas... It was still sitting out here in the canteen, so I occasionally used it. Each time I did, its delicious pizza sent my taste buds to Heaven (It always produced exactly what type of pizza I was craving).

So this was similar... But what was that supposed to mean? Could this bowl produce an endless supply of pizza?

"No, of course not. It makes soup, not pizza. The soup is extremely delicious, loaded with various ingredients... Isn't that right, Dr. Bright?"

"Indeed. Good call comparing it to The Never-Ending Pizza Box. In the case of A Gift from Dad, this bowl can fill endlessly with delicious soup the person sitting before it is bound to love," Dr. Bright said.

Fill endlessly? They said that so casually, but it was a really big deal... I had no idea how that worked, but that was precisely what made it an SCP object. Yet having grown fairly accustomed to such anomalies, I was beyond freaking out or making wisecracks over something like that at this point. Instead, I silently listened to their explanation.

"Furthermore, the soup that springs forth in the bowl has mild healing properties for those who eat it," Dr. Bright said, looking disappointed by my unenthusiastic reaction. "While it isn't a cure-all to the same degree as Panacea, simply eating the soup from A Gift from Dad will completely cure minor ailments and injuries. To top it off, you're enveloped in a sense of contentment while eating it, forgetting any and all dark emotions, such as loneliness and fear."

"Ahh, we could certainly use that at the moment," Iris said, looking at Dr. Bright in mild surprise, before smiling. "You heard we were upset and went through all that annoying paperwork just to bring A Gift from Dad to us? You can be pretty thoughtful sometimes, Doc!"

"Wah ha ha! But of course! The SCP Foundation brags to the entire world about how I'm such a nice guy!" Dr. Bright boasted proudly with their head held high and chest puffed out, their comment clashing with that hot body.

Hm... Seeing as this was Dr. Bright we were dealing with, I simply assumed they had a dirty trick up their sleeve. Was this actually a genuine act of kindness done out of the goodness of their heart? I still couldn't fully trust them...but we'd never get anywhere if I doubted every little thing.

"Feel free to help yourselves, kiddos," Dr. Bright said with a dazzling smile, before pushing SCP-348 in front of us with both hands. As they pushed the bowl, that mad scientist said somewhat ominously, "After this, I'm going to have you two—especially ▮▮▮—experience something a bit shocking. The ordeal is too harsh to challenge when you're emotionally spent; I need you to feel reasonably better."

"Ordeal? What sort of trouble are you planning to get us mixed up in this time, Dr. Bright?" Iris asked. The expression on her face screamed, "I knew it!" Why, she even heaved a sigh, as if relieved. Honestly, there was no way this troublesome researcher would do anything out of the goodness of their heart.

As such thoughts ran through my head, I happened to glance down at SCP-348... I have no idea when it first started, but somewhere along the line, liquid began filling the ceramic bowl.

"Oh, wow! It really does fill with soup on its own," Iris exclaimed, sliding her chair back some in surprise.

Seeing as it continued to rise at the same speed, the soup appearing in A Gift from Dad was probably meant for me. Despite not having an appetite all morning, simply the smell of it made me feel famished. It smelled great. I bet the soup would taste amazing.

I watched the bowl fill for a while, ultimately coming to a stop once the soup hit a certain point. It appeared to be a simple soup with odd-sized vegetable slices and the type of meat sold on discount at grocery stores.

Hold up. Something about it looked familiar... I could swear I've had this soup somewhere before...

"Go ahead. Have some, ▮▮▮▮," Dr. Bright urged, watching me with keen interest.

They looked so excited, I was struck with a strange sense of resistance, but I braced myself for whatever might happen and pulled the bowl closer. With a spoon in one hand, I began to sip.

"H-How is it? If it tastes bad or makes you feel weird, spit it out, okay?" Iris said worriedly, but for better or worse, there was nothing strange about the taste of the soup filling my mouth. It wasn't as if it was amazingly wonderful, but it was nowhere near bad enough to spit out, either. It was normal soup.

A familiar flavor that tasted just right spread throughout my mouth. I was certain I recognized this seasoning. I'd had this soup somewhere before.

"Well, according to SCP-348's test results, young subjects generally enjoy the soup produced, stating it reminds them of their parents' cooking," Dr. Bright offered. That would certainly explain it.

Sure enough, this tasted exactly like the food my

parents made every day. It was home cooking... That would explain why it felt so nostalgic.

My parents... My family... Suddenly overwhelmed by sadness, tears welled up in my eyes. Family. They were part of my former life. It all felt very distant from me now. I was currently living somewhere awfully far from them. I was unable to bear that new reality; it weighed down on me relentlessly.

The soup was definitely good. It healed the soul, filling me with happiness by simply putting a spoonful in my mouth. But that wasn't enough. I couldn't take this any longer. Suffering a severe case of homesickness, I desperately wanted to see my parents—my family. Mom, Dad, my familiar old home...

I wanted to go home. At the very least, I wanted to talk to my family, if only to say a few words. I broke down against the flood of emotions; unable to hold them back, they turned into tears that streamed down my cheeks. Damn, this was embarrassing! I couldn't believe I was crying... But I was bursting with such nostalgia and sorrow, I honestly thought I was going to lose my mind.

"▮▮▮▮? A-Are you okay?" Iris asked, looking at me worriedly. She gently dabbed at my cheeks with one of the paper napkins placed on the table. I let her wipe my cheeks as I drowned in my tears.

What was I doing in this place? I'd given up on going back, telling myself this was simply how things were, accepted my fate, and even grew comfortable with my new environment. But as it clicked that the life I always took for granted had slipped far out of my reach without my even realizing it, I began to tremble in apprehension and fear.

"Uh-huh, I see. I thought that might be the case," Dr. Bright said with a knowing expression on their face, as if they'd read my mind.

With a wry smile, they pointed at A Gift from Dad, their flashy red fingernail standing out a mile. "Look, ██████. Now that you've consumed the soup, isn't a message materializing on the inside of the bowl?"

I didn't notice until Dr. Bright pointed it out, but on the inside of the simple bowl—A Gift from Dad—Japanese characters had at some point begun to reveal themselves. Hmmm, I wondered what the message said...

"Heh heh! This is one of the fascinating features regarding SCP-348... Upon finishing the soup, the message that appears will be in the language most familiar to the drinker of the soup. It isn't guaranteed, but can be observed with high frequency," Dr. Bright said.

Leaning in, Dr. Bright peered into the bowl. "What does it say? The messages it displays are typically warm words of comfort... Or rather, they are the most important message or warning the drinker of the soup's parents wanted to pass on to their child."

Embarrassed over having a woman's face so close (Dr. Bright outwardly looked like an absolutely gorgeous bombshell), I felt oddly flustered as I listened to their explanation. "Previous cases have included 'Don't forget to brush,' 'I'm glad you're happy,' and 'Thank you.' In tune with SCP-348's plain appearance, the messages are often simple... What type of message did you parents have for you?"

Hm, I tried to imagine what my parents wanted to say to me most right now... Since I was probably being treated as a missing person, I bet it would be along the lines of "We're worried about you" or "Where are you now?" Expecting to find a message along those lines, I casually looked into the bowl.

As the line of characters entered my eyes, I was shocked. The message written on the inside of A Gift from Dad said, "I'm so proud of you for never skipping school."

......

...What?

What was that supposed to mean? I haven't gone to school in ages. But it was true that before I wound up in this eerie SCP Foundation research facility, I had perfect attendance and no tardies. Overall on the healthy side, I wasn't undisciplined enough to play hooky. In reality, I was only attending school out of habit. Nevertheless, my parents often dropped words of praise for maintaining such a pristine track record. They've outright told me in person the exact same thing that was written in A Gift from Dad. I could still remember the hint of pride in their smiles...

Er, so what did this mean? Was this message what my parents in the past, not the present, wanted to convey to me...? It wasn't horribly appropriate for me at the moment. In fact, it outright didn't apply.

"No, the message displayed in SCP-348 is supposed to be a message that your parents currently want to pass on to you. Hm, this is most fascinating. Yes, I believe it will support my theory," Dr. Bright said.

With a broad grin, they offhandedly claimed, "It's just as I suspected. ██████, apparently, you aren't a resident of our world."

Uh, what...?

MILESTONE
[MIRROR WORLD]

SCP-105.

Special Containment Procedures: SCP-105 is implanted with a tracking device and is currently housed at Site-17. SCP-105 is currently allowed Class 3 (restricted) socialization privileges with approved site personnel, granted based on continued good behavior and cooperation with Foundation personnel.…→For details, refer to the section for SCP-105

WHO ARE YOU?

Confidential

THE FOUNDATION DATABASE IS CLASSIFIED
ACCESS BY UNAUTHORIZED PERSONNEL IS STRICTLY PROHIBITED
PERPETRATORS WILL BE TRACKED, LOCATED, AND DETAINED

Content relating to the SCP Foundation, including the SCP Foundation logo, is licensed under Creative Commons Attribution-Sharealike 3.0
and all concepts originate from http://www.scp-wiki.net and its authors. SCP Foundation: Iris Through the Looking Glass, being derived
from this content, is also released under Creative Commons Attribution-Sharealike 3.0. To view a copy of the license, please visit
https://creativecommons.org/licenses/by-sa/3.0/ or contact Creative Commons, PO Box 1866, Mountain View, CA 94042, USA.

LATER THAT DAY...

After we finished our mysterious breakfast, we relocated to Dr. Bright's lab. I wasn't sure if it was because I ate the emotionally soothing soup from SCP-348 or if Dr. Bright's excessively cheerful disposition was rubbing off on me, but my entire body felt warm and fuzzy. I wasn't in the best of spirits, though. Dr. Bright's earlier statement nagged at the back of my head.

"Excuse me, Dr. Bright." Apparently of a similar mind, Iris hesitantly spoke up, while the researcher lined the paper bags of souvenirs off to the side. "May I ask what you meant by your earlier comment? What did you mean when you said that... 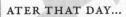 isn't a resident of our world?"

"Oh, I'll be sure to go all over that; don't you worry. I don't like being enigmatic for the heck of it. I'm afraid that for better or worse, I'm not all that great at picking up on the mood, as anyone will tell you." Dr. Bright elegantly sat on a chair and turned to face us, a surprisingly serious expression on their face.

Iris and I were sitting shoulder-to-shoulder on the bed in our usual spot, putting us directly across from the mad scientist.

"Now then, where should I begin?" Dr. Bright mused, a contemplative expression clouding their face as they made a show of seductively crossing their legs.

"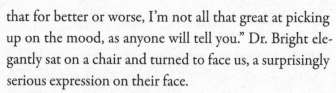, we—if I may be so bold—we, the members of the SCP Foundation, have kept you under observation to identify your special characteristics, while simultaneously investigating your origin to the point of obsession."

Well, I guess that was a given... After living in this SCP Foundation research site for as long as I had, I didn't bat an eye over the revelation. Such was their purpose as the SCP Foundation. It was their goal to investigate, research, secure, contain, and protect anomalies that extended beyond the realm of rational thought.

Within the course of the very first day I strayed into this research site, all of my personal possessions, including the clothes on my back, were confiscated and analyzed through and through. Everything I said and did was watched and observed. I'd had to undergo countless physical exams as well. Analyzed to the DNA level, everything about me was laid bare.

"That's what you'd think, isn't it? It's completely within the power of the SCP Foundation to do that. We possess the necessary knowhow, experience, and drive. You were rather compliant and honestly divulged personal information, making you an easy test subject to work with in those regards." Dr. Bright frowned, as if they thought there wasn't any fun in that.

"Based on the investigation's findings, we've learned that true to your appearance, you're an overall unspectacular, normal boy. Aside from your unique ability to enter photos, there is nothing particularly special about you. You're the painfully average type of guy—from average intelligence to physical capabilities to appearance—I'd never want you for my boyfriend," Dr. Bright said, adding their unnecessary personal opinion.

Their face turned serious as they continued, "That was what everyone thought. Even I was starting to lose interest in you personally, if not in your abilities. But just to play it safe, I searched for supporting evidence regarding your investigation...and came across an incredible fact."

Dr. Bright suddenly thrust their face up close to mine and smiled impishly.

"A field agent went to the city in Japan where you lived, according to the statement you gave. Seeing as you were worried that your family would be upset over your disappearance, it was necessary to at least inform your parents of your wellbeing. Of course, this was all heavily motivated by the ulterior motive of conducting a background check," Dr. Bright said.

"Were ███████'s parents worried about him...?" Iris asked, trying to be considerate of my feelings, but Dr. Bright shrugged with a grin.

"Not in the least! No one even noticed ███████ was missing, not even his own parents, school teachers, or anyone else who knows him in any way. No one was worried as they went about their *normal, everyday lives* as if nothing had happened," Dr. Bright answered.

That...was actually a bit shocking. In reality, I wasn't all that special of a person; it wouldn't matter whether I was around or not. But I never doubted that at least my parents would freak out and search for me if I suddenly went missing.

Did people hate me more than I realized...? Was I a pathetic loser, unloved by everyone?

Seeing me wallow in self-pity, Dr. Bright laughed merrily, "Sorry! I phrased that poorly. It was only natural for those associated with you to act normally. For you see, you never went missing."

Huh...? What was that supposed to mean?

"This is hard to explain, but you are still there. You're still going about life like normal in the city where you lived in Japan, ███████. You seemed to be enjoying an overall happy youth in your own right as you bounced between home and school day after day." Dr. Bright looked me square in the eye as they continued spouting nonsense. "I was there—in the city where you lived—until just this morning. I flew over and met 'you' myself. I made it seem like a chance encounter and spoke with you, if only briefly. I simply couldn't believe someone else's findings, so I went all the way to Japan to check a few things personally."

Oh, so that was why Dr. Bright was gone for so long. They were actually conducting a legit investigation. Going by that stack of souvenirs, they made several stops across the world along the way. I wouldn't be surprised if they did it on the side while tackling one of their bazillion other projects.

"Not only do I interact with you personally, I've possessed a large, diverse pool of people. I have more life experience than anyone else out there. I believe I have a good eye at recognizing people, believe it or not," Dr. Bright stated, forthright and solemn. "From what I saw, the ███████ in that city in Japan was the same person as ██████ here before me. Just to make sure, I pretended to trip in order to touch the one I saw in Japan and get a skin sample. I've run DNA tests, but they give the exact same results."

"Huh? Wh-what does that mean?" Iris asked. She looked completely bewildered, like it didn't make any sense to her. "Is an identical impostor of ██████ stealthily taking ██████'s place to steal his identity and become him?"

"While that is a possibility, I think it's safe to reject that hypothesis. No science in the world could create a clone that is completely identical. Even if it was possible, there is no point. Who would benefit from stealing the identity of a normal Japanese senior high boy?" Dr. Bright pointed out.

Hmph! I felt like they were belittling me, but in reality, it was just as Dr. Bright said. Of course, the life I considered normal would probably look like Heaven on Earth in the eyes of someone like a war orphan... Nevertheless, the number of people leading far more luxurious lives than I rivaled the number of stars in the sky. It'd still leave the question: Why would someone choose to steal *my* identity?

"This has nothing to do with clones or impostors. I analyzed his psyche and movement pattern, and not even the greatest of actors could recreate ████ to such perfection," Dr. Bright said, presenting their argument like a master detective. "It's hypothetically possible to make a body identical to yours with the aid of any number of SCP objects, but it wouldn't have your mind. At the very least, people would notice minor discrepancies. But the boy I spoke with when I flew over to Japan was you through and through, ████."

"So, um, seriously what does that mean? You said you weren't going to be enigmatic, so stop putting off the conclusion like it's so profound, Dr. Bright!" Iris snapped harshly at the end, growing impatient.

With a wry smile, Dr. Bright nodded and said, "In short, the ████ here before us is a guest visiting from a parallel world. If you look at it that way, all of the dots connect, so I'd like to favor that hypothesis."

A parallel world... I've heard those words several times throughout my time participating in Dr. Bright's experiments here at this SCP Foundation research site. There wasn't just one world, but countless worlds simultaneously existing at once... Most were overall extremely similar, but various circumstances could bring about innumerable discrepancies, small and large.

The parallel worlds were usually independent of each other, not interacting at all. But there were instances where a variety of things collided together to connect worlds... maybe? At least, that was how I remembered Iris explained it to me when I asked her about the unfamiliar words.

Those words came up when we discussed my unique ability to enter photos as well. It wasn't as though I was going to the point in time the photo was taken. In other words, I wasn't traveling to the past, but to a parallel world of the past, or something like that.

Since I was going to parallel worlds, nothing I did in the photos had any effect on our current world. So I couldn't go back and prevent a horrible tragedy from occurring.

"Uh-huh. ████, your abilities also support this hypothesis. You possess the ability to enter parallel worlds though photos," Dr. Bright aptly added, as if they were reading my mind. "Upon figuring that out, the rest was easy. The world you're originally from isn't the one we're currently on. From our perspective, it's a parallel world inside a photo."

"Oh, I get it... That's why you said ████ isn't a resident of our world, isn't it?" Iris said. Quicker on the uptake than me, she sounded convinced, nodding.

A moment later, it sort of sunk in. This was a parallel world and there was another version of me who existed here. That other me was still carrying out a normal life typical of a senior high school boy—the normal life I resigned myself to before I wound up in this world.

And that would explain the message in A Gift from Dad. It was meant for the me of this world, not the me here thinking about all of this stuff. Here in this world, I was probably attending school every day like usual. That was why my parents offered those words of praise. To be fair, the bowl had no way of knowing I was a different person visiting from another world...

In order to strengthen their hypothesis, Dr. Bright went out of their way to have me eat from A Gift from Dad. Plus, it comforted us while we were feeling down, effectively killing two birds with one stone. Though in reality, there was still a good chance they were merely toying with us. Dr. Bright was that type of person.

As I was half-heartedly considering the surprisingly trivial meaning behind the prior events in the canteen, Iris closed her eyes and groaned quietly, "The ███ next to me is a visitor from a parallel world? No, I probably pulled ████ out of a picture—out of his parallel world—just like I do during all of our experiments."

Iris opened and closed her hand several times and sighed deeply. "I feel simply awful. I've torn you from the world where you belong, haven't I? And then I had the nerve to keep you here because I'm lonely and say I think of you as family... Man, I'm terrible!"

Iris... I didn't feel there was any need for her to blame herself. At first, I only stayed here because I had nowhere else to go, but I was here now of my own free will. I chose to be at Iris's side, as her good roommate. And as family, if she didn't mind me thinking of her that way.

I poured all of those feelings into squeezing Iris's hand, which made her give a slightly relieved smile. I could feel the warmth of her small hand.

Perhaps I was a traveler visiting from another world who shouldn't exist on this one. But I didn't regret the rather lengthy time I spent on this world where strange SCP objects existed as a matter of course. I didn't consider myself unfortunate. Not when I always had Iris kindly smiling at my side. I felt satisfied. I was happy. Nevertheless...

"Of course, a man's life—his soul—can never be held down by another. No one has that right. Although it's a bit ironic coming from the owner of Immortality...in a funny sort of way." Dr. Bright sounded surprisingly serious, not nearly as jovial as their words might imply.

"You're free to live the life you choose in either world, ██████. I'm certain the SCP Foundation's higher-ups would want to secure an entity as precious as you, but I personally want to leave the choice in your hands. What will it be? Are you returning to your old world? Or would you like to stay here forever?"

Uh, but I didn't see why they would bother to ask if...I wanted to go home. Was there a way to get back? Did they know of a method to return to my old world...?

"Going back should be easy. I haven't verified it yet, so this is still conjecture, but I believe you just need to go back into the photo you first popped out of. That photo-world is the parallel world you're originally from. It's your world, ██████," Dr. Bright said...and then pulled a photo out of the breast pocket of the lab coat they always wore.

A hint of nostalgia rose within me at the sight of the photo. It displayed countless rows of dingy library stacks. It showed the library where I consulted that occult-loving, weird upperclassman about the Girl in the Photos. That felt like years ago; it was almost like I was catching a glimpse of a previous life.

Unlike Iris with her supernatural powers to view the pictures she took as moving images, I saw it as a simple still image. In the center of the library stacks, ██████████-senpai was out of focus due to flailing around. There was a book she dropped in her surprise.

Oh, that was right! The title of that book was *Through the Looking-Glass, and What Alice Found There*. So this was how the picture over there looked from this world. The sight of somewhere from my memories began to fill my heart with a longing to go back. But my life here at the research facility was happy, too—and had its own kind of fun.

I wished I could pop back home, if only briefly. I wanted to see my parents and friends from school. I wanted to shoot the breeze, study, attend club activities, laze about watching TV while eating snacks from the convenience store, and enjoy that boring, invaluable normal life.

If I had to choose which world to live in, that would be tough. I couldn't stand the idea of never seeing Iris again, and I'd miss interacting with all the fantastic SCP objects. Now that I took a second to look back, my life here was truly fun and exciting every single day.

"Well, I haven't verified this, so I can't say for certain, but when you return to your world, coming back probably won't be an issue! If you follow the same process—meaning Iris touches you in the photo and pulls you out—you should be able to return to this world," Dr. Bright said with a wink after fondly watching me debate over what to do as if I were a cute kid. "You can freely travel between the two worlds. Iris is the only one capable of dragging you back, and I'm sure she wouldn't use that ability if you never wanted to return... In other words, you can come back as much as you want, so long as that is what you and Iris desire."

From their seat in the chair, Dr. Bright elegantly spread out their arms. "With that in mind, what would you like to do? I've said this several times now, but you get to decide for yourself. I will leave this to you, ███████. As a reward for participating in so many valuable experiments all this time, I shall allow you to choose." Dr. Bright spoke in a rather patronizing matter, but I could sense the kindness and warmth in their words. My heart was filled with the same warm fuzzies as when I ate the soup from SCP-348.

"Well, I'll personally be a bit sad to see you go back," Iris said, placing her hand over mine this time and leaning close to peer into my eyes. "But it isn't as if we'll never see each other again. From the sound of it, you can come back to play whenever you want. If you want to return to your old world, I won't stop you."Despite what she said, she threaded her fingers through mine as if hating to let me go.

Iris offered me an innocent smile and said, "I can no longer see my true family, the one that I'm related to through blood. So I think you should go see yours while you still can."

But I considered Iris family now, too. I poured that sentiment into squeezing her hand back. I also poured my feelings for her into it.

I would return to my old world. Even if just once. Even if only for a short time. While I was there, I wanted to see my parents and friends and tell them about my experiences in this strange world. There were a bunch of wacky, insane incidents that happened while I was here. That occult-crazed senpai was bound to eat these stories up. I was going to share my story about how I fell into the world of SCP objects.

"Then you should do just that. Do whatever your heart decides, 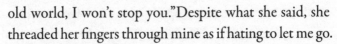," Dr. Bright said. With over-exaggerated reverence, they offered the photo to me. "Try to be quick about it. This photo was deemed an entrance to a parallel world, attracting the interest of a bunch of bored researchers. It's a test subject in its own right! I've swapped it out with a fake to buy some time, but it was a pain in the neck sneaking this out."

"If you keep breaking the rules, one of these days, you're going to get yourself terminated, Doc," Iris said, exasperated.

But Dr. Bright loudly laughed it off, "Wha ha ha! If that happens, maybe I'll go seek refuge in ███████'s world! But I'll need to make you horrendously indebted to me, first."

"It's hard to tell whether that's a joke or not in your case," Iris retorted with a chuckle, finally loosening up a bit.

She reluctantly let go of my hand and stood up. Turning to face me anew, Iris offered me a slight bow before saying, "...Well, I guess this is goodbye for now, ██████."

As she waved her hand, she said, "Bye-bye. Thank you for becoming my family."

The pleasure was all mine. I was so glad I met Iris.

We said, "See you later," and I placed my hands on the photo.

The smell of the air changed. Within the blink of an eye, I was back in my old world. It felt the same as when I entered the photo-world during all of our experiments, so I wasn't particularly stunned or anything. It was surprising how much I'd grown accustomed to this.

Apparently, I jumped out of the photo. The brief second suspended in the air made it difficult to land on my feet. Planting them squarely on the ground, I barely managed to catch my balance.

"Oh, whoa!" The shrill cry hurt my ears.

Turning toward the sound of the voice on reflex, I saw 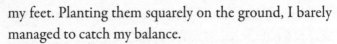-senpai standing diagonally in front of me, so close I could touch her if I held my arm out. From her perspective, I just appeared from thin air, so it was no wonder she was surprised. She reeled back, whacking her head against the stack directly behind her. The impact sent several books tumbling to the ground. A cloud of dust filled the air.

"Huh? What? What gives? What's going on? What just happened?" It felt like I hadn't seen ████████-senpai in ages as she threw question upon question at me, completely indifferent to the books she knocked down.

I could feel her breath on my cheeks. Oh, yeah. She was the type of person who would inadvertently enter my personal space... I felt like I was a bit more comfortable with the opposite sex after my co-ed life with Iris, but certain things simply made me feel awkward.

I was trying to squirm away from Senpai as she bore down on me. Unfortunately, there was nowhere to run in this cramped space lined by library stacks. Senpai pounced on me like a predator and began shaking me by the shoulders.

"Hey! C'mon, didn't you just vanish? And then you reappeared! Or was that my mind playing tricks on me? No, I saw it with my own two eyes! Gyaaah! Shoot, I just saw a real paranormal phenomenon! ♪" she cried, absolutely ecstatic. If she saw an SCP object, I bet she'd faint from excitement.

At any rate, even though I spent several months in the other world, I was gone for less than a few seconds here. Perhaps since the photo was a still image, time didn't pass while I was in it.

I didn't really understand how that worked. I should report as much as I could remember and have researchers who were several dozen times smarter than me look into it. Then I could ask what they thought. That was easier, and it made me extremely happy that it was an option... I was thrilled that I could return to that world and talk to Iris in the future.

Seeing as time didn't pass any in this world...there was no worry that I put my parents and everyone out by disappearing without a trace for so long. It was great this had a happy ending where no one was sad or upset.

Wait, hold up. There was still no guarantee I could return to that other world. It wasn't like we had already proven I could bounce back and forth between the two worlds. Not to mention, Iris was the only one capable of pulling me out of the picture. Although the odds were less than one in a million, if she didn't want to see me again, that would be the end of it. She could sever our bond and my connection with the other world from her side.

Pathetic as it was, I was suddenly filled with apprehension. I hastily began searching for my connection (that photo) with the other world! Dropping to my knees, I started to shuffle through the books scattered on the floor.

"Oh, oops! I made a mess! Let me help!" Senpai offered as she excitedly squatted under the false impression I was enthusiastically cleaning up the books that got knocked down.

She picked up the copy of *Through the Looking-Glass, and What Alice Found There* lying next to her and looked at me. "You have to give me the dirt later! I want to unravel the paranormal phenomenon that I saw! And you're a key player! I won't let you off the hook...!" Senpai exclaimed. It was scary how she panted from excitement, but more importantly...

A photograph was peeking through the pages of the book in ████████-senpai's hand. I carefully took the book from her and flipped it open with my heart racing. Tuning out senpai's ramblings until they were nothing more than background noise, I stared at the photo in the book. My heart was filled with expectation.

For some odd reason, lately, whenever I cracked open a book in this world, I would find a photo stuck inside. It was always of a cute girl. In the past, I didn't know that girl's name. But I knew now. And I would probably remember it for the rest of my life.

Iris. Brought together in a world both near yet far, she was someone dear to my heart.

"Oh, what's up with that photo? Where did it come from? Who the heck is that girl? Do you know her? Who are those people around her? Yikes! Isn't there something freaky about that cat?!" Noticing something strange about what Senpai screamed in my ear, I looked back down at the photo.

As illogical as ever, some time seemed to have passed in the photo. Iris wasn't the only one in it now.

First off, there was Dr. Bright standing unnecessarily proud with their head held high. I wasn't sure if they were simply passing by or if Iris asked them to come, but Dr. Goldman and Dr. Selkie were also there. Finally, there was even Josie the Half-Cat with half its body missing. She was held in Iris's arms.

I felt deeply touched as I looked at the photo. In the past, Iris was the only one who appeared in the photos here in this world. But now it included the people and SCP objects I met and interacted with during my time

at that strange research facility. Above all else, Iris was smiling. Her smile was filled with affection directed toward me.

The things I experienced in that world weren't a dream or illusion... I felt that keenly now. They would always remember the time we shared, and I would never forget. And if I wanted, I bet they would welcome me back to their world...with warm smiles like the ones in this picture.

I could return to my other home, where strange SCP objects existed all around us.

—END OF FILE

SCP OBJECT CREDITS (TEXT)

"SCP Logo" by Aelanna.
Based on the "SCP Logo."
http://www.scp-wiki.net/dr-mackenzie-s-sketchbook

"'Iris'" by DrClef, edited by thedeadlymoose.
Based on "SCP-105 – 'Iris'" and the SCP Foundation Japanese
Branch translations of "SCP-105 – 'Iris.'"
http://www.scp-wiki.net/scp-105
http://ja.scp-wiki.net/scp-105

"Immortality" by TheDuckman.
Based on "SCP-963 – Immortality" and the SCP Foundation
Japanese Branch translations of "SCP-963 – Immortality."
http://www.scp-wiki.net/scp-963
http://ja.scp-wiki.net/scp-963

"The Clockworks" by DrGears.
Based on "SCP-914 – The Clockworks" and the SCP
Foundation Japanese Branch translations of "SCP-914 – The
Clockworks."
http://www.scp-wiki.net/scp-914
http://ja.scp-wiki.net/scp-914

"The Old Man" by DrGears.
Based on "SCP-106 – The Old Man" and the SCP Foundation
Japanese Branch translations of "SCP-106 – The Old Man."
http://www.scp-wiki.net/scp-106
http://ja.scp-wiki.net/scp-106

"'Able'" by Kain Pathos Crow.
Based on "SCP-076 – 'Able'" and the SCP Foundation Japanese
Branch translations of "SCP-076 – 'Able.'"
http://www.scp-wiki.net/scp-076
http://ja.scp-wiki.net/scp-076

"The Never-Ending Pizza Box" by Palhinuk.
Based on "SCP-458 – The Never-Ending Pizza Box" and the
SCP Foundation Japanese Branch translations of "SCP-458 –
The Never-Ending Pizza Box."
http://www.scp-wiki.net/scp-458
http://ja.scp-wiki.net/scp-458

"Builder Bear" by Researcher Dios.
Based on "SCP-1048 – Builder Bear" and the SCP Foundation
Japanese Branch translations of "SCP-1048 – Builder Bear."
http://www.scp-wiki.net/scp-1048
http://ja.scp-wiki.net/scp-1048

"Carnival of Horrors" by DrClef.
Based on "SCP-823 – Carnival of Horrors" and the SCP Foundation
Japanese Branch translations of "SCP-823 – Carnival of Horrors."
http://www.scp-wiki.net/scp-823
http://ja.scp-wiki.net/scp-823

"The Coffee Machine" by Arcibi.
Based on "SCP-294 – The Coffee Machine" and the SCP Foundation
Japanese Branch translations of "SCP-294 – The Coffee Machine."
http://www.scp-wiki.net/scp-294
http://ja.scp-wiki.net/scp-294

"The 'Eye Pods'" Author Unknown.
Based on "SCP-131 – The 'Eye Pods'" and the SCP Foundation
Japanese Branch translations of "SCP-131 – The 'Eye Pods.'"
http://www.scp-wiki.net/scp-131
http://ja.scp-wiki.net/scp-131

"Grammie Knows" by Dexanote.
Based on "SCP-517 – Grammie Knows" and the SCP Foundation
Japanese Branch translations of "SCP-517 – Grammie Knows."
http://www.scp-wiki.net/scp-517
http://ja.scp-wiki.net/scp-517

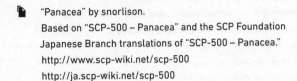

"Panacea" by snorlison.
Based on "SCP-500 – Panacea" and the SCP Foundation
Japanese Branch translations of "SCP-500 – Panacea."
http://www.scp-wiki.net/scp-500
http://ja.scp-wiki.net/scp-500

"Young Girl" by DrGears.
Based on "SCP-053 – Young Girl" and the SCP Foundation
Japanese Branch translations of "SCP-053 – Young Girl."
http://www.scp-wiki.net/scp-053
http://ja.scp-wiki.net/scp-053

"Josie the Half-Cat" Author Unknown.
Based on "SCP-529 – Josie the Half-Cat" and the SCP
Foundation Japanese Branch translations of "SCP-529 – Josie
the Half-Cat."
http://www.scp-wiki.net/scp-529
http://ja.scp-wiki.net/scp-529

"A Gift from Dad" by Zyn.
Based on "SCP-348 – A Gift from Dad" and the SCP Foundation
Japanese Branch translations of "SCP-348 – A Gift from Dad."
http://www.scp-wiki.net/scp-348
http://ja.scp-wiki.net/scp-348

SCP OBJECT CREDITS (ILLUSTRATIONS)

"'Iris'" by DrClef, edited by thedeadlymoose.
Based on "SCP-105 – 'Iris'" and the SCP Foundation Japanese
Branch translations of "SCP-105 – 'Iris.'"
http://www.scp-wiki.net/scp-105
http://ja.scp-wiki.net/scp-105

"The Never-Ending Pizza Box" by Palhinuk.
Based on "SCP-458 – The Never-Ending Pizza Box" and the
SCP Foundation Japanese Branch translations of "SCP-458 –
The Never-Ending Pizza Box."
http://www.scp-wiki.net/scp-458
http://ja.scp-wiki.net/scp-458

"Josie the Half-Cat" Author Unknown.
Based on "SCP-529 – Josie the Half-Cat" and the SCP Foundation
Japanese Branch translations of "SCP-529 – Josie the Half-Cat."
http://www.scp-wiki.net/scp-529
http://ja.scp-wiki.net/scp-529

"Immortality" by TheDuckman.
Based on "SCP-963 – Immortality" and the SCP Foundation
Japanese Branch translations of "SCP-963 – Immortality."
http://www.scp-wiki.net/scp-963
http://ja.scp-wiki.net/scp-963

"Builder Bear" by Researcher Dios.
Based on "SCP-1048 – Builder Bear" and the SCP Foundation
Japanese Branch translations of "SCP-1048 – Builder Bear."
http://www.scp-wiki.net/scp-1048
http://ja.scp-wiki.net/scp-1048

"Neko Desu. Yoroshiku Onegaishimasu" by lkr_4185.
Based on "SCP-040-JP."
http://ja.scp-wiki.net/scp-040-jp

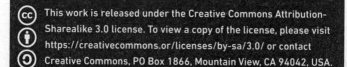
This work is released under the Creative Commons Attribution-Sharealike 3.0 license. To view a copy of the license, please visit https://creativecommons.or/licenses/by-sa/3.0/ or contact Creative Commons, PO Box 1866, Mountain View, CA 94042, USA.

SCP FOUNDATION
IRIS THROUGH THE LOOKING GLASS

Experience these great light**novel** titles from Seven Seas Entertainment

See the complete Seven Seas novel collection at
sevenseaslightnovel.com

Experience all that SEVEN SEAS has to offer!

Visit us online and follow us on Twitter!
SEVENSEASENTERTAINMENT.COM
TWITTER.COM/GOMANGA

SCP FOUNDATION
THIS PAGE INTENTIONALLY LEFT BLANK

SCP FOUNDATION
THIS PAGE INTENTIONALLY LEFT BLANK